The HALLOWEEN IN ME

E. R. BILLS

This volume is dedicated to the noble spirits who made me who I am and will stay with me forever.

contents

Foreword — vii

1. The Halloween in Me — 1
2. Minerva's Vision — 23
3. Tarry Tornado — 39
4. Recumbent Female Nude — 61
5. The Amulet — 79
6. The Judge — 105
7. A Dark White Postscript — 115
8. Pendulum Grim — 149
9. Nature Calls — 167
10. Fandango — 193
11. Nia — 209
12. Rugby Players Eat Their Dead — 227
13. Warren — 247

PREVIOUS APPEARANCES — 261
If you enjoyed this book... — 263

It was always there, really.

From my earliest memories of childhood and well into my youth, there was Halloween in me.

There was no specific reason for it, or at least not one that I could easily pinpoint or isolate. You can't isolate darkness—it isolates you. I knew that if nothing else at a tender age. But I never felt the worse for it.

If you have Halloween in you, you're capable of singular empathy. You're capable of sympathizing with victims and monsters. And if you can see both sides of a Thing, you recognize it (if you're honest), even in yourself. I don't know if I'd challenge the millennia of fragmented folklore or organized religion that claim evil exists, but I would—as Albert Camus maintained—suggest that ignorance is more prevalent than evil and that most monstrosity springs from it. I would even say that ignorance is more dangerous than evil because it breeds monstrosity in broad daylight

Our better angels are not always proponents of light and rarely spring from lightness. Some are borne of darkness or recognitions of darkness, like All Hallow's Eve. Others inhabit darkness like a second skin, a protective buffer. It's the only place they're safe.

one
the halloween
in me

It's not the horror, but the human element that makes this story so appealing to me. The narrative explores the possibilities of the afterlife. Although there are hints of cosmic horror, including an idea of what the afterlife might be like, it's the desire of humans wanting to stay connected to each other that makes the story so heartfelt and enjoyable.

--**Madison Estes**, horror writer and editor of *Road Kill: Texas Horror by Texas Writers, Vol. 6.*

"HAUNT" is such a harsh word. It's a word the dead prefer not to hear or use.

I didn't exactly understand that before, but now I do, as I stand in the dark next to the fruitless Bradford pear tree in front of my house. I'm waiting to catch a glimpse of my children. It's certainly not my intent to *haunt* them.

My departed state is even more precarious than my previous one. And it is the result of something that happened a couple of years back. I distinctly recall the conversation. It was one of those moderate stalemates you often encounter in the first decade of a marriage. We would have learned from it, I think. But for better or worse—I tried to do what I thought was right.

"That doesn't make any sense," I sighed into the phone. "Mr. McShay died several months ago."

"No argument from me," Jackie replied from the other end of the line. "I just thought you should know."

"Okay," I said. "I'll see what I can find out."

Sheesh, I thought. Was someone else living there? Had they rummaged through Mr. McShay's attic? I thought he took the Halloween figures apart every year.

Ever since my wife Jackie and I moved back to the old neighborhood, she complained about the McShay place. "It's a little weird," she said. "He puts a lot more effort into Halloween than he does Christmas."

This perspective frustrated me. I didn't like seeing Christmas decorations up in October. In fact, I considered it bad taste and almost inconsiderate.

I loved my wife dearly, but the free-spirited co-ed I'd been smitten by at a Bad Mutha Goose concert in Austin in the spring of 1987 seemed to become a little less open-minded with each passing year. She was becoming her parents. And she wasn't the only one.

Friends, relatives, old teammates—wild as March hares back in the day, but now, middle-aged, reverting back to whatever default settings—political and/or religious—their parents had programmed into them when they were young. We had rebelled passionately against this prospect in college, but now our contrarian instincts were going the way of the dodo. Out with the new and in with the old. Jackie was even starting to make comments about me missing church.

I pulled into our driveway later that afternoon and parked. I stepped out of the car, and the first October wind hit me. I stopped and stared north.

Halloween would be here soon. The weather would change and then we'd have our night.

They'd have *their* night. The kiddos.

Or at least they used to have it.

We had real Halloweens when I was a kid. Spooky, full-throated free-for-alls. That's why Halloween was my favorite holiday. But the thrill of it was much diminished. My wife preferred taking the kids to the Fall Festival (It really got my goat--they wouldn't even refer to it as a Halloween Festival!).

Held at a local church, the Fall Festival included an overnight lock-in for the teenagers. But what teenager wanted to be locked up in a church gym on Halloween?

Wasn't the equivalent leaving them in a graveyard for Christmas?

I was offended by this usurpation.

I took a deep breath of the October wind, then turned and surveyed the McShay place four houses down on the other side of the street. Mr. McShay's oak trees were barely affected by the breeze, but, sure enough, a couple of Halloween figures were out in the yard. They were narrow and mildly menacing, even from a distance.

"Shit," I said.

My best friend growing up had been Terrence McShay. *Terry.*

He'd lived in that house until he joined up for Desert Storm. His dad was a Vietnam vet, and a stint in the military seemed to be a point of family pride. Terry went to Kuwait, and I went off to college.

Terry and I spent every Halloween together growing up, and his house was always the scariest in town. Mr. McShay was an electrician and, early every October, he'd bring scrap metal conduit, fittings and boxes home and build figures in his yard. He'd pull out his 1/2" bender and construct skeletons out of electrical metallic tubing (EMT), creating striding legs and flailing arms. Then, we'd dress them in old clothes or anything else we could find lying around.

The first year, Mr. McShay created only one figure. He erected an EMT skeleton for a mummy, driving the legs into the ground to keep it upright. Then, he padded the abdominal area, placed a Styrofoam wig head on top and wrapped the entire affair with athletic tape that was torn in half all the way through the roll, giving it the proper width and a head start on fraying. It was startlingly realistic in the dark, especially in a light wind. The mummy's wrapping curled and twisted. You half expected him to grab you or reach out and follow you.

The next year, Mr. McShay had two figures and the year after that, three or four. Sometimes they wore life preservers or brandished fake plastic knives or hatchets. Later, there were soldiers.

After a while, Mr. McShay would stand up ten to twelve figures every Halloween, starting with a few in early October and increasing the number until All Hallows' Eve. One year, they were all cowboys. Another year, they were all soldiers. One even wore a flight suit. It was wickedly off-putting to pass the McShay place after Terry's dad had added a figure or two. It always startled me—and I lived right down the street.

The kids in our town loved the McShay set-up and, before long, even people from out of town were dropping by. Mr. McShay started purchasing dry ice and placing ceramic casserole dishes with it around the front yard, covered with fallen leaves. It created an eerie Halloween ambiance. A couple of years after that, he added a strobe light. It made the figures look as if they were moving. And sometimes unsuspecting (and suspecting) passersby claimed they had.

The rag-tag, twisted figures leaned in unnatural and grotesque postures in the breezes and wisps of dry ice fog rose to make the whole affair look like a horror movie graveyard.

On Halloween night, the younger kids would stand on the street curb and trade dares about going through the McShay yard or up to the house for candy. If you'd already mustered the courage to do it and been scared yourself, you'd hang back or sit on a curb across the street, a wily veteran, and watch the other kids as they worked up the nerve to go earn their treat. It became a rite of passage.

Some of the newbies were so terrified that their parents had to practically drag them up to the front door. But we could tell even grown-ups got the willies. They just hid it better.

In the early days, we helped Terry's dad bend the EMT conduit and build the figures. But as we grew older, hit puberty, got interested in girls or baseball, we became less involved. Mr. McShay pressed on by himself, making monsters, "Halloweening" the yard as he'd put it. And though we might have developed other interests, we still made appearances come Halloween. The dry ice, the strobe light and the swaying figures—we acted too cool to admit it—but they were as scary as ever.

Terry was killed in Operation Desert Storm. I was still in college. I missed that Halloween at the McShay place and several while I was living in Austin.

I didn't forget about All Hallows' Eve, though. I was just busy with other things. When I'd talk to my parents, they'd fill me in on what Mr. McShay was doing and how many figures he had up. As far as I could tell, Mr. McShay hadn't lost a step. Kids still came from all over.

The years flew by and eventually my parents passed away, followed shortly by Mrs. McShay.

When I brought my wife and kids to live in the neighborhood a couple years back, Mr. McShay was still around. And he was thrilled to see me. He claimed he hardly knew any of the new residents on the street. He said he thought they didn't know what to make of him, especially on Halloween. But the kids still came around and that was all that mattered.

We talked about Terry and baseball. We shared memories of some of the old Halloweens in the neighborhood. Mr. McShay loved our visits, but sometimes his eyes would well up and he would turn away. I'd give him a minute to shake it off and act like nothing happened. I felt bad for him. We both missed Terry.

The second Halloween after we came back, Mr. McShay got sick; but the figures still went up. Jackie acted a little disappointed. I guess she was hoping his illness would preempt the ghoulish assembly.

The following year, Mr. McShay was in a nursing home. I didn't go to see him as much as I should have, and I felt bad about it. But when the first October breeze came, we were again greeted by ghostly figures on his lawn.

Jackie was not amused. Worse, it annoyed her that our kids were fascinated by them.

I was quietly ecstatic. Not just for myself, but for the kids, too. I wanted them to have the same great Halloween memories I had.

I was also curious. Was Mr. McShay hiring out the figure assembly and placement? He had a younger brother I'd met and visited with a few times, but I couldn't remember his name. Was the brother taking care of it?

I went to see Mr. McShay before Thanksgiving that year, just before he died. I asked him who had put up the Halloween figures in his yard and he smiled, but said he didn't know. We visited briefly, talking about baseball and the weather, and then he asked me if I'd seen Terry. I assumed he was confused. I told him I hadn't, and he surprised me. He assured me I would. He told me I'd probably meet "Shank" as well.

I barely remembered the name. Shank was one of Mr. McShay's old Vietnam buddies. He had died in the war. Mr. McShay never talked about it much. Terry told me Shank had saved his dad's life.

"They'll try to enlist you," Mr. McShay said. "Be ready."

I nodded and smiled.

I assumed Mr. McShay was losing his mind.

Two weeks later, he was dead.

I saw his brother Seamus at the funeral. He laughed when I asked him about the Halloween figures. He didn't know anything about it. He said he remembered the old Halloweens at his brother's and said it was sad. He was putting the place up for sale, but he had some misgivings. He almost felt like he was destroying a local landmark.

The morning after my wife notified me of the appearance of Halloween figures in the McShay yard, she phoned early again. On her way out to work, she'd noticed another figure. She wondered if I'd found out anything.

"Not yet, honey," I said. "But I'll investigate today."

When I got home, I stopped by the McShay place to get the realtor's name from the "For Sale" sign. But there was no sign. It was gone.

I had planned to ask the realtor about the Halloween figures. I assumed the house must have sold.

The figures swayed in the breeze.

I got out of the car, went to the front door, and knocked.

No answer.

I knocked again, then froze. Just over my right shoulder, one of the figures moved. I spun around and glared. It was dressed in black coveralls and wearing a hockey mask. An homage to Michael Myers from John Carpenter's *Halloween*. I could've sworn it moved.

Not swayed. *Moved.*

A chill ran through me. A core-shaking chill like I hadn't experienced since I was a kid. It felt good and bad—but it was probably just my imagination. Had to be.

Grinning, I turned around. It was silly of me. I would have sworn to it, but maybe I'd just misjudged its position when I walked up. That was the only plausible explanation.

No one answered the front door, so I walked back to the car. I gave the "moving" figure a respectable berth, but the experience made me grin again. It was just the Halloween in me. Some of the old McShay magic.

For the rest of the week, I quizzed the neighbors about the Halloween figures inexplicably popping up. No one had a clue. Most considered Mr. McShay's Halloween interests unseemly and strange. When I played devil's advocate and observed that some folks went overboard with the Christmas decorations, my neighbors looked at me like I was unseemly and strange. And possibly a slanderous heathen. Public sentiment had clearly shifted, and it seemed like Mr. McShay and I were the dodos. I realized then that it was just me.

"Who's doing it, then?" Jackie asked.

"I don't know," I said. "But it's not his brother."

"Well, who else could it be?"

"I'm not sure."

"I'm sorry. I'm not trying to be a curmudgeon. It just reflects badly on the neighborhood."

"Why?"

"Because it's a pagan holiday."

"That's not fair. And that's not exactly true. Halloween is like a mobile costume ball for kids. And it's all play-pretend."

Jackie decided to drop it. But her fixation on the subject was frustrating.

She'd been a little sneaky, or I'd been a bit obtuse. I realized she had anticipated McShay's death would curtail Halloween decorations in the neighborhood. Jackie had been playing the long game. She knew her views on the subject would benefit from attrition. The return of the figures was forestalling this outcome.

That Saturday night, I was up late. I couldn't sleep. Jackie was already in bed.

I sat up and watched old scary movies on TV until two o'clock in the morning. I even let the kids stay up (our little secret). It was a fun thing to do every once in a while. For Halloween to have any hope of survival, it was necessary, even.

After I put the kids to bed and went to make sure the front door was locked, I was startled by a lone, dark figure swaying in our front yard. Another chilling quake shook me to the very center of my being. It took the breath out of me.

I closed my eyes.

It was dark. What had I really seen?

I looked again. It was still there. *And it was facing the house.*

The figures usually faced the street, the direction that trick-or-treaters approached from. Why was this one facing our house? Why was it in our yard?

The hair on my arms stood up.

Was it the black figure wearing a hockey mask?

I couldn't tell. Too dark. I wondered if it could see me.

I backed away from the front door slowly, never taking my eyes off the figure. After a couple of steps back, I could hardly see out of the front glass, but I noticed my reflection. I halfway expected my hair to be white. But it wasn't.

I smiled, mustering bravado. It really was just the Halloween in me. There was no other explanation. My imagination was running wild. But things were getting out of hand; it wasn't like me to get so rattled.

I went back to the door and peered out the glass. There was nothing there. The lone, dark figure was gone.

Maybe it had never been there. Or maybe it was just a kid from the neighborhood goofing around.

Shaking my head, I opened the door.

There was nothing in my front yard. But now there was an extra figure at the McShay place.

"Not cool," I said to no one in particular.

The next day, I walked down to the McShay house and knocked on the door and, again, got no answer. None of the figures moved, but there was another in addition to the one I'd noticed last night. I hoped there was a logical explanation. Either way, I was unnerved.

Over the next couple of weeks, I was busy with work or the kids' practices, and I didn't have time to sort out a logical explanation for the return of the figures, so I avoided thinking about it. My wife helped the children plan their non-Halloween costumes for the local Fall Festival. More "creatures" appeared at the McShay place and a drive through our neighborhood gave unsuspecting visitors a mild scare. The figures were slightly sinister and foreboding, and it took a few days to get used to them. As always, they looked out of place among the manicured lawns and picket fences.

I didn't know who was doing it, or why, but I was secretly pleased. Jackie was frustrated. The figures had startled her more than once. I kept my enthusiasm guarded. The neighborhood wasn't going to be the same without Halloween at the McShay place. Where was the harm in one last "Hurrah?"

Halloween fell on a school night, making the Fall Festival all the more practical.

The kids enjoyed the festival's inflatable playhouses, caramel apples and trickless treats. The bobbing for apples station of the mini-midway was the least visited—the parents didn't want the kids to get their costumes wet. Not a scare in the place. To me it was just plain depressing.

We returned home around ten o'clock. and the trick-or-treating had frittered out. Just a few stragglers here and there.

Against my wife's wishes, I had left a big cardboard box full of candy on the front porch. It only seemed right. The box was empty, and I was glad. I tore the box into small pieces and threw it in the recycling bin.

I went inside, helped tuck the kids in and told my wife I'd come to bed later. She nodded off quickly, so I decided to go back outside.

The weather had been perfect: low sixties, high fifties, no rain, light wind. It felt the way Halloween was supposed to feel. I missed watching the costumes go by, the gags, the excited kids.

The ghostly mannequins were still out at the McShay place. No dry ice or strobe lights, but they were still there, swaying in the breeze. All Hallow's Eve was their dominion.

I abruptly started toward them.

It would be melodramatic to say I was drawn there, but I did feel a yearning, a nostalgic tug.

As I walked, I felt like a kid again, fourteen, ten—eight. I smiled and laughed. Halloween had always been our night.

I approached the McShay place feeling like a big man, scared, but thrilled. Mystified, but also knowing—knowing as much as the parents, as much as other grown-ups. That was the thing about Halloween. It wasn't just the cheeky trick or treat threat. Kids were empowered and grown-ups were taken down a notch. They didn't know what was around the next corner any more than we did. They definitely didn't know what was happening at the McShay place. We were almost equals for a day. And in the possibilities created by uncertainty, there was magic and mystery again. It was a feeling I missed.

The McShay figures swayed. There were thirteen—a baker's dozen. A witch, a sunken-ship survivor (complete with a discolored, orange life preserver); a caped figure, maybe a vampire; a headless doctor, his stethoscope ear pieces still clasped to his stump of a neck; the figure dressed in black coveralls with a hockey mask; and the rest were soldiers. Mr. McShay always had soldiers. A sailor with a sailor's hat on his skull, a fighter pilot, a diver. The diver was new. I'd never seen a diver there. A diver in a frayed scuba suit and cracked mask. Very cool.

There was also a tall Marine in desert camos and a regular Army soldier.

Our improvised graveyard playground had tested our courage when we were kids, and we'd proved ourselves, again and again. Now, it was being offered to a new generation whose parents seemed to spurn the gift. I couldn't. I wanted it for my kids.

I gazed in awe, transported through time. Then, one of the figures grabbed my wrist.

I instinctively jerked my arm back; but the figure didn't let go. It was the Marine in desert camos. His face—a cracked skull—was expressionless. I struggled to free my arm, but the skeletal hand wouldn't release it.

I watched then, stupefied, as another figure, the one with the hockey mask, stepped forward. This unmistakable display of volition gave me the impetus to free my arm from the creepy Marine's grasp.

"What the—"

"Bryan," the hockey mask said. "It's me."

I recognized the voice. I knew that voice. It—

"It's me. *Terry.*"

My head swam. I leaned too far one way and almost collapsed. The hockey mask grabbed my shoulder and steadied me.

"Stay with me, Bryan," the hockey mask said. "I'm real. This is real."

"Terry... *how?*"

"Dad, Bryan. It was my dad."

"But—*you died.*"

"Yes. But this—*Halloween*—it allowed me to come back. To visit."

Back. Visit. "With your dad?"

"Yes."

"Why? What's happening? I don't understand."

"Take it easy, man."

"Why are you wearing a mask?"

"It would be too much, Bryan. *For the kids,* I mean. And you wouldn't recognize me. There wasn't much left after..."

"Oh," I said, still bleary but recalling the way my friend had died. "Who's the Marine?"

"Dad's friend. *Shank.* Remember? Shank's been coming back since we were kids."

I could only offer a weak "Jesus" before I leaned again, irretrievably, and fainted.

When I came to, I was still lying in the McShay yard, and two trick-or-treaters were standing over me. Captain America and a Ninja Turtle.

"Are you okay, Mister?" the Ninja Turtle inquired.

"We thought you were dead," Captain America said.

"No," I answered. "Just frozen in ice."

They didn't get my joke.

"I'm all right," I continued, sitting up.

"Whatcha' doin' on the ground?"

"I just got tired." I looked around. "Listen, I don't think there's any candy left here tonight."

"Do you know the people who live here?" asked the Ninja Turtle.

"I used to."

"Who put up all the monsters?" Captain America queried.

"My uncle says a demon from hell lives here," said the Ninja Turtle.

"Your uncle is full of crap," I replied.

"That's not nice," Captain America said.

"Who said I was nice?" I sold it with a glare, suddenly wishing the kids would leave.

"I'm gonna tell my dad," warned the Ninja Turtle.

"Listen," I said. "I'm a dad. And the man who lived here, he was a dad, too. Not a demon."

"How do you know?"

"Because I grew up here. And he was my best friend's dad."

The wind was gone from my sails. These two boys were probably best friends, just like Terry and I had been... or were.

Thankfully, Captain America and the Ninja Turtle moved on. I stood up slowly. The Marine dressed in desert camos and Michael Myers were motionless again, but not for long.

"That was a little overboard, don't ya' think?" Shank said. His voice was deep and low.

"I think I'm losing my mind," I replied.

"No," Terry said. "It's just a lot to take in."

"My mortgage payment was a lot to take in. Hearing you'd been killed in Iraq was a lot to take in. *This* is not something you just take in. I don't even know how to process it."

"McShay always said you was a good egg," Shank muttered.

"What's happening?" I responded. "How is this happening? Why?"

"Can we talk in the backyard?" Terry asked.

If I was just talking to phantoms in my head, it made sense to do it where no one would see. "Sure."

We went to the backyard and stood in the shadows. The rest of the figures remained motionless.

The back yard was just like I remembered it, only smaller. We'd treed a squirrel or two in the old oak in the far corner and slept outside on old army cots more times than I could count.

"I'm sorry, Bry," Terry said. "I know this is a shock."

"Is it really you, Terry?"

"Yes."

I struggled with it and thought for a moment.

"What baseball card did we fight over right here on this very spot when we were ten?" I asked, testing him.

"Nolan Ryan's 1979 Mets card. Topps, I think."

"Damn," I said. "*It is you*. How?!"

"Dad."

"Okay. But how?"

"I was first," Shank said. "I'll explain it the best I can."

Shank looked around and then lowered his head. "It was after the war," he said. "Or what happened to me there. I was in a place I can't describe. I saved McShay, Terry's dad, yeah... but I did some other things, too. Bad things. War does that. And one day, I just lost it. I lost my shit and didn't stop losing it 'til a grenade launcher fragged me. *Benito Finito*. But the day I died was not a relief. No light, no tunnel. I was just on a different plane. Fighting the Vietcong was nothing compared to being at war with myself, battling my own demons. I had been my worst self. I was my own dull, sad, crazy monster, and I was stuck. But when I moved along that plane, I thought a lot about McShay. Thinking about Terry's dad kept me going. We'd had some laughs. We were friends. He was a good guy, and I wondered what had happened to him.

"It was an eternity before anything changed, but it did change. I kept moving along the plane and one day I just saw McShay. He was building something. Right there in the front yard. I couldn't explain it, but I was happy to see him.

"I watched him. I saw Terry when he was young. *I saw you.* And I just stayed. I quit fighting with myself. I quit wandering. I just hung around.

"Right before Halloween came, I came out. I came out to McShay just like we came out to you tonight. He was shocked, but he bawled his eyes out. He hugged me and held me in a way that made me feel like I was actually here. And I sort of was—just like we are now.

And that's how it went. Year after year. Only Halloweens, mind you. I came back and hung around for Halloweens."

"The dry ice was Shank's idea," Terry said.

"Really?"

"Yep," Shank said. "That was after I'd been back a few times. It was fun. *It was so much fun.* So, I got this reprieve every Halloween. A break from what might as well be called hell. Just a chance to visit."

"And then I came along," Terry said.

"Yeah," Shank nodded. "Hated that. Your poor dad. No man should have to bury his son. I was worried."

"It was tough," Terry agreed.

"Yeah," Shank said. "After you—after you were gone, your father asked me if you were out there. He asked me if I could find you. I said I'd try. And I enlisted some friends. Your dad just wanted to see you again, Terry."

"That's when the extra army men began showing up?" I speculated.

"Yes, sir."

"That's why they looked so real."

"Yep. Because they were. We were. And we eventually found Terry."

"What happened, Terry?"

"IED. Never saw it coming. A click and a boom. Died instantly... dumbfuck that I was. I should have gone off to college with you."

"McShay never forgave himself," Shank said.

"It wasn't his fault," Terry said. "I kept telling him that."

"I talked to him a while back," I interjected.

"Yeah?"

"Yeah. He actually tried to spill the beans about this, but I had no idea what he was talking about. Terry, you know I loved him. But I thought he'd finally gone off his rocker. He even said y'all would recruit me."

"He was radio silent on the subject for decades," Shank said. "Can't blame him for slipping a little or wanting to confide. He was worried."

"Worried about what?"

"Worried about what would happen to us."

"Oh. Yeah. What will happen?"

"He's gone, Bry," Terry said. "*He's gone.* Somebody will buy this house and we'll be gone. We won't have a place to go. We'll lose this."

"Oh. *Oh.* Right. I wasn't thinking."

I stared at the back of the McShay place and then looked in the direction of my house.

"Does it have to be Terry's house?" I asked.

"Not necessarily," Shank replied.

"Can it be my place?"

"That's a lot to ask," Terry said. "Things have changed."

My eyes welled up. "No, they haven't," I said. "Not for me."

"War's over when we're here," Shank said. "Halloween's our R&R now."

"I want to help," I said, wiping my eyes. "I want to do it. We can have it at my house."

"You sure?" Terry asked.

I nodded.

Terry and Shank walked me back to the front yard, and we hugged. Then, they assumed their positions.

"See ya, Bry," the hockey mask said.

"See you," I replied. "Next Halloween, right?"

"We'll be there," Shank muttered. "We've never lost anybody on this detail."

The next morning, all the figures in the McShay yard were gone.

The "For Sale" sign was back up by Thanksgiving and the place sold before Christmas.

The new owners put up gobs of Christmas lights and a cardboard sleigh.

In early October of the following year, I bought a 1/2" EMT bender at a pawnshop, some EMT and some boxes and fittings. I put up two figures the first weekend of October and a couple more the week after. I dressed one in old jeans and a frayed, long-sleeve hoodie; I outfitted the other with my college graduation cap and gown. I may have been the only one, but I felt like I'd outdone myself.

When Jackie got home, I braced for the worst.

"What is this?" she demanded.

"Just getting into the Halloween spirit."

"Well... *get out of it.*"

We didn't talk anymore that evening. And the next day we ignored the subject.

That night I stood at the front door and stared at my creations, wondering when they might be joined by a figure I had not created. I slept very little that weekend.

I checked for "strangers" every morning as I left for work. I was pleased to find the figures I'd put up were disconcerting even in daylight; but there were no nocturnal additions. I began to fear that I'd have to put up all the figures myself. Had my reunion with Terry really happened?

Jackie was fit to be tied. I tiptoed around. Finally, the subject was broached one evening in bed. Jackie was lying on her side with her back to me. I slid over behind her but kept my hands to myself.

"I don't understand this," Jackie said.

"What do you mean?"

"This obsession with Halloween."

"I'm not obsessed. I just like it. I love it. It's the best holiday there is, especially for the kids."

"It's not even a real holiday."

"Says who?"

Jackie got quiet.

I continued. "Look, Hon. I love Halloween. Always have. It's about mild mayhem and friendly mischief. It's an opportunity for even the stuffiest people to take the night off, be weird, have some fun. Where's the harm in that?"

Jackie didn't respond. That meant we were either trapped in a bitter stalemate or she just didn't feel like arguing. I hoped it was the latter.

I retreated to my side of the bed.

On the evening of October 22nd, I cursed myself for a fool. Looking out my front window, it seemed it had all been a figment of my imagination.

Only then did I notice an extra figure outside.

It startled me, but I wasn't frightened. In fact, I was relieved. I quickly went out into the yard.

"This is sweet," a Marine in jungle camos said. Shank was back.

"Where's Terr—"

"Right here," Terry said. He was a janitor with a ratty mop.

"You made it."

"Was there ever any doubt?" Terry replied.

I hugged him. "I'm so glad," I said. "I'm just... so glad."

"Wouldn't miss it."

The last week before Halloween was a blur. More figures appeared in the yard. I picked up a fog machine and a strobe light. Jackie didn't like it, but didn't say much. Her silence was strange, but I didn't want to antagonize the situation. I'd even been going to church steadily for a couple of months to stay in her good graces.

Jackie made Fall Festival plans, and I mounted the strobe light. I also made a special trip to a party store. I liked passing out candy on Halloween, but I knew you could buy plastic eyeballs, spiders and cheap plastic vampire teeth in bulk and thought it would be cool to hand those out along with the candy.

My kids were fascinated with the Halloween figures, and, as it turned out, also enjoying a growing celebrity status at their school. Other kids were asking what it was all about and making plans to drop by.

A few days before Halloween, I decided it would be fun to join the "creatures" in the front yard, so I bought myself a costume. Jackie was perturbed but patient. I wanted more than anything to introduce her to Terry. It was the best way to explain. I just didn't know how she would take it. It was easy to imagine the encounter going south. Fast.

In the wee hours of the morning after midnight before All Hallows' Eve, I heard a tap on our master bedroom window. It was Terry. I met him out front. He was the only figure standing.

"Nice neighbors you got," said Shank from the ground.

Two men had come through the yard with bats, smashing the figures.

"Sorry," I said. "I don't know who would do such a thing."

"If I wasn't already dead," Terry said, "that probably would have killed me."

"I thought about shoving those bats up their asses," Shank added, "but we didn't want to get you in any trouble."

"I appreciate that," I said. "I'm still relatively new to my neighbors. Anything like this ever happen to your dad, Terry?"

"No. Never."

"A lot more humbugs in the neighborhood these days, I guess."

On Halloween night, Jackie was pleasant and agreed to let the kids hang out in the yard before the Fall Festival. It wouldn't really be dark by then, but I didn't complain. I knew the kids would be able to see the yard again after the festival.

Everything was going well. The figures swayed, the fog machine belched creepiness, and the strobe light trapped it all in an old-timey flicker-show frame. The kids that came through were thrilled and, though I couldn't see Terry's or Shank's faces, I sensed their grins. They were having fun and so was I. And that's what it was all about.

Looking back now, I know I should have seen the vandalism the night before as a warning. I should have taken it more seriously. When Mr. Jake showed up, I knew we were in trouble.

Mr. Jake had been a drunk when Terry and I were young. I'd seen him at church a few times recently and assumed he'd sobered up. I didn't recognize him when he first started pacing in the street, but soon he was saying things loud enough that I caught pieces of them, and then he was drunkenly shouting.

"This... is... a... house... of... *Satan! SAY-TAN!* This is a House of Satan!

When I finally heard him and realized who he was, the trick-or-treaters near the house were already scattering. I took my mask off and approached him in the street. He started to scream about the house again and I said hello.

"It's me, Mr. Jake," I continued. "It's Bryan Nichols. Do you remember me?"

"No," Mr. Jake said. "*Yes.* What are you doing here?"

"I live here."

"In the House of Satan?"

"No, Mr. Jake. This is my house. It's Halloween. We're just having some fun. I thought I might pick up where Mr. McShay left off."

"We thought that would be an end to it," he said. "This is a Christian town now. Why are you doing this?"

"Mr. Jake, you know me. I grew up here. This is what we did when I was growing up here. Those Halloweens are some of my best memories. I want my kids to be able to experience it."

"Well, it's a Christian town now," Mr. Jake repeated, jerking his head. "Can't you see? We're... We're—we're trying to keep it that way."

"Mr. Jake," I replied. "Are you okay? You seem confused."

"I'm not the one's confused. You're making a spectacle."

Mr. Jake's seriousness made me uncomfortable. Were we really debating this?

"It's Halloween," I said.

"I know it's Halloween, but Halloween isn't what we thought it was back then. It isn't good or wholesome."

"Says who?"

"Says me. Says lots of folks."

"Well," I said, my frustration growing, "Lots of folks have their own yards. I have mine. Don't you think it would be better if we tended to our own yards and minded our own business?"

"This is town business," Mr. Jake quipped. "Spreading deviltry is town business."

I was tempted to laugh, but I didn't want to upset him further. His sincerity stumped me, and I was annoyed.

"Well," I said. "If it's town business, pass an ordinance."

"We will. But you need to listen."

"No, Mr. Jake," I responded pointedly. "You need to listen to yourself."

Mr. Jake looked at me hard, and I reciprocated accordingly. "Happy Halloween," I said.

Mr. Jake stared at me a moment longer and then turned toward his truck. I put my mask back on.

The people who had gathered in the street to watch quietly dispersed. Mr. Jake had ruined the entire vibe.

And he wasn't finished.

As I reentered my yard, I couldn't see the headlights approaching. The strobe light was still flashing.

Mr. Jake drove his truck into my yard and mowed down several of the figures before I realized what was happening.

I heard a passersby scream. Then, I felt several impossible cracks and landed on my back.

Shank abruptly straightened bolt upright, reached into the cab of Mr. Jake's truck and grabbed him by the neck. I couldn't make out exactly what happened next, but the truck veered sharply, slowed down and rolled into a neighbor's house.

Not realizing I was actually among the figures that Mr. Jake had run down, the passersby tried to attend to Mr. Jake at the household next door. Terry and Shank came to my side.

"What happened?" I said. I could feel something poking through my rib cage.

"I went bobbing for apples," Shank replied. "Adam's apples. I don't think Jake is going to make it."

"Am I?"

"Hang on," Terry said, lifting my head. "Just hang on."

"Medic!" Shank screamed. *"Medic!"*

"Jackie is going to be so pissed," I said, spitting up blood.

"Easy, buddy," Shank said.

Shank looked at Terry as he took my hand. "It's gonna be okay," Terry said. "It's gonna be okay."

Terry was wrong. And he's admitted as much.

It was just something you say when you know things aren't going to be okay and there's not a damn thing you can do about it. I didn't hold it against him. He was just trying to make me feel better, allow me to go easier.

Now, I'm on the other side as All Hallows' Eve approaches. And the Halloween in me—it's all I have left.

Terry and Shank were able to get me back here, but we have no—for lack of a better word—venue to play, no refuge to inhabit.

Still, Halloween springs eternal.

My presence isn't a haunting. It's a longing.

I lost consciousness before my family arrived home from the Fall Festival and I never got to say goodbye.

I know my kids were fascinated by all the Halloween figures before Mr. Jake's rampage, but I realize what happened probably soured them.

Even so, I hold out hope.

I want to reach out. I want to let them know I'm here. I hope Jackie blames me and not Halloween. It's the only way I'll ever be able to be with them again.

I just know my kids will outgrow the Fall Festival someday and have a Halloween of their own. I'm happy to wait.

I've got nothing but time.

two
minerva's vision

This is a tale of tragedies. The tragedy of injustice, the tragedy of endings, and, worst of all, the tragedy of beginnings that come too late.
—**Mario E. Martinez**, horror writer and author of *San Casimiro, Texas: Short Stories, A Pig Named Orrenius & Other Strange Tales*

IN MINERVA'S VISION, clouds gathered on the western horizon, maybe somewhere north. They approached quickly, rising, expanding and turning. But then the burgeoning mass peeled back and separated into large wisps, revealing snatches of darkness. Blackness.

Minerva pushed it out of her mind.

This was why she could no longer work at the China Palace.

Minerva sat in a hard, plastic deck chair on the back porch of her mother's old one-room *choza*, less than a half mile from the Rio Grande. *Choza*. That's what her mother, Isabella, had called it, and that's what it was. A shack.

Minerva stared at her gloved hands.

Her real name wasn't Minerva. Minerva was her stage name, Roman or Greek or something; she couldn't remember. Her real name was Maria. Maria Salas. Minerva was a fake name, a prop—like her gloves.

Minerva was born with only two digits on each hand. She suffered from ectrodactyly disorder. It was also known as cleft hand, split hand malformation and lobster claw syndrome. That was why she had a fancy name, a carny name. As a young girl she had toured the northeastern border of Mexico and traveled through Texas, Arkansas, Louisiana and Mississippi as Minerva the Lobster Girl—in Mexico, Minerva, *La Niña Langosta*.

The gloves were extra-large so her large, abnormally shaped digits could squeeze into the thumb and ring finger of each glove. The other glove fingers were filled with silicone caulk or wood glue, depending on the type of glove. When the caulk or glue dried, they allowed her hands to look somewhat normal. It hadn't mattered when she was a carnival attraction. But in the ordinary world, working at the China Palace, it was a problem. The sight of her hands could put customers off their lunch.

People often didn't notice her birth defect, because Minerva was physically striking otherwise. She was tall, slender and dark-skinned, with bewitching green eyes. Her favorite aunt kidded her that she had *ojos de un diablo*. The eyes probably came from her father, an unknown gringo, a john. Her mother had worked as a prostitute.

When Minerva's mother, Isabella, was little, she had fetched buckets of water from the Rio Grande for the *choza* where she and her parents lived on the Mexican side. They couldn't have known it then, of course, but the water was poisoned with chemicals from the gringo communities upstream, in Texas and New Mexico. Pesticides and fertilizers and mining waste. Later, when Isabella worked with her parents in the fields, the gringo farmers sometimes sprayed the crops while the laborers were still working. No one had known what that spray might do to them or their children.

Isabella married when she was young. A hardy man from Guanajuato. But Minerva's older brother was born with his internal organs outside his body, dying soon after his birth. Isabella's husband's family had blamed her. They said her womb was polluted. They believed she had been tainted by the hand of a *bruja oscura,* a dark witch. That's why Isabella became a prostitute. No one wanted to make a *monstruo* with her, a monster, another freak. Most didn't even want to work with someone who made a *monstruo*.

Minerva was an accident, but her mother was extremely protective of her. Isabella worked long, hard hours at a bordello to take care of Minerva. It wasn't Isabella's idea for her daughter to join a carnival. Minerva thought of it. She just wanted to help. And being a *criatura* in the freakshow tents never bothered her at all. In that environment, she was with her own kind. Her friends and lovers were loyal, protective, and kind. They were together. *Juntamente.* And she was heartened by their togetherness.

But then her mother became ill. The same poison that twisted Minerva's genetics had eaten up her mother's insides. Minerva left the carnival and came home. She took a job at the China Palace as a dishwasher.

Slowly, Minerva became fascinated with the fortune cookies. Even though they were prepackaged and shipped in from the Chopstick Food Company in Chinatown, in New York, she thought they were magical. She asked the busboys to save them if patrons didn't open them with their meals. She took paper bags of them home and read them. Eventually, she started looking up recipes.

Minerva began making her own fortune cookies for her mother. Homemade fortune cookies with real Mexican vanilla, from scratch. The cookies contained messages Minerva had written herself, in Spanish. Then, one Christmas Eve, she gave the owners of the China Palace some of her homemade fortune cookies as gifts. They loved them. They loved them so much that they created a new position for her. They made her the China Palace's fortune cookie maker. They put her in charge of the whole fortune cookie operation. It became a staple of the eatery.

Minerva had never been so happy. This new vocation eventually became her entire focus.

Minerva studied the guests as they came in, imagining which patron should get which cookie. Then, she started creating fortunes for each individual guest at each table. Though she insisted the mixes be fairly fresh, the cookie batter could be pre-mixed in several batches throughout the day. At lunch she would guess the size of the crowds to determine how much batter to utilize and then start the cookies in the oven on lightly buttered sheet pans. While the cookies were baking, she would study the patrons. When the cookies were out of the oven, she wrote the patrons' fortunes, then she gently folded the cookies over the extended ridge between her two opposable digits. Her cleft hands were perfectly suited for the task. The final step involved placing the cookies folded-ends down in the cups of muffin tins until they cooled. This ensured that they held their shape until they hardened. To-go orders didn't get homemade cookies. Only dine-in patrons.

Minerva's fortune cookies became wildly popular and soon began to increase China Palace traffic. Most Asian food connoisseurs hardly ever ate the fortune cookies themselves—they just cracked them open to read their fortunes. But Minerva's homemade fresh fortune cookies were delicious, so good that the messages (in most of the patrons' native tongue) were initially just a bonus. Then the fortune cookie notes themselves became popular. It was one of the worst-kept secrets in the Valley.

Minerva's cookies helped the customers. Her cookies warned them. Not in dire ways, but with pleasant admonitions and suggested prudence. She tried to keep a low profile, but there were whispers. Some believed she had *segunda señal*—second sight.

But that was over now. It had to be.

Minerva still occasionally visited *la choza*, and this was one of those days. Her mother had died several years before and now Minerva wondered if she really had been tainted by the hand of a *bruja oscura*. She had always tried to use her *visión profética* for good, but today there was only bad. Something Minerva did not want to see. That's why she couldn't work at China Palace anymore. Minerva could not lie to the customers. And it would be even worse to tell them the truth.

Minerva went to the kitchen sink inside to see if the water was still working. It was. She bent over and splashed some up to her lips to see if it was good. It was cool and refreshing. She retrieved a glass from the cupboard, filled it halfway, and drank it. Then she undressed.

Minerva had tried to live her life in a way that wasn't harmful or hurtful to others. It was not a conscious decision; just the way of her family and the people she cared about. She possessed natural dignity. There was no pride in it—it simply was.

Minerva would face what was coming naked and unashamed, without regret.

"You know what your problem is?"

Berl Becker smiled. "My editor?"

"Funny, but no," said Becker's editor, Thomas. "It's that ego. It's that holier-than-thou attitude."

"Holier than thou? I just do my job, Tommy. I'm just trying to do my job."

"Your job isn't starting a crusade," Thomas replied. "Your job is reporting the news."

"I report the news. I report it and you ignore it."

"It's not that simple, Berl. *You know that.* The world doesn't revolve around *Berl Becker.* Or Thomas Luchar, for that matter. How long have you been here?"

"Three months."

"How's your Spanish coming?"

"It's getting better."

"Ninety-seven percent of the population here in Brownsville speaks Spanish, Berl. Getting better doesn't cut it. Laid-off journalists are pounding the pavement everywhere. You're lucky to have a job."

"I know. I do know that. But I don't have to like it."

"Well, you'll like this even less."

"What?"

"Your next story. That Chinese food joint down on Levy Street is going to stop serving fortune cookies."

"Oh, well. *Stop the presses.*"

"Don't start, Berl. It's the most popular Chinese food place in town. It's been there for years and the regulars are upset. It's your next assignment."

"Really? That's how you're gonna handle this? Loaning me out to the food beat? *How can a Chinese eatery stop serving fortune cookies?*"

"That's the story, Becker. That's what you're getting paid to find out."

Thomas was correct. Newspapers were shuttering left and right. The median age of the average newspaper subscriber in America was sixty-five. Any newspapers that were still alive and kicking owed that fact to the Baby Boomers. Boomer loyalty came with a catch, however. Several catches.

They didn't like bad news. They didn't like reporting that challenged or seemed critical of their worldview (or implied they might not have a worldview of substance). They didn't like hearing about global warming or evolving gender roles. They exhibited a more than mild disdain for young people, in general. And minorities. And some older citizens of minority groups didn't care for the younger members of that group, either, or recently emigrated members of that group.

Berl knew that the *Brownsville Beacon* had to be mindful of its largely mindless readership. He could also see why Thomas decried his arrogance. But he couldn't help but bristle at all the fluffy, hand-patting "human interest" pieces he was forced to churn out to soothe the rubes. He considered it an editorial sin and a threat to the *Beacon*'s long-term prospects. He would swallow his pride, though. A lame story was still a story. He would be a good soldier; he owed Thomas that.

Brownsville wasn't the most likely place to plunk down and start a Chinese restaurant, but Kim and Tran Lee had hung in there and the China Palace was relatively popular. Especially with the locals. It was a nice break from tacos and enchiladas. The citizenry embraced the Palace, and it evolved into a community favorite. Becker subsequently learned that, for years, the Palace had offered a unique hometown touch. The restaurant began making homemade fortune cookies with the messages written in colloquial Spanish. Berl could see why the Palace's decision to not offer fortune cookies anymore was creating such a stir.

Berl had a passing acquaintance with Kim Lee, so he didn't call ahead. When he got to the Palace, his progress was slow.

"I would rather not talk about it," Kim said. "It is a sore subject."

"How so?" Becker queried. "You're just going to stop serving fortune cookies. They're not even really Chinese. The first ones appeared in California. San Francisco, I think."

"Be that as it may, Mr. Becker, it is part of our tradition here at the China Palace."

"Call me Berl."

"But you misunderstand, Mr. Berl. We will still offer fortune cookies. They just will not be homemade."

"Oh. Well. That's not bad, is it?"

"Yes and no. It will not be the same."

"Okay. English instead of Spanish. Pre-cooked or pre-produced instead of homemade. It won't be the same... *but it kind of will be the same*, right? It's a cookie. But it's not even really dessert."

"You do not understand, Mr. Berl."

"Fair enough. But I'm trying to."

"The popularity of our fortune cookies was due, yes, to the fact that they were homemade, and, yes, because the messages were written in Spanish. But those were—well—these matters were not the only issue."

"I'm sorry, I've misunderstood. Can you please tell me what the other issues were?"

Kim was frustrated. There was a large, ornate bowl of plastic-wrapped fortune cookies on a prep counter near the cooking area. Kim grabbed a handful and handed them to Berl. "Choose one, Mr. Berl. Please choose one and open it."

Berl chose one and handed the others back to Kim. Kim set the remainder on the prep counter.

Berl removed the plastic, opened the cookie and examined the message. It was printed on a tiny piece of paper no more than two inches wide and one-half inch from top to bottom. The type was tiny, too. It informed him that "An interesting investment opportunity is in your near future."

Kim grabbed another off the prep counter and held it out to Berl. "Try another one."

Berl took it, removed the plastic covering, and cracked it open. He read it aloud. "'Close friends are seeking you for your sound advice.'" Berl cocked his head. "That's certainly questionable."

Kim smiled and then gestured toward the remaining fortune cookies. "You make my point," he said. "These are mass-scripted and formulaic. Very mundane. Sterile. Minerva's were more personalized."

"Personalized? Okay. Any thoughts on replacing her?"

"Mr. Berl. You still do not understand. Perhaps I misspoke. Minerva's fortune cookie notes were personal. *Personal and specific.* To the individual."

"Huh? How is that possible?"

Kim shrugged his shoulders and thought for a moment. "I am not Chinese, Mr. Berl. I am from Hong Kong. Hong Kongers believe that certain things should never be given as gifts. It can even be as simple as the names of some of these things being pronounced like other things, bad things, that sound the same. In Hong Kong, this is enough to make them bad omens. Do you understand?"

"Yes," Berl replied.

"Good," Kim said. "In Cantonese, 'to give a clock' is pronounced 'song zung.' These words sound the same as those we use to say, 'to prepare for the end.' They refer to the way we pay our respects to a loved one near the end of their life."

Kim nodded at Berl to make sure he was following him. Berl nodded back.

"That's why we never give clocks as gifts," Kim continued. "Because they are a reminder that time is running out."

"Okay," Berl said, somewhat perplexed. "But what does this have to do with Minerva? Or fortune cookies?"

"That, Mr. Berl, is something only she could tell you." Kim smiled. "But our customers love her. She is a singular spirit. She will not be replaced."

Kim told Berl that Minerva didn't own a cell phone, but had a landline at the small house she kept on East Monroe Street near the Immaculate Conception Cathedral. He also mentioned Minerva's mother's place.

Berl returned to the *Beacon* offices and rang Minerva's house repeatedly. He never got an answer. Not even an answering machine. Then, he located one "Isabella Salas," the mother, deceased, on the Internet White Pages. He rang that number as well, but it was disconnected. He took note of the address of the mother's residence and then pilfered two pieces of gum from the top, right-hand drawer of Thomas' desk. It was an ongoing prank he cherished. It reminded him of the good ol' days in newsrooms of yore, when the press was still referred to as the Fourth Estate.

On a hunch, Berl decided to drive over to the mother's place. As he pulled up, he noted that the house wasn't much. In fact, he was fairly sure it didn't even have electricity, and the day was turning into a real scorcher. There was a Chevy Malibu out front. He parked behind it. The car looked to be in good shape and there was very little dust. Someone was probably home.

As he stepped out of his car, he noticed the clouds drifting through the blue sky, their images reflected before him in the tilted windshield of the Malibu.

Berl knocked on the front door. He heard a light creak in the wooden floor inside and waited.

Minerva answered the door wearing only a Day-Glo yellow G-string.

Berl swallowed the gum he'd pilfered from Thomas's desk.

"There's no air conditioning," Minerva said.

"I, uh, see that," Berl managed.

"Who are you?"

"I'm Berl Becker with the *Brownsville Beacon*."

"Why have you come?"

"I've... been assigned... I'd like to talk to you about fortune cookies. Homemade fortune cookies."

Minerva looked him up and down. "Let's go to the back porch."

"Sure."

Berl followed her through the small house, observing her shoulders, the small of her back and everything that was not hidden by her G-string.

The back porch was just as hot, but it afforded them the occasional, mild breeze. Berl could see trees running along the Rio Grande in the distance. There were two deck chairs, and Minerva took a seat in the one on the right. It was then that Berl noticed her "hands."

It looked like the index and middle fingers on each hand were missing. Each thumb was long and broad and, like normal thumbs, opposable. The ring and pinky fingers seemed to have merged and resembled a second thumb. One broad fingernail. These merged digits also appeared to be opposable. Minerva's hands were essentially comprised of two large opposing thumbs with her dark skin and the customary wrinkles. She noticed him noticing.

"I have gloves if my hands make you uncomfortable," she said.

"No," he replied. "I'm fine."

"Good," she said. "Most people find them disturbing. *Muy desagradable.*"

"That's probably because they see them when you have more clothes on."

Minerva smiled. "Whoa, *gringo*. Are you hitting on me?"

"Berl. Or Becker—please."

"Burl? Like Burl Ives, the Snowman? In *Rudolph the Red-Nosed Reindeer*?"

"The same. But with an 'e' instead of a 'u.'"

"I remember that movie. I loved Rudolph. But you're a long way from the North Pole, *gringo*."

"Call me Berl, please.

"Okay. Berl."

Minerva's nipples and belly were slick with perspiration. The heat was brutal. The sweat was pooling in her navel. Berl could hardly look away from her and she knew it. Her green eyes held him almost sympathetically.

"I came down here to be alone," she said. "But I'm glad you found me. I think it might be good." She held her misshapen hands out and opened them wide, calling attention to her nudity. "Don't be shy, Berl. Make yourself comfortable."

"I'm not sure that's appropriate," he mumbled.

Minerva shook her head and rearranged her chair so that it faced his. Then she stared into his eyes.

"I thought I would face this all alone," she said. "I was okay. I thought I was okay with it. But now you're here. And I think I'm more okay with it."

"Okay with it? Okay with what exactly? Quitting your job?"

"No. I'm not okay with that. I didn't want to do that. I had no choice."

"No choice?"

"I was not going to lie. I couldn't."

"Lie about what?"

"Lie about their fortunes. Or my fortune. Or yours."

It was hard for Berl to study her. Her breasts were small and perky, with perfect, brown areolae. Sweat-soaked strands of dark peach fuzz ran above and below her pooling navel. She was slender and slightly muscular. The front of her Day-Glo yellow G-string was now more yellow than Day-Glo yellow, because it had soaked through. He thought he had even caught the scent of her sex.

The heat made Berl sweat.

Minerva made his teeth sweat.

"Take yours off," she said, her green eyes never leaving his.

Berl held her gaze.

He removed his shirt and then used it to wipe the perspiration away from his brow.

"Now we're both skins," Minerva said.

"Skins?"

"Shirts and skins. The way the boys used to split up in teams to play."

Berl remembered. "Are we on the same team?"

"We're on the only team now, *gringo*. All of us. Every living thing."

"Berl, *please*. Please call me Berl. What do you mean, 'same team?'"

"*El fin viene*. We're all going to die."

"*Die*. In the philosophical sense? Or in the abstract future tense?"

Minerva studied him. His face, his blue eyes. His chest. His broad shoulders. "Death is not abstract," she corrected. "In the soon sense or in the soon tense."

"Why did you quit working at the China Palace?" Berl inquired.

"I told you already. I wasn't going to lie. Take off the rest. Please."

Berl was gawking at Minerva, and she knew it. She had to be at least ten years younger than him. And she was hiding very little. Except —*what was it E. E. Cummings called it?* The "shocking fuzz of your electric fur." But she probably shaved that—if she could. It might be hard for her to hold a razor with her—it might be difficult.

The shocking feel of her electric pudenda.

"It doesn't really matter now," Minerva said. "But I'll tell you everything. Just take off your pants."

Berl pulled off his shoes and socks and then removed his trousers, folding them neatly and stacking them on his shoes. He was still put together well for a man approaching forty. His boxers were light blue cotton and soaked with sweat. He sat back down.

Berl focused on a spot just beneath Minerva's sweaty left breast. Just below the alluring curve, he could make out the delicate beat of her heart. It was a rhythmic tremor in her glistening perspiration.

He was suddenly erect.

They stood up simultaneously and began to kiss. Berl leaned down to run his lips and tongue over her breasts. Minerva slid her cleft hand into his boxer shorts and seized his manhood.

They made love on the cracked concrete of the back porch.

She hadn't shaved.

Still completely nude, they were back in their chairs, which they'd moved so they were sitting side by side and facing the Rio. Every caress seemed new. There were no wasted gestures.

Minerva stared at Berl, her green eyes gentle and sparkling. She squeezed his normal hand in hers and turned back to the river. Berl squeezed one of her thumbs in return. He was seized by an unexpected silliness.

"It had been a while," he said. "Wow."

"For me, too," Minerva replied. "It was nice."

"Yes, incredible. *Increíble*. Is that the right word? I feel giddy. It's embarrassing. It's embarrassing to feel so..."

"*Contenta. Muy contenta.*"

"*Sí.*"

"It's the way I wanted to feel," Minerva said. "I just didn't know it."

Berl raised his arms and clasped his hands behind his head. "We waste a lot of time, don't we?"

"Yes," Minerva replied. "We do. Do you have anybody? Close, I mean?"

"No.

"Do you have any children?"

"No. You?"

"No."

"That's hard to believe."

"Is it?" Minerva turned to Berl and smiled. "Thank you."

She turned back to the Rio and leaned forward, taking a deep breath. "Oh, *mi nuevo amor*," she continued. "Now for why. Why we are here. Do you still want to know?"

Berl ran the fingertips of his right hand down and back up Minerva's spine and then traced a shoulder blade. "Yes," he said.

"I may have lied to you," Minerva replied. "I don't know if I really wanted to talk about it or think about it before. But you're here now, and I don't mind. It won't matter anyway. Are you sure?"

"Yes," Berl repeated. "It's my job."

Minerva smiled.

"I have visions," she said.

"Visions?"

"Visions. I see things ahead, in front. I see things in front of some people. Not all, but many people. Many customers of the China Palace. At first, I was just making the fortune cookies with translated sayings from the store-bought kind. But then I started thinking up my own. I didn't know exactly what was happening or what I was doing or how I was doing it, but I remember when I realized. *Un día guardado es un día Ganado. Visite a un médico con regularidad.* I wrote it in a cookie for a man and woman who had come to eat. They were married. 'A day saved is a day earned. Visit a doctor regularly.' That's good advice for anyone, yes? But the couple came back a few days later. The man had been experiencing heart palpitations and was on the verge of having a heart attack. He went to see a doctor, and the doctor caught it. The doctor gave the man medicine and put him on a special regimen. They came back and said I saved his life."

Minerva took Berl's hand again and continued.

"It started like that. I was not sure it was true. I started to look over the customers when they came in, before they ordered. Not all of them carried signs of what was in front of them—what could come. Those customers got the normal messages, the typical stuff."

"Catch-alls."

"Yes. Catch-alls. But some. I saw something ahead of them. In front of them. It wasn't always bad. I wrote about it and placed it in their cookies."

"*Deus ex crustulum.*"

"What is that?"

"It's Latin," Berl said, grinning. "It means 'God in the cookie.'"

Minerva balled her thumbs and punched his shoulder playfully.

"Ow."

"I'm not God, *pendejo*," Minerva said. "Or a goddess. God is not even God. And he's definitely not me. I am only me." She grinned, but it faded quickly.

"The other day," she continued, "I stopped seeing anything different. What was in front of every customer was the same. No customer's future was different from any other. All the patrons of the China Palace had one future, the same future. And it was also the owners' future. And it was also my future. So, what was the point? Why keep making the cookies? It would only be lies."

"And you still see it, this future?"

"Yes.

"Are you afraid?"

"I was, yes. But now... I thought I would face it alone. But I am glad you came here. I am happy that I am not alone."

"No. You're not alone. But we're practically strangers."

"That may be what I like about it the most. No history. *Sin equipaje*. No baggage. *Como primitivos*."

Berl waited for her to translate.

"Like primitives," Minerva said. "The last man and the last woman will be the same as the first man and the first woman. Naked and afraid. Worried about what will happen next. But not alone."

"I like that," Berl replied.

Minerva smiled. "Do you like me?"

"I do."

"Do you love me?"

"I think I might. As much as anyone can love a stranger, I suppose. Is it really over? Is everything really ending?"

Minerva's eyes softened, and she nodded once. Berl lowered his gaze momentarily and then met Minerva's again. "Of course," Berl continued. "Of course, I love you."

"I think I might love you, too," she said. "There's no better way to spend the time we have left. *Así debería haber sido todo el tiempo.*"

Berl smiled and waited.

"That's the way it should have been all along," Minerva translated. "For all of us."

"*Estoy acuerdo,*" he said. "I agree."

"*Estoy de acuerdo, mi amor. Estoy de acuerdo.*"

"Oh, right. Right. I was close."

———

When the moment came, Berl and Minerva were sitting in their chairs, holding hands, not a stitch of clothing between them.

Berl was so full he thought he might burst. Full of life and happiness, and, strangely, hope. Even at the end. Even in the face of what would come.

Minerva told Berl that it was funny that he was the one who appeared at her mother's door. That she had always identified with Rudolph the Red-Nosed Reindeer. That Rudolph was, like her, different. A freak. Minerva felt that they had played a similar role, and she felt a kinship.

"But you don't have a red nose," Berl teased.

"No," Minerva responded, smiling. "But I do have red lobster claws." She snapped her opposable thumbs together like pincers and they both laughed.

Then they kissed.

"You made me think of Rudolph," she continued. "After I really hadn't in a long time. It makes me feel good. And now I've fallen in love, like in all the best stories. It's a happy ending. And not one I ever thought I'd have."

"Me, either," Berl said. "It does feel good."

The clouds piled up quickly, then. From the south. Berl and Minerva hardly noticed.

The clouds rose, expanded and turned above the Rio Grande.

The clouds roiled and burst, noiselessly peeling back and separating into colossal, rising wisps. Darkness was revealed and a cool void began rushing in.

The atmosphere was no longer in congress with the Earth.

As Minerva and Berl stared into each other's eyes, the blue sky evaporated into space.

Blackness descended.

And cold silence.

three
tarry tornado

Once a college football player myself, I never thought the Texas football state of mind was tethered to any practical reality... "Tarry Tornado" is like a ghostly spider probing the gossamer hinterland of the Lone Star football psyche.

--**David Robledo**, Fulbright STEM-H research specialist and Faculty Affiliate with the Institute for Coastal Adaptation & Resilience at Old Dominion University

IT'S A STRANGE ACCOUNTING, memory.

The experiences we remember, the moments we forget. The details we miss.

What mercifully fades or fortuitously dissipates in our cerebral ether; or what wrangles us endlessly and denies us peace. Psychological debits and credits that keep us in the red or black, and ultimately tally who we are or what we've become.

Most folks don't sweat the bookkeeping or collect their receipts and pay little heed to their own stats. But some track every dime. I was one of the former until July 26, 1999.

I remembered Clifton Baird vividly.

I'd all but forgotten Coby Nettles.

On a sunny Saturday morning one week earlier, I was cruising the county roads around my hometown, Tarry, Texas, south of Stephenville. I'd been with the Erath County Sheriff's Department for a little over a year and, before that, the Walker County Sheriff's Department in Huntsville for six years. I had a wife, Maria, and two kids: Barret, in the first grade, and Brittany, in kindergarten. Maria and I were looking to leave our small home in Stephenville and get a place in the country. Windshield time on patrol was useful on that front; I could scout out promising possibilities for a move while keeping an eye on the rural communities in the area, killing two birds with one stone.

I'd gone to school in Tarry and had a sort of love/hate relationship with the place. When I was young, I couldn't wait to get out. Now, I liked the idea of raising my kids in a town where everyone knew everyone else, and folks could still leave their front doors unlocked. I may also have grown a little nostalgic.

My senior year at Tarry, I'd received some all-state buzz (in retrospect, unwarranted), and I accepted a walk-on opportunity to play football at Sam Houston State University. I attended a year on my own nickel and then earned a ride. In high school, I'd played running back. At SHSU, I played slot back, returned kickoffs, and so forth, until my junior year, when I tore up my knee. Still, I finished college and got my degree. Football had been a means to an end. I'd never had illusions of going pro; I was plenty quick, but not big enough.

Saturday mornings in Erath County were usually quiet and, by lunch, I'd wandered out on State Highway 6 and was coming up on an unincorporated community known as Clairette. It was just a speck on the map, and there was absolutely nowhere to eat. It was practically a ghost town.

I passed an old white van, well off the shoulder on the other side of the road, and noticed the driver's side window was rolled down. It being July in Texas, this wasn't entirely worthy of my notice, but there was a buzzard on the ground just below the door. I decided to pull over and investigate, thinking maybe the driver was sleeping one off and the buzzard was simply getting ahead of itself.

The moment I stepped out of the cruiser's air-conditioning, I knew I was wrong. The reek of death assaulted my nostrils like smelling salts, and I spotted two more buzzards in the tall grass on my side of the road a quarter of a mile back.

As I approached the van, the nearest buzzard took off. The odor got stouter, and I noticed the flies. They were inside and all around the open driver's side window. They scattered when I took the last few steps and peeked in through the opening.

The driver of the van was as dead as a doornail. His body was draped over the blood-soaked middle console, but there was no damage to the vehicle. The driver was big and thick, with huge shoulders that seemed stuffed into his bloody white t-shirt. The way his torso was positioned, I didn't realize why the center console was so blood-soaked at first. There was also blood on the headliner of the van and the driver's seat headrest.

I walked around to the front of the vehicle and spotted the source of all the blood through the windshield.

The driver's head was missing.

My hunger pangs dissipated.

* * *

After I called it in, I continued to examine the site. I inspected the van, and I walked the immediate perimeter. The back of the van contained one green, paint-splattered, eight-foot, fiberglass ladder, one ancient, six-foot wooden ladder, an unrolled, faded orange extension cord and a rusty toolbox.

The driver's head wasn't in the van.

The driver's head wasn't near the van.

There was very little blood on the driver's side door, inside or out. A dozen sagging droplets, maybe.

There was no way he got out this far with that haircut, I thought. "And anybody tried to reach in and slice this big bastard's head off," I said to myself. "There'd be blood everywhere."

An attacker would have left smudges on the door, surely. As big as the victim's neck was, the assailant would have needed a bow saw to finish the job.

I turned my attention to the two buzzards that, by then, had been joined by the third. They were twenty feet off the road, about a hundred yards back.

It didn't make sense, but I had to check.

The walk was short. The heat was already beginning to rise off the patched, rural highway asphalt in blurry waves. It was going to be a hot one. I had soon crowded the buzzards and sent them packing. One looked like it'd taken off with a house sparrow's egg in its beak, but it gulped it down before it was ten feet in the air.

It wasn't a sparrow's egg, of course. It was one of the victim's eyeballs.

I'd found the victim's head. It was lying on its side.

The buzzards had consumed a considerable patch of the van driver's face, leaving portions of his skull and facial musculature visible. The driver's other eye had been picked at, but not removed. The sunny-side cheek was in tatters, but I could tell the big fella still had a prominent jawline before his death.

It still didn't make any sense.

I walked over to the road and looked both ways. There were a few splashes of thick, dry blood about ten feet down, cutting across the median at a diagonal. A couple of sets of tires had driven through them.

It was peculiar, a real head-scratcher. My stomach grumbled.

I hitched up my service belt, which constantly required hitching because it held my gun, an additional gun magazine, a baton, a flashlight, handcuffs, and mace. Some days I felt like going by an athletic supply and purchasing some hip pads, like the kind we used to wear in our football pants. The duty rig felt like it weighed fifty pounds, and then there was the vest. As I wiped the first sweaty brow of the day away with the back of my right hand, I wished I'd donned my hat.

Body in the van, head in the grass, spatter in the road—but, excepting the console—not much blood in or around the vehicle.

"What am I missing?" I mumbled.

I studied the farm road again.

About fifty feet back from the diagonal blood spatter, I saw what looked like the end of a piece of string. Not kite string—pull string, probably nylon. It was lolling in the almost imperceptible breeze right next to a half-filled, two-liter bottle of trucker piss at the edge of a stretch of grass.

I heard the ambulance in the distance and turned back to the decapitated head. I suddenly felt a strange sense of déjà vu.

Had I been there before?

What was different?

What seemed the same?

***

When the EMTs arrived, I took them to the driver's corpse, pointing them in the direction of the head. Then I grabbed some temporary boundary posts, a rubber mallet, and a roll of yellow police tape and roped off the pertinent areas. The department radioed that the crime scene team was on the way.

I took pictures of the blood spatter on the street in case we got any more traffic. I didn't have the equipment or the manpower to block the road off—I would have to divert cars as they appeared.

I walked down to the string.

There was a secure loop in the line (achieved by a double-tied granny knot about sixteen inches back) and it was caked in blood. That's why it wasn't more affected by the light breeze. It was anchored by the drying blood, probably even stuck to some of the grass.

I glanced further down and spotted a wooden fence post that the other end of the string seemed to be attached to.

"Oh," I said.

The post was another fifty feet away, but there was at least a hundred feet of pull string coiled and folded between the post and the end of the line at the edge of the grass.

"Not murder," I continued. "Suicide. *Damn*."

The dead man had tied one end of the pull string off to the post, got into the van and then granny-knotted a noose around his neck. Then he drove away as fast as he could. When the speeding van reached the end of the slack in the pull string, the loop jerked the man's head off neatly and cleanly. Like a nylon guillotine.

The driver's head cleared the window and bounced across the street and into the grass. The van eventually came to a stop off the road after the headless driver's right foot slipped off the gas pedal. The vehicle rolled the extra hundred yards on its own.

When back-up arrived, I brought them up to speed and told them I had to get food. As I turned and started walking to my cruiser, I heard one of the EMTs say, "We have a winner!"

I kept walking.

"Found a money clip in his back pocket," he continued. "His license was tucked in with a few bills."

"Who's Mr. Potato?" the other EMT inquired.

"Clifton Baird."

I stopped and turned. "Clifton Baird," I said. "It says Clifton Baird on his license?"

"Yep."

"What year was he born?"

"1964."

"Shit," I replied. "You're kidding."

"Nope."

Clifton Baird. *The Tarry Tornado.*

Baird had been a couple of years ahead of me in school, and he was the complete package. He was a tank that ran like a gazelle. A widely coveted blue-chipper. He could outrun any of us, but he often went out of his way to run over us. He wasn't a bully in the traditional sense, and I don't think he ran at us with any animosity. He just thought it was funny.

He was a man-child in late elementary school and a full-grown man in junior high. A lot of the older boys—especially the so-called "studs" —tried to pick on Baird at one time or another; it never went well. Particularly for them. Girls and women twice Baird's age hit on him.

The younger kids, including me, couldn't really relate. He seemed more like a figure from Greek mythology. He was enormous. He was too physically mature. Later, in high school, he led Tarry to three state championships in football during his freshman, sophomore, and junior seasons. And, despite the fact that he was a stand-up start, he never lost the one-hundred-yard or one-hundred-meter dash at a junior high or high school track meet (as I recall, the transition from yards to meters occurred between junior high and high school). Baird could outrun most of our teammates backwards—*backpedaling*. He was the stuff of legend. But he was also just a big, goofy country boy. We realized that when we started to catch up with him in size. He'd just had a crazy head start.

As I contemplated his demise, it occurred to me that we had all forgotten that sometimes. Maybe our impressions and expectations of him had been unfair, if not outright wrong.

Still, Baird didn't seem to have a care in the world until his senior year.

I was a sophomore and on the JV football squad. Since we weren't a big school and didn't have a big program, the JV often played dummy defense for the first team varsity offense. To be fair, we all actually practiced together, and Baird was a bulldozer amongst Tonka toys. He didn't show off, but he didn't pull up either. Our head coach seemed to approve. He operated under the assumption that it might toughen us up.

In retrospect, I think he was wrong. I remember kids crying during practice. Young men were called out and embarrassed. Players were shamed. Today they call it "toxic masculinity". Back then they called it football.

In the course of one late two-a-day, full-pad practice before school started his senior year, Baird got the handoff on a veer call and took off just outside a good lean from the right tackle. Unfortunately, however, a small, over-achieving, dummy-defense linebacker named Coby Nettles recognized the play, tripped as he cleared the defensive end, and collided head first with one of Baird's piston-like knees. It struck Nettles square in the crown of his helmet.

There was a sickening crack, and Coby Nettles collapsed like a sack of potatoes. He was unconscious and, as players gathered round, an assistant coach sprinted to the office and called the county's local fire station EMT. When Nettles came to, he started puking, but he couldn't turn his head. He almost drowned in his own vomit. He started coughing and choking and the coaches turned him sideways.

The image was horrific. Nettles' head seemed to stretch away from his shoulders at an impossible angle. Other players started puking as well.

Practice ended and the rest of the two-a-days scheduled that preseason were canceled. There were only three days of work-outs left anyway.

Baird was visibly distraught.

The gruesome collision hadn't been intentional, but it got to him. In a town the size of Tarry—as I said—everybody knew everybody. Baird and Nettles hadn't been best buddies, but they were friendly. Just like Baird and I. We'd been around each other all our lives. Pee-Wee football, T-ball, Little League Baseball, Pony League. The Tarry Queen burger shop. The Tarry Tundra snow cone stand. The Future Farmers of America (FFA). The Fellowship of Christian Athletes (FCA). Vo-Ag. We all saw each other every day at school; we all saw each other at the usual places over the summer.

What happened to Nettles affected Baird. The coaches tried to tell him it wasn't his fault, but he had problems shaking it. He sat through pep talk after pep talk, nodding his head, smiling obligatorily and flashing facsimiles of that air of gridiron invincibility, seemingly ready to smash through the dozens of walls of hapless defenders he would shred his senior season.

As I looked back, however, I suddenly recalled him gritting his teeth a lot. And he didn't run as recklessly as he had before, or at least not with the same ferocity. So, that final championship season never happened.

The Tarry Tigers went into the 1984 season ranked number one in the 3A division. There was even a big picture of Baird on the District

15AAA page of Dave Campbell's *Texas Football* magazine. Our coaches answered questions about a four-peat in every interview, but they were modest and conspicuously low-key. They knew Baird was struggling.

Baird didn't run over anyone that season. He simply ran away from tacklers. It was electrifying and fun to watch, but he no longer presented a one-two punch. It wasn't noticeable at first, but, especially later, it was glaring.

Our coaches began to berate him, but to no effect. We only made it to the quarterfinals that year, and Coby Nettles never returned to classes. He was home-schooled the rest of his junior year and the entirety of his senior year. He later earned a GED, but never recovered enough to get a job or have a normal life. And around town, very few people even talked about it. Nettles' accident had spooked the school's star player and hamstrung the Golden Goose. The chief topic of interest regarding the incident had only been how much and how long it would affect the team. And, by proxy, the town.

Baird's scholarship offers thinned out after his underwhelming senior season, but he still found himself suiting up for Texas A&M. He had some great games against players his own size and seemed to regain what most football coaches refer to as a mean streak. Getting away from Tarry definitely helped.

Baird was drafted in the fifth round by the New Orleans Saints. It was a consensus opinion that the Saints sucked back then, but it was still exciting to see a guy we had suited up with playing on Sundays. He didn't last long. Only two seasons. Rumors suggested that he had a substance abuse problem.

After the pros, Baird kicked around in New Orleans and then started roughnecking in Midland. He was out there for a while but, a few years ago, his grandmother died in Clairette. She had left him her place.

I had heard that he had returned and lived there, but that he also kept to himself. I respected that. People in small towns seem to have no sense of how much their expectations can weigh on their kids. I assumed

Baird just wanted to keep a low profile. But I also learned that he'd never married or had kids. That was a surprise.

Most of the bona fide old high school football heroes and would-be heroes that I knew could hardly wait. Their time in the sun gone and largely forgotten, there was nothing they looked forward to as much as handing the ball off to the next generation. It was practically considered a civic duty, especially in Texas. But sometimes existence jukes you with a hip or head fake so effective that you watch the rest of the play on your ass. Sometimes circumstances make you, well... more circumspect. Like my knee at SHSU. Like Baird's collision with Nettles.

Things didn't go according to plan. Things changed.

I was okay with it. But what if I hadn't been?

Baird had further to fall. What if he had put all his eggs in one basket?

For all I knew, Baird only had one basket. And maybe just one egg.

Another deputy and I went out to examine Baird's place after his death. The crime scene evidence clearly suggested suicide, but we still had to investigate.

The old house was located just off a main farm road and had a sand-stone block exterior with a few pieces of petrified wood mixed in here and there. I had always liked those old mish-mashes. They looked home-made and more pioneer. The house was mostly empty, and it didn't look like Baird had done much in the way of upgrades since he inherited the place. The aging hardwood floor was warped in spots and there were cracks in some of the crumbling plaster walls. A dated box TV/VCR set in the living room was on and televising an old football game. And there was an old wheelchair sitting in front of it.

I turned the TV off. We assumed the wheelchair had belonged to Baird's grandmother.

The faucet in the kitchen sink had a slow drip, but the dishes in the yellowing plastic dish drainer next to it had been hand-washed, stacked neatly, and were dry. There was a jug of relatively fresh milk and a jar of homemade plum jelly in the fridge. Half a loaf of white bread and a jar of peanut butter were in the pantry. Not much clutter. Baird's bed was even made.

We also noticed sheets and a pillow on a long, faux antique couch. It looked like Baird had been sleeping in the living room and sometimes watched TV in the wheelchair. At the foot of the TV, there were two shoeboxes full of VHS cassettes. They were labeled with dates and opponent names: December 10, 1982—Gilmer Buckeyes; September 18, 1981—Glen Rose Tigers; September 11, 1981—Comanche Indians, November 20, 1981—Refugio Bobcats; and so on. Some nights Baird must have sat up and watched reruns of his high school games.

It saddened me. In fact, it suddenly seemed intensely depressing.

I had played in some of those games and stood on the sidelines for some of the others. It occurred to me that what Baird had had back then was maybe the most he'd ever have. Or all he believed he'd had.

Was that why he had done it?

His suicide was not spontaneous. The string, the post—and everything staged on a long stretch of straight country road. He had put some thought into it.

Out on the back porch, on a large wooden cable spool that was lying on its side, we found a cracked bong. A half-smoked joint rested in an ashtray. Under the bong was a piece of white notebook paper, folded in half. Baird had used the large, wooden cable spool for a table. It was surrounded by a few heavy-duty camp chairs in various stages of collapse. I retrieved the folded paper from underneath the bong and examined it.

Dear Coby,
Please leave me be. I'm sorry for what I did. I'm sorry for how things turned out. I didn't mean anything.
Cliff

The pen used to write the letter wasn't on the makeshift, round table, but the note looked recent. I wondered if Coby Nettles was still living in the area.

I called the department and spoke with dispatch. Dispatch informed me that Coby had lived in the area but passed away two years earlier.

"Baird must have been losing it," I said.

I had a friend at the county Medical Examiner's office, and he knew that I had been acquainted with Baird, so he rang me after the autopsy.

"Your boy was taking a beating," he said. "*Before* the haircut."

"Is that right?" I replied. "Do tell."

"He was covered with fading and fresh contusions, especially the lower extremities. Shins, knees, ankles."

"What do you make of that? You saying someone worked him over? *In Clairette?*"

"Guy that big? I don't know. With no defensive bruises or cuts, I doubt it. But he was an aging Clydesdale, otherwise. Maybe he was just clumsy."

"I certainly don't remember that about him," I said.

"Just letting you know."

"It's strange."

"Yep."

I thought back for a moment to our examination of Baird's place. I didn't remember any obvious trip hazards. Then again, he was a stoner. But that didn't make everything make sense. In my somewhat limited experience with potheads, I knew they didn't usually hit the bong and start two-stepping around their living rooms by themselves. They usually turned on the TV and curled up on the couch with a stale bag of Doritos. The VCR tapes made more sense, but the bruises?

Was he back on Gulliver duty? *Were the Lilliputians in Tarry still tilting at lost championship trophies?*

Baird's funeral was the following Wednesday. There were lots of familiar faces there, including classmates and old-timers. People that remembered Baird for what he had been: the Tarry Tornado, the legend.

Baird's ex-girlfriend, Heidi Johnson—now Heidi Glanville—was in attendance, and she was crying. She'd been in Nettles' class. When she saw me, she gave me a big hug. "I can't believe it," she said.

"Me neither."

"We need to talk after," she added, regarding me with weary eyes.

I nodded.

Three former teammates showed up: Ricky "Bigsy" Briggs, Trent "Tarzan" Sarvis, and Kevin "Coop" Cooper. Bigsy had been an all-district offensive tackle, Tarzan had been an all-region tight end, and Coop had played center. Bigsy and Coop had both had hands in Baird's record-breaking yardage totals, and Tarzan was consistently wide open because opposing defenses stacked the line to stop Baird. Bigsy had done some blocking for me, too, and his nickname suited him. The halfback veer to his side was almost always money. We immediately assumed our locker room lingo.

"As I live and breathe," Bigsy said. "Fast Lane, *Lane Fisher*... How's it hanging, son?"

"Ask your wife," I said.

"We're divorced," he remarked, grinning.

"Well, tell her to stop calling me," I replied.

Briggs laughed, and Tarzan hugged me. "You cut your hair, Tarzan," I observed.

"You can still slap my ass," he smiled.

I pushed Tarzan away playfully. "Doing the grown-up stuff," he continued.

"I can't hold that against you," I answered. "That shit's going around."

"Not for me," said Coop. "Ain't found the right one for my seed."

"I thought for sure you'd get hitched up with Savannah Kentry," Bigsy said. "I thought it was a done deal."

"She found the Lord at Abilene Christian," Coop replied. "And he's hung like a whale."

"The original Moby Dick," Tarzan quipped, and people started looking over. We toned down our snickers immediately.

"I can't believe Baird eighty-sixed himself," Coop remarked, out of the side of his mouth, when we had reassumed the proper level of solemnity.

"I heard you found him," Tarzan said.

I shrugged my shoulders. "I did. I didn't realize it at first, but yeah. It was a shock."

"It doesn't even seem real," Bigsy replied. "Dude was a monster truck. Unstoppable."

"Except by his own bad self," Coop answered. "It was crazy what happened."

"The other day," Tarzan asked, "or that last day of two-a-days back in '83?"

No one answered.

The service was short and sweet. I reacquainted myself with a lot of old Tarry and shook several leathery hands. The school district had dropped down to the 2A classification. More and more old-timers and fewer and fewer youth. It was the way of things in small-town Texas.

A secondary coach I hardly remembered and wouldn't have remembered if I hadn't seen his face, was a nice surprise. "Coach Leonard," I said, smiling.

His hair was long, white, and mildly unkempt, but he was still lean and wiry. And he had the palest green eyes I'd ever seen. I didn't remember them.

"*Lynyrd Skynyrd*," Bigsy chimed in, reaching out to shake Coach Leonard's hand. "Where's your old boss?

"I lost track," Coach Leonard said. "I got out of coaching not long after you boys graduated."

"What you been doing with yourself?"

"Just teaching. Granbury. About to retire."

"Social studies?"

"History, now."

"You look good."

"You're too kind, Bigs. And it's truly a sad day."

"It is," Tarzan agreed.

"We put too much on him," Coach Leonard admitted. "All of us."

"We did," I said. "We really did."

We chatted with Coach Leonard for a bit and then bid him farewell. Bigsy was headed back to Fort Worth, Tarzan to Dallas, and Coop to Decatur. Since it was more or less on all of their ways back, we agreed to meet for lunch in Stephenville.

Heidi was waiting next to her car. She'd driven in from Abilene, where she and her husband ran a Southwestern décor furniture store.

"I heard you've been with the Sheriff's department for a while," Heidi said. "I didn't know who I should talk to. Or who I should tell what."

"What's wrong?"

She hesitated.

"I have to say something," she said. "But I don't know how it will sound. It sounded crazy to me. That's why I haven't talked to anybody yet."

"Okay," I responded. "It's okay. What's on your mind?"

"Cliff. *Baird*. I don't know... I think... *I think he was seeing things.*" Heidi looked around and then leaned in. "I thought he was confused at first, or maybe just making things up. We hadn't stayed close over the years, but we were still friends. And I thought maybe he was lonely and being stupid, maybe trying to rekindle something by getting me to come out."

"Okay," I said. "Lame, maybe." I remembered the stack of VCR tapes under the TV/VCR. "It turns out he was human, like the rest of us. It happens. What did he say?"

"It's crazy, I know. But he talked a lot about Coby. He said that—*he claimed*—Coby was there."

"Here? Nettles? He said Nettles was here? After he passed away?"

Heidi's eyes welled up, and she wiped them with the back of one of her long, slender wrists. "That's what he said. I thought he might be going crazy. It didn't make sense, right? But now. Oh, now. Now I don't know."

"It's definitely strange," I replied.

"I know what it sounds like," Heidi said. "I know it's crazy. But I had to tell somebody."

"What did Baird say, specifically? Do you remember?"

"He said he was back. Coby. One time when we were on the phone, he said he had to go. He said Coby had come in the room. It was just a week or so ago."

"That sounds crazy."

"Yeah. Completely. But he believed it."

"Did he say anything else?"

"I don't know if it had anything to do with him killing himself or not. But he was scared, Lane. I mean, Deputy Fisher. He was really scared."

"Lane is fine. But you know Coby died a couple of years back."

"Yes. Of course. And it was bad."

"Bad?"

"His mom was his caretaker. Full-time. Just her and him after Coby's dad passed. Just her and him out in the country off Meeker's Gap Road. There was nobody else. And when she died, Lane... when she died, Coby starved to death. *In his wheelchair.*"

"Oh, my God."

"He died out there all alone. They didn't find him for weeks. It was a double funeral. And I was one of the few who showed up. It was horrible, but nobody cared. They had no interest in dredging up that stuff, especially so close to two-a-days starting. They didn't want it to get in the players' heads."

Heidi gave me her card and told me to call if she could help. On the way to Stephenville, I couldn't get Coby out of my head. Or Mrs. Nettles. I think she might have been a den mother for our Cub Scout troop when I was younger. And Coby. What a terrible way to go.

After Coby left and Baird graduated, I hadn't given either of them much thought. I was too concerned about my own high school football legend—as lackluster as it was compared to Baird's. Football season, off-season, two-a-days. And basketball and track sprinkled in between. I didn't hear mention of Coby again for years. But it was always a short subject.

I recalled the old farts I'd seen at the funeral. Four state championships in a row would have been a state record.

Had the Nettles family become pariahs after the accident? Had the town blamed the Nettles family for the "letdown" of Baird's senior year?

I noticed my shoulders and biceps had tightened and my hold on the steering wheel of the cruiser was a death grip. My teeth were clenched.

I slowed down and eased up, took a deep breath, and exhaled. Then I dialed Heidi on my flip-phone.

She was as eager to talk as I was.

"I keep thinking back," Heidi said. "Before."

"Before what happened to Nettles," I replied, remembering.

"Yes," Heidi said. "Yes. It was terrible—for Coby and his family most of all. Cliff, too. He was never the same."

"I remember that." I recalled it very clearly.

"He was so fun-loving. So carefree."

"He had the world on a string," I observed. "But it changed on him real fast."

"I just still can't believe it. It was an accident. But I don't think he ever forgave himself."

"I think you're right."

"He was never the same," Heidi continued. "Not as long as I was around."

"I heard a crazy rumor that they were thinking about putting a billboard up a few years back," I said. "Announcing to the world that the town was the 'Home of the Tarry Tornado.'"

"Yes. I heard that, too. It didn't go anywhere. Cliff wanted nothing to do with it. In fact, he talked about suing the town if it went forward."

"Really?"

"Yes. And that was before Coby started coming around."

Bigsy and the others were waiting at a hamburger joint on the Erath County square in Stephenville when I arrived. They already had a table. I told them about the town's plan for Baird's commemorative billboard and they were surprised.

"Baird wasn't Earl Campbell," Coop said. "He had his day, and I was privileged to witness it. For sure. But he flamed out, plain and simple. I hate it. But that's what happened."

"It wouldn't have happened," Bigsy said. "It was just a freak accident."

"It was," Tarzan agreed. "But do you remember all that shit they laid on him—on all of us? The Zig Ziglar bullshit? The 'I'm okay, you're okay' crap?"

"It helped some of our teammates," I said. "They bought in."

"That's my point," Tarzan replied flatly. "They were sold short. We were sold short. Positive thinking can't give you what Baird had. You can't fake it or fool anyone but yourself... and the power of positive thinking can't cure a broken neck, either."

"I know that," I said. "I couldn't agree more. But they got more out of some of our teammates than I ever thought was possible. Remember the Kray brothers? The coaches couldn't make 'em mean, but they were functional defensive ends for a while. The one couldn't do three push-ups and the other probably had a 6.8 forty time, at best. But they were serviceable. They even managed to get themselves prom dates—maybe even girlfriends."

"It's true," Bigsy said. "They'd probably still be virgins without old Zig."

"I *zagged*," Tarzan scoffed. "You've either got it or you don't. They didn't have it. They're lucky they even survived. Remember that bull-in-the-ring bullshit, your goddamn head on a swivel? The coaches never bore down on them. They knew better. They bore down on Baird like he was Atlas or something... and just fluffed most of our teammates up.

It was all smoke and mirrors. And when the *Friday Night Lights* routine was finally over, they were back to being what they had been all along—what they would be for the rest of their lives. *Normal.* Mediocre. Or worse—*ask Nettles.*"

Coop finally spoke. "I ain't gonna lie," he said. "They had me believing. It was all ridiculous, of course. But it was their job, and they certainly weren't doing anything but carrying water for the town. It's like that in every town, at every high school. The whole country is just a pep rally and a big game, every four years. It's just what we do."

When a waitress finally came over, we told her to come back around in a few minutes.

"That's heavy," Tarzan remarked.

"And true," I said. "I never thought of it that way. But it's true."

"So, what?" Tarzan replied. "Nettles was just collateral damage? Baird was just a talented dud?"

We all sat silent for a moment.

Bigsy nodded his head. "I know it's easy for us to say, because we have lives. But if the most important thing you accomplish in your whole life is in high school, I feel sorry for you. There's a lotta living to do after that. And, hopefully, you have something more important to accomplish and look forward to. That's not how the coaches or the town sold it, but they were all full of shit."

We skipped the lunch, exchanged handshakes and hugs, and vowed to get together soon. We were all sincere, but I doubted it would happen. As I said, existence had a way of juking you—juking all of us.

I decided to head back out to Clairette.

Baird had no siblings, no children and no will, and I wondered what would happen to the house. When I pulled back up, the intermittent blocks of petrified wood shimmered in the sun like diamonds. Heidi told me Baird left a spare key under a rusted-out spittoon next to the front stoop. I grabbed it and re-entered the house.

The TV was on again. But the wheelchair wasn't in front of it.

I walked over to turn the television off and recognized a play. It was

Baird, big number 49—I hadn't thought about his jersey number until then. Mine was 19. It looked like a game against Stephenville, preseason maybe. Stephenville was 4A back then, a much bigger school than Tarry. And there was Baird, blasting through the line, shedding linebackers, crumpling safeties. It was at least an eighty-yard run. The sound on the old VHS cassette was terrible, but I could hear the crowd cheering—and that's when one of the wheelchair's metal footrests clipped my left ankle and knocked me over.

Someone was in the house. I grimaced in pain but turned onto my side and reached for my firearm. The wheelchair footrests slammed into the center of my spine, and I wailed.

Breathing heavily, I rolled over flat on my back. The wheelchair was occupied by a twisted, emaciated form that I hardly recognized. His eyes were sunken and dark, and he wheezed as his shallow breath passed though cracked lips and a drawn-up mouth.

"Coby," I said.

And then I passed out.

When I came to, the TV was back on, and the empty wheelchair was sitting next to me. I felt like somebody had hit me in the back with a bat, so I laid there for a minute. For once, I wished I'd have worn my bullet-proof vest.

I wasn't sure what exactly had happened, or maybe I just couldn't, or wouldn't, allow myself to believe what had happened. Or maybe the whole thing was a figment of my imagination.

I sat up and used the arm of the wheelchair to stand. I was a little shaky. I decided I might need an ice bath when I got home.

Except for me, the house was vacant.

My assailant was gone. Or invisible.

I was undecided on the matter. I preferred the former explanation to the latter, but I suspected my preference was more wishful than honest or relevant. A wheelchair had knocked my feet out from under me. A crippled, dead classmate had *tackled* me in a wheelchair.

It wouldn't make it into my report.

I checked the bedroom and the back porch to make sure the place was empty. Then I limped through the living area, pausing when I heard a noise in the small kitchen. I couldn't make out who or what was behind the sound, but I didn't try for very long. A *Tarry Testament* yearbook was laid on the nearest Formica countertop.

I examined it.

It was Baird's, from 1981. It was open to the blank pages in the back and it looked like everybody in the high school at that time—teachers, coaches, and students—had tried to sign it. The right-hand page had comments from both me and Nettles. Mine was bland. "Looking forward to playing ball with you again next year," I wrote. I'd tried to be cool instead of gushing. I had, after all, considered myself the heir apparent.

Nettles had poured it on thick. "You're a legend, Cliff. It's exciting to know you and great to be your teammate. Can't wait til next season!"

I held on to those comments and looked back.

I remembered that play, that moment, that collision—it was like the way people always described a car wreck after the fact. It happened in slow motion.

Everything about that instant had moved in slow motion, for all of us and for the whole town. But it never really ended for Baird or Nettles. One was crippled and eventually starved to death. The other took his own life.

I'd just been lucky. It had been a cakewalk for me. But Baird.

And worse, Nettles.

There was no way to square it. Not even Baird's suicide was enough. The whole town had failed Coby Nettles and Clifton Baird. The whole damn culture. There was no way to make it right.

Coby," I said. "*Coby*. Are you here?"

There was no answer.

"Nettles? It's me. Lane Fisher."

More nothing.

"Coby, if you're here... or you're somewhere. Hey, man. Cliff's gone. And he was sorry. *Real sorry*. And I'm sorry. I'm really sorry."

I turned off the TV and ejected the VHS tape. I put the tape in one of the shoeboxes and replaced the lids on both, stacking them neatly in front of the TV. I put the key back under the spittoon and then I left.

As I drove away, it occurred to me that very little had changed.

Here they were—here we were—all these years later.

Still bouncing off each other, still colliding.

And for what?

That's the thing about Greek myths, mythology, and football legends. We all grow up hearing the stories. In small towns like Tarry they become inviolate. A code almost.

As if they were worth dying for.

———

I never told Bigsy, Coop, Tarzan, or Heidi or anybody else about going back to Baird's house. Nobody would have believed me anyway.

I crossed old Tarry off the list of potential communities Maria and I were considering moving our family to, and I didn't even have to explain it. We eventually settled in Granbury.

If he participated in sports, Barret would be a Granbury Pirate instead of a Tarry Tiger. And Brittany would be a Lady Pirate.

Since the move, I've driven by Baird's place dozens of times and, occasionally, after dark. The house is supposed to be vacant, and it looks like the electrical service has been disconnected.

But sometimes when I've passed by at night, I swear I've seen a light emanating from inside the house. A fluid half-glow, like the light of a TV screen.

I've stopped the cruiser and backed up twice, just to make sure.

I've been thinking about going in.

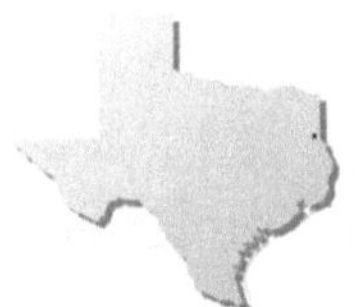

four
recumbent
female nude

This story gets into the mind of a sadistic predator in a way that will turn your stomach. It reminded me of some of Stephen King's darker stories and a little bit of Matt Shaw. Having said that, the story doesn't feel like shock for the sake of shock, which is a problem in many horror stories. It doesn't shy away from the dark subject matter, but it doesn't feel exploitative, either... This story perfectly illustrates the objectification of women... Despite the fact that this story is so disturbing that I had to set it aside a few times before I could finish it, I feel like this is one of the best horror short stories I've read in a long time.

*--***Madison Estes**, *horror writer and editor of* Road Kill: Texas Horror by Texas Writers, Vol. 6.

WHAT WAS LOVE?

Caleb hadn't felt it with another living, breathing, human being. He had experienced carnal desires, yes. Lust. But he didn't confuse them with love and, on the occasions when he had sated his desires, he hadn't done so with, well, living flesh.

He had read up on the subject of love once, though.

Caleb always diligently endeavored to separate himself from the ranks of the mis- and uninformed, and on the question of love, the theories of matching hypothesis and genetic fitness rang truest to him—but not *for* him. The latter explanation discussed the reasons behind conventional human attraction and coupling; but it didn't address his own, less conventional, libidinal impulses. The former ignored the common wisdom of "opposites attract," which was a profound concept to Caleb. What was more opposite than the living and the dead? Both theories seemed a little simplistic in contemporary terms, and neither applied to Caleb. He felt no kinship with the living. It wasn't their fault —he just wasn't attracted to them.

He loved Frankenstein or, more specifically, the unnamed monster of *Frankenstein*. Nameless, friendless—anathema to the living.

Feared. Hated. Misunderstood.

Caleb felt kinship with the creature the first time he saw it on TV, played by Boris Karloff. He ached for this rudimentary being, felt its frustration, experienced its pain.

His eyes welled up just thinking about it.

And, again, in *Bride of Frankenstein*. Rejection, loneliness. Unimaginable despair. To be the only one of your kind—the first, last and only Mohican—the only other choosing nothingness over sharing your plight. It was beyond heartbreaking. It was soul-crushing—or, perhaps better put—spirit-crushing, especially if you hadn't been born (or reborn, as it were) with a soul.

It was the ultimate affront. An insufferable existential pronouncement. And yet the monster crept on. Caleb was convinced the creature still inhabited the icy climes of the North Pole—what was left of them, that is.

The monster's dilemma became Caleb's passion. Creating a suitable mate. Born dead but living. Not the stuff of B-movie pretenders, but the real deal. The authentic living dead.

Necrophilia had its shabby charms, but Caleb wanted more. Killing women and then having them was not particularly delectable for him. Killing for lust seemed wrong. But killing for companionship this was almost palatable. This, he could almost rationalize.

Victor Frankenstein's method on TV, however, was entirely unsound. When you mixed and matched and cobbled together a corpse —even if you spent hours or days meticulously reconnecting tendons, nerves, arteries and bone tissue—the charges of electricity steadily applied to "jumpstart" life shook the sutures and connections apart. Even if Caleb used pins in the bones, superglue and ten-pound-test fishing line for the stitches.

Caleb needed a whole person. A recently deceased, whole person. White, Black, brown or other, preferably female. And ideally someone he didn't have to murder.

Freshness was key, and this was tricky. Bodies prepared by funeral homes were injected with formaldehyde. It preserved them—he'd lain with two or three. But formaldehyde precluded reanimation. Pure formaldehyde was a highly combustible gas, and the vapor from liquid formaldehyde solution was explosive. Applying electricity to a dead body recently injected with formaldehyde solution was extremely ill-advised.

This severely limited Caleb's pool of candidates. In fact, off the top of his head, only Old Order Mennonites got away with refusing formaldehyde as part of funerary arrangements. Typical Mennonites employed the same funeral homes, morticians, and cemetery services that regular Protestants used. Another exception Caleb had heard about pertained to people living out in the country on family land. If they owned a certain amount of acreage, they could designate a cemetery plot on their property and have their remains interred there, *au naturel* with no preservatives. But how would he go about locating pretty or quasi-pretty girls who lived and had recently died on plots of land large enough for private interment? And how could he gain access?

Caleb's desire provided him with a serious quandary. Where was he going to find a fresh mate that he didn't have to kill?

Maybe he was better off alone, indulging in infrequent, low-hanging —but less than delectable, not to mention forbidden—fruit. It had sustained him thus far.

It just had a terrible aftertaste. And stigma.

Kendra was a teenage runaway. She was stupid and brash. She said as much herself.

Now she sucked off old men at truck stops. But it was better than being brutalized by her stepfather. She didn't know them, and she wasn't sharing a roof with someone who also brutalized her mother. And besides, it never took very long. She was young and pretty, even on bad nights. The oldsters couldn't help themselves. They couldn't hold it. It was like siphoning stale Krazee Stix. Except they tasted like spoiled mayonnaise after a menthol cigarette.

Kendra only worked a few hours a day, a few nights a week, but she had her own apartment and even a dog. She didn't have to spend forty to fifty hours a week tied down to a real job. And her roommate could work the same spots and they could give each other referrals. Plus, they had each other on the side.

Kendra had light skin, natural blonde hair, and prominent cheekbones. She was slender, but less so in the right places. Her roommate was a fuller-figured brunette. A lot of the old truckers liked variety and the illusion of conquest. They wanted to take their masculinity back, jumpstart their libido. They popped a little blue pill an hour before they parked and it "paid off like a slot machine." Kendra could get one off the first time without even removing her halter top. And they'd pay double for a second round, where sometimes she stripped down to her panties. Or she and her roommate would get them off one after another, swapping trucks. Sometimes she even threw on a MAGA hat. Nothing made withering old farts cum like a quasi-teenage girl in a MAGA hat.

Two or three hard swallows, and she was usually done for the evening. Two conquests for the johns, who felt like real men again, and less bitter. It was white-trash lucrative. Once or twice a john had gotten rough, but no worse than her stepdad. The most dangerous thing about the job were the old-school lot lizards. Half of them were meth-heads, and they didn't like the competition.

Kendra didn't smoke and kept her drug use to a minimum. The local junior college sometimes crossed her mind, but mostly she just slept in, goofed around and hit a bar after work. She didn't keep many boyfriends, and she'd never been in love. But it wasn't a problem.

She was getting by.

Patty had had enough of Kendra and her roommate.

Patty had been swallowing trucker paste for twenty years and these "young, candy-ass bitches" were putting a serious dent in her pocketbook.

"Those twats probably don't even know what a pocketbook is," Patty hissed, nursing a stale Budweiser. "I'll show those sluts."

Sure, she could sell her ass down the road in Niggertown. It even paid better, sometimes. But rarely at her age. And she preferred her own kind, and eensie-weensie white-trash trucker dicks, to Mandingo sausage. She practically had to pack a lunch for all the time it took to get some of those bucks off. And they usually rearranged her plumbing. She didn't have the stamina or enthusiasm she used to, and the truckers were her bread and butter. She decided she would have to take matters into her own hands.

Patty had had this one regular, Lonnie, who usually came through once a week. Phoned ahead. He liked to take his girls away from the truck stops, and he had this spot out on a dark, wide county road on the outskirts of town. He called it his "fuck spot." He would pick his girls up at places like Fast Fuel Stop and take them there. Kendra was his new girl, and Patty knew that if she spotted Lonnie's truck at his fuck spot, Kendra was with him.

Even hopped up, Patty knew deep down that it wasn't Kendra's fault. But business was business. The upside of the truck-stop ass trade was that a lot of it ran without pimps. But that could also be the downside. If Patty had a pimp, he would protect their business. The local trucker-suck industry was entirely free market. She had to protect her interests. She had to eliminate the competition or at least send a message.

Yes. She would send a message.

And the next time Lonnie came through, she would be the one slurping his glue. And things could get back to normal.

Caleb felt the stigma attached to necrophilia was wildly unfair.

A Baylor University drop-out in his early forties, Caleb had recently read about an all-American frat boy on the West Coast who had gotten a seven-month probation after humping an unconscious co-ed behind a dumpster. And a New Jersey teenager who actually filmed himself raping an unconscious teenage female and shared the cellphone video of the act via text with his friends, including the caption "When your first time having sex was rape."

A judge in the latter incident determined it was not rape, wondering aloud if it even constituted "sexual assault." The judge noted that the young perpetrator had come from a good family, made good grades, and was even an Eagle Scout. And this simply didn't square with the traditional definition of rape, which, his Honor defined as a sexual assault by a stranger at gunpoint.

Caleb was appalled. He knew if he got caught, it wouldn't matter that he had made pretty good grades and been an Eagle Scout. Or that he never would have filmed one of his conquests, although he knew "conquest" wasn't the right word. "Relations" was a better word. His relations with corpses were no worse than these boys' relations with unconscious, living women. In fact, in Caleb's mind, what those boys did was worse. Corpses were insensate.

"Much worse," he said, as he cased the Fast Fuel Stop station on the outskirts of Big Spring. He knew that some of the girls that worked the back lot were runaways and if he borrowed one, she might never be missed. Which would be ideal.

The wait was the rub. He really didn't want to kill the girl who would become his living dead mate. He might be able to rationalize it, but it set a bad precedent. It was a bad idea. That was probably the real mistake on Frankenstein's monster's part.

Some of those eighteen-wheelers were pretty high off the gravel, though.

Caleb sat up. What if one of the girls fell stepping out and broke her neck? It might be perfect.

No, he thought. Fixing a neck would be almost impossible. Even dead girls needed healthy necks.

"Omigod," Lonnie exclaimed, his neck thrown back, his right hand buried in Kendra's hair.

Kendra was still sucking. Lonnie was empty, but she knew he liked for her to put on a show. She moaned and sucked harder.

"Omigod, little girl. Oh shit. You win. You got me." He loosened his grip on the back of Kendra's head and ran his fingers through her hair.

Kendra released his member and raised her head a smidgen, picking one of Lonnie's public hairs away from her tongue with the index finger of her crank hand.

"Oh, Daddy," she cooed, sitting up. "That was a hot one."

"*Mmm-hmmm*. But you know you don't have to play that way with me, Kay."

"Sorry. Habit, I guess."

"It's alright. It *was* a good one." Lonnie removed a few bills from his short-sleeve shirt pocket and handed them to Kendra. "Would you like a smoke?"

"No. I'm alright, honey."

"You're more than alright. You oughta be on a white-sand beach somewhere, giving young boys heart attacks."

"Maybe someday," Kendra said. "Thanks."

Lonnie lit a cigarette and took a long drag. Then, he left the cigarette in his mouth and used both hands to pull up his trousers and cover himself.

"How come you don't wear underwear?"

"Habit," Lonnie replied, smiling. "I sit on my ass all day in this truck. I don't need no skivvies. They're just something else to creep up my ass or cramp my fruit basket."

"Fruit basket?"

"My banana—and those two Parker County peaches."

Kendra laughed.

"I ain't playin' Kay. Underwear can bruise the goods. 'Specially if you ride around all day as long as me."

"I believe you."

Lonnie took another long drag off his cigarette. Kendra took a drink of her lukewarm Mountain Dew and swished it around through her teeth.

"Kay?"

"Yeah?"

"You know, I got at least half an hour left on the old flagpole."

"Yeah. Wanna go for two?"

"I was thinking of shooting the moon."

"Well, we better get started, Daddy—I mean, *baby*."

"No, Kay. I'm talking about changing it up. I'm talking about screwing the moon."

"Whataya mean?"

"Girl, I like you. You know that."

"Yes."

"Well, I would give you three hundred bucks, up front, to fuck yer ass."

"Baby. You know I don't like the brown."

"I know, I know. I'm just sayin'... five hundred, then. Lemme fuck yer ass."

"*Lonnie.*"

"I know, I know."

Lonnie finished his cigarette and tossed it out the driver's side window.

"You can't fault me for trying," Lonnie continued. "I can't help it. Your ass, Kay, it's a national treasure."

"Aww, thanks Lonnie."

"I mean it, kid. And I was just kidding about the boof-job. I just like talking about it. I have a buddy who says his wife's ass is the tightest pussy he ever had. He carries on and on."

"But her ass isn't a pussy," Kendra said.

"Well, you and I know that, Kay. Of course. I never done that to a woman. Like I said, I just like talking about it."

"You have any juice left?" Kendra replied. "You wanna go for two?"

"Oh, hell. Not tonight, sweetie. You got me good. I'll get you back to the station."

"Okay, baby. That's fine, too."

"You know I like you?"

"I know. I like you, too. And your fruit basket."

Caleb began to wonder what he was doing at Fast Fuel Stop. What were the chances a girl would fall out, or off, of one of the trucks? And then what trucker wouldn't notice and just drive off? There were too many ifs and buts. "If ifs and buts were candy and nuts," he mumbled, "we'd all have a Merry Christmas."

Still, Caleb continued to scan the darker areas of the lot with his night vision binoculars. They had built-in infrared lights and a night-time range of three hundred feet. A whole football field. But he wasn't catching anything useful or intriguing. All he had seen so far was a heavyset lady step out of a truck cab, drop to the ground, and puke between two sets of trailer tires.

The idea of driving through downtown interested Caleb, but what were the chances he would find a girl walking alone to run over (or clock with his door), with no witnesses? Somewhere the whole thing wouldn't be caught on a traffic cam?

Being a sexual deviant was easier in the old days, he decided. Being a criminal, too. But he didn't really think of himself as a criminal.

Caleb hadn't reduced himself to sex dolls yet, but he had considered it. Briefly. Screwing inorganic objects seemed much worse than screwing the dead. They were organic, at least. Even if they were no longer animate.

Caleb also liked the feel of real human flesh. Dead human flesh. Beauty couldn't exist in anything that wasn't fleeting. Some real life, probably dead, writer or philosopher, had written that. Or maybe it was a poet.

What was more fleeting than dead human flesh? It was much more susceptible to rot and decay than living flesh.

Patty was waiting for Kendra when Lonnie returned and parked his truck. Kendra's car was sitting on the other side of a different truck. Patty grabbed a tire iron she kept tucked behind the passenger seat and slipped out of her old Isuzu Rodeo SUV. She crouched behind the second truck.

Just as Kendra came around the back end of the truck trailer, Patty sprang into action and struck Kendra hard in the back of the head with the lug-nut end of the tire iron. Kendra collapsed immediately. Patty leaned over and hit her on the side of the head again, just to be safe.

Patty grabbed Kendra's purse, made sure the money and Kendra's phone were inside, and then scurried back to her Rodeo. Lonnie drove away on the other side of the second truck, none the wiser.

Caleb couldn't believe his luck.

He dropped his night vision binoculars and drove over. He got out of the car and took a look at the girl. She was wearing a short red tartan skirt that barely covered her butt and a tight midnight blue t-shirt that looked like it had an old Keith Haring print on it. Maybe the "Dancing Dog." There was some blood on the gravel beneath her head and even better news—it smelled like she had shat herself. If she wasn't dead, she was probably dying.

Caleb wrapped her head in a towel and laid her on an old shower curtain he kept in the trunk of his gently used Nissan Altima.

When he arrived at his house, he was whistling. It was that goofy Cher song, the one that, once heard, took a couple of days to put out of your mind. His good fortune made him feel like singing. He belted out the chorus line about life after love.

Caleb pulled into his two-car garage and made sure the door closed behind him. Then, he got out and set up a plastic, six-foot folding table in the center of the empty bay. He opened his trunk, wrapped the girl in the shower curtain, and transported her to the table.

She was still breathing.

Caleb raised one of her arms and dropped it. It fell abruptly and without hesitation. Her extremities appeared to be areflexic. He grabbed an LED flashlight and opened one of the girl's eyelids. He shined the beam into the eye and the pupil didn't dilate. She was probably brain dead, and the rest of her body would soon follow. He opened the other eyelid.

The lights were on, but no one was home.

Caleb undressed the girl carefully and then cleaned up the blood and excrement. Her figure was petite and attractive. Her milky white breasts were ample and firm, exquisite, really. And her comely face had been left undamaged by her assailant's attack.

Caleb was not usually attracted to the living, but the girl was gorgeous. Breathtaking, in fact. He placed her clothes in the washer and transported her to the spare bedroom. He kept a queen bed in there with plastic cover sheets. He laid her on it and put a pillow under her head. Her legs had parted, and he could just see her labia majora.

She lay there, completely nude. Serene. Like an Egon Schiele model. "Recumbent Female Nude with Legs Apart"—but with no stockings.

She was beautiful.

Caleb couldn't resist.

He leaned in between her legs and licked her gently. Then, he left the room and grabbed a condom.

Patty drove to the new Whataburger on the interstate and parked. She took all of Kendra's cash and slipped it into her pocketbook. She turned off Kendra's phone and placed it in the glove compartment. In a couple of days, she would text Lonnie as Kendra, and tell him she was out of the "business" and for him not to call her anymore. Patty was sure that the next time Lonnie came through town, he would call her and things would get back to normal.

Patty wiped the blood off the tire iron with several Kleenexes that she had discovered tucked in Kendra's purse. She stepped out of her Rodeo, stuffed Kendra's purse into Whataburger's outdoor trashcan and went inside for some taquitos.

After Caleb was finished making love to the girl, he placed a fresh comforter over her and snuggled up alongside her. He wasn't used to a warm body. But hers fit like a glove. He enjoyed it and this surprised him.

He listened to her shallow breathing.

He was quiet and a little fearful. What had come over him? He had strayed. He almost felt adulterous.

Was he changing?

When he woke up in the guest room in the middle of the night, the girl was gone.

He flew out of the bed and looked around. The girl's pillow had blood on it and there were smudges across the plastic sheets.

Caleb found her on the floor on the other side of the bed. She was on her stomach and her head was lowered. She was shifting her weight from side to side at her shoulders. She wasn't moving forward or backward—just shifting her weight, mimicking a crawl, but unable to use her arms or legs.

Caleb left the room and put on his favorite robe. He felt guilty. The only reason he had had sex with her while she was still alive was because he thought she would be dead by morning. This complicated things. He cursed his weakness.

He retrieved his LED flashlight and reentered the guest bedroom. He sat down in front of the girl and watched her. She made no ground but continued to rock from side to side at her shoulders. She was trying to crawl, but seemed to have forgotten how.

Caleb switched on the LED flashlight and slid a hand under her chin. He pushed her hair away from her face and raised her chin slowly, training the flashlight beam on both eyes, one after another. Her pupils did not dilate. The girl was blind, and her failed movement was a reflex. Or the girl was brain-dead, and her movement was a physiological impulse. It wouldn't do, but he didn't want to hurt her. He kissed her forehead.

He picked her up and placed her in the bed on her back. She seemed to calm, so he left the room and closed the door.

Kendra's last coherent thought regarded Lonnie. They had a good working relationship and sometimes he was funny.

With a few more steady johns like Lonnie, maybe she could attend Howard College. Or become a hairdresser or something. Perhaps it was time.

Then a loud, solid crack. And darkness.

Her truncated thought processes began receding into the folds of her brain. The consciousness that comprised Kendra's identity was soon gone. Forever. What was left was primal and low. Emanating mostly from her medulla oblongata.

She would teeter. And she might even be able to lean toward the sun.

Caleb was concerned. Two days in and the girl wasn't dead. She was weak from a lack of food and water. And gaunt. And she was back on her stomach again, in the bed. Rocking back and forth at her shoulders.

He watched her bare ass for a long time and then left for another condom.

He took her from behind and then laid on top of her with his full weight. Maybe she would suffocate.

She didn't.

He rolled off of her and laid on his back at her side. Her face was turned toward his. He began to talk.

"My name is Caleb. What's your name?"

The girl didn't answer. She simply stared absently.

"I really don't know what to do with you. No offense, but I was hoping you might expire. Nothing personal."

The girl stared.

"I'm in uncharted water, here. I've never been with a living, breathing girl before." Caleb smiled sheepishly. "You are still breathing, right?"

The girl stared.

"I love your body. I love your breasts. I know that sounds corny.

We're practically sweethearts now, though. But I still wanted you to know."

Caleb slid down the bed and placed his right cheek on her ass cheek. She was a living, breathing, Egon Schiele nude. A still life. But she was starting to smell. It was coming from the wounds in her head. He was careful to clean everywhere else.

"I'm going to give you a name," Caleb continued. "Is that okay?"

The girl didn't respond. Caleb thought for a moment.

"How about Katya? I'm pretty sure it's a Czech name. Maybe Russian. But Slavic anyway."

The girl stared.

"*Katya*. I like that."

Caleb smiled and got up.

Was this true love?

It wasn't laughable. Caleb knew that he wasn't the first person ever to fall in love with a still life. And a masterpiece besides. Da Vinci's *Mona Lisa* or Botticelli's *Venus*, for example. Men had been falling in love with them for centuries. But what he had with Katya was even better. They were technically cohabitating. And they were faithful to one another.

By the fourth day, he'd been with Katya more times than he'd ever been with another woman. And he was beginning to think she was quasi-sentient.

When she rolled over and began shifting her weight back and forth at her shoulders, he usually took her. And when he was done, she stopped. It seemed to calm her.

Her pupils were still unresponsive, but her body wasn't.

He'd tried to brush her teeth the night before, but one fell out. She wasn't looking healthy. Which, yes, was technically the plan.

But he was having second thoughts.

He was thinking about feeding her. He was even thinking about dropping her off at a hospital.

If they fixed her up and healed her head wounds, the sky might be the limit. Sure, she was technically brain dead. But it didn't matter to him. He imagined their future.

If she survived, she would probably wind up in an assisted-living facility. He could follow the news and find out her whereabouts. He could figure out which facility she was staying in. He could pretend to visit and make her "acquaintance." He could hang around. He could say he knew her from the truck stop. He could even eventually say that he loved her—which he was beginning to think wasn't a lie—and that he wanted to spend time with her. Be with her.

He could push her around the assisted living facility in a wheelchair, talk to her, take her to get fresh air. If no one claimed her, he could step in. He could make an arrangement with facility staff. He could sit with her. With technology these days, they might even be able to conceive a child. If they fixed her up, Caleb was sure Katya could do it.

Wouldn't that be something?

On the fifth day, Kendra's body was starving, dehydrated, and weak. Her lips were beginning to crack and the wound in her head was infected. The cognitive processes that had previously constituted Kendra were still entirely absent, never to return, and whatever neuro-logical impulses that still echoed weakly in her being were base and primal. She was reptilian, at best, and blind to boot. It was this dark, primeval stasis that Caleb disturbed.

Caleb decided that he wanted to make love to Katya in the missionary position, face-to-face and breast-to-breast. And he wanted her to hold him as he looked into her beautiful, vacant eyes. The back of her head smelled rank now, anyway.

And if they were going to make a baby, he decided they should do it before he dropped her off at a hospital. It was the best way to insure there were no hitches.

Caleb was beginning to evolve. His taste for living human flesh had gained purchase. It was a new experience, and it was all due to Katya. And they might have a baby. A child of his loins and her womb. He was excited. It was almost better than *Frankenstein*.

Caleb had an idea for the occasion. He would make love to Katya missionary-style, but he would zip-tie her wrists in front of her beforehand. Then he could crawl into her arms before they consummated their love. It only made sense.

When Caleb climbed onto Katya and into her forced embrace, he didn't wear a condom. Katya was dehydrated, so he spit on his hand three times to lubricate his member. In a matter of moments, they were making Iago's "beast with two backs." But Caleb's Desdemona simply stared.

It didn't diminish his affection.

Just prior to the moment of Caleb's ejaculation and orgasm, however, the physiological effects of Katya's dehydrated body and unattended head wound synchronized to make her entire frame begin to shake. Caleb paused in mid-thrust. He wasn't sure what was happening.

Katya's musculature suddenly contracted violently. She suffered a massive seizure, and since her arms were bound, they pulled in and up, constricting Caleb's chest just below his shoulders.

He was shocked. He couldn't believe it.

Had she regained consciousness?

Katya's immediate, vise-like grip forced the breath out of Caleb and remained too constricted for him to take another. She was literally squeezing the life out of him, blocking the flow of air to his lungs. And he couldn't break free.

He could hear the tendons and muscles in Katya's arms straining and popping, but she didn't let go.

Caleb began to panic.

He couldn't breathe.

He attempted to break free, but Katya's seizure hadn't run its course. He grunted airlessly and became faint. While Kendra held Caleb close, he squirmed and twisted and saw stars.

He tried to scream.

five
the amulet

Every child is born knowing life is but a dream. Every adult forgets. The things we call good luck or magic, the things we call miracles, are spontaneous reminders from the unconscious that we are dreaming. Lazy dreamers habitually default to the familiar. "The Amulet" tells us that magic exists if we choose to see it. There is nothing but magic here! We can amazingly and successfully navigate the dream. We can dream with lucidity, and accept responsibility for shaping our dream to our benefit.
—**Armando Sangre**, San Antonio horror writer

"I SHOULD RUN you over with my pick-up truck," the post stated. It was a response to a piece I wrote for the *Panther City Press* (*PCP*).

It wasn't the worst threat I'd received, but significant enough for my editor to forward it. I was mildly amused. I'd have to be more careful at traffic intersections and double-check both ways. Maybe keep an eye out for a truck flying the Stars and Bars.

I decided to ignore it. And I definitely wouldn't mention it to my wife.

The strange room was a neo-rococo decor boudoir, a designation that most of the boys would never understand or be able to articulate in their lifetimes. In the vernacular of their world—Fort Worth in the late 1950s —it was simply "fancy feather" or maybe "high hat." Especially the British furniture, which was primarily early 19th century. But there were also two ancient Greek vases, one vase from the Orient, two Saxon candlesticks and a cabinet breakfast set composed of Wedgwood stoneware. The centerpiece was a well-worn, but sturdy Victorian daybed, draped in a multi-colored, rich Iranian rug and scattered with scarlet cushions. None of these items were particularly appealing to the young men, but one thing caught the leader's eye. An amulet on an ornate table next to the daybed. Probably silver but tarnished —weathered.

Unbeknownst to Tommy Bell—the orchestrator of the small gang's break-in and already a renowned southside brawler—the amulet, which was shaped like a crude, flat pear and dotted with Greek letters and arcane symbols, dated back to the Byzantine period. It was retrieved from the western edge of the Sea of Galilee in what is now part of Lebanon. Bell hadn't known that the Greek letters spelled out the Hebrew name for God, $I \, A \, W \, \Theta$, or "Yahweh" in the English alphabet. He hadn't known the strange symbols were magical etchings inscribed to ward off "demons" and the curse of the "evil eye." One side of the amulet featured a rider, a halo encircling his head, on a galloping horse, thrusting a spear into the breast of a female figure lying on her back. The other side depicted an eye pierced by swords and arrows. The besieged orb also appeared to be encroached upon on all sides by lions, a serpent, a scorpion and carnivorous birds.

Bell possessed no knowledge bearing on the symbolism of the amulet—he just thought it was cool.

I wasn't aware of any of this growing up.

My parents were both hardworking, upstanding, middle-class Americans; but nothing had been given to them. They had it tough, and it left an impression. They wanted more for themselves and more for their kids, and they worked hard to get it.

As a child, I didn't know very much about that, either. I learned about these things later, when I was an adult, and, later still, when I had kids of my own. There were several other things I should have known, but before I could learn them, my father died. He was seventy-one. I was forty-six.

That might sound ridiculous, I admit. Forty-six years in the varying but fairly consistent orbit of a parent should be ample time for you to get to know them and know them well. But that wasn't the case for my father and I. There was a gulf between us that sometimes verged on enmity. Some people said we were too much alike. I don't think he or I believed we were much alike at all—and, in the end, we were both wrong.

At the age of fifty-seven, my father complained of a mounting pressure in his head, and he was subsequently diagnosed with a craniopharyngioma—a benign tumor near his right optical nerve. The tumor was surgically removed, but it left him blind in one eye and disrupted his brain chemistry. He survived another fourteen years, some of them good ones; but they were hard on my mother, and my father and I never got around to talking about everything. I didn't hear about the amulet until right before he died and even then, completely out of context.

My mom told me she woke up at three o'clock in the morning and my father wasn't in their bed. She said she found him in the living room on the floor next to their brown leather couch. There were brass brads along the bottom of the couch, and he was removing them one by one with his fingers. He told her he was looking for a necklace medallion. An amulet. He said he couldn't remember what he did with it. His fingernails were bloody, and he seemed confused. She had no idea what he was talking about. Mom helped him get back to bed, and he didn't remember anything about it the next morning.

Tommy Bell, Sr., passed a couple of weeks later. I wrote his obit and thought I did a nice job, but I also felt bad. The day my father died, I was working on a series of bombings that occurred in Fort Worth in 1953. I'd actually discovered a local TV broadcast hard-copy describing one of the incidents on the microfilm machine at the central Fort Worth Library. Dated November 17, 1953, the story, titled "Negro Blast," started: "Fort Worth's race friction continues to flare. This morning, another negro home was blasted in the Riverside neighborhood on the city's east side..." The broadcast ran seven days after my father's eleventh birthday, and the same year he met my mother.

I'd pitched a piece on the incident (or series of incidents) to *PCP*. I'd been writing for them for a few years by then, enjoying the freedoms of an alternative newsroom. It was a good place for me to stay out of trouble, or not get in trouble for troubling a publication's readership. The circulation was smaller, but the readership was generally younger and more open-minded. I'd never been very good at keeping my head low, so I felt comfortable there. I was a Fort Worth native after all, and writing for *PCP* allowed me to dig into the town's history, particularly with regard to how it impacted the present. I'd never heard of these bombings before, and that surprised me.

I wondered if my dad would have remembered the story.

Probably not, but he was no longer around to ask.

My dad had a friend named Mort—Morton—whom he'd run around with as a teenager. Mort was a couple of years older than my father, so he was getting on in years, maybe seventy-five or seventy-six.

Mort had been a Navy man for a short time and, occasionally, a few years or so after my dad passed, I'd have a beer with him at the original Poop Deck, on the corner of Seminary Drive and Granbury Road. He'd talk about the old days, and my mom and dad, whom he loved like a brother and sister. He and his ex-wife had been the only attendees of my parents' wedding. I'm pretty sure they came to my small wedding as well.

When I got to the Poop Deck around 5:30 p.m., Mort had already had a few beers and was holding a newspaper clipping. I sat down and ordered an Amstel Light.

"You still drinking that *Europiss*, TJ?" he teased. It was a long-running joke. Actually, two long-running jokes. I was Tommy Bell, Jr. Not Thomas or even Tom. I was Tommy, Jr., so "TJ." And he knew why I drank Amstel, as well. But I played along.

"You've been to Amsterdam," I said.

"Yes, sir. Dutch women. That was another life."

I laughed. "Me, too. Just not exactly in the Netherlands."

"Oh, that's right. Shit. The Greek Islands. My brain cells are getting soggy."

"That's why I drink Amstel *Light*," I kidded.

"Yes, well. I guess it's better than the clap.

"Depends on who's giving it to you, right?"

"You little shit," he mumbled. "It's getting where you know all my comebacks better than me."

"I'm sure you've forgot more than I'll ever learn. What's that?" I asked, nodding at the clipping.

"Just something I forgot," he replied. "Just something I came across when I was emptying some old boxes in the spare room."

"Oh, yeah?"

"Yep. Got me to thinking about your old man..."

"Really. What? Was I adopted?"

Mort almost spit beer. "Ha! You know better than that. You're a chip off the old block."

"I didn't use to think so. But now..."

There was a mild ruckus at a pool table in the rear. Mouthing, pushing, wingmen stepping in—fisticuffs averted. The usual.

Mort sneered, "Rookies."

I smiled. I was used to it.

Mort took another sip of his beer and turned his attention back to the clipping. "Your father was a hard man," he said. "But he had his reasons. He didn't have it easy."

"I know."

"And no one who hung around him very long had it easy, either." Mort added.

"I'm aware of that, too."

"Of course," he said. "I know you know. But you gotta' understand.

It's just the way things were in those days. Tommy and his brothers, all of us—we never had much. We grew up poor. Dirt poor. That was really the thing most of us had in common. Poor people were really looked down on where we lived back then, and some kids... well, let's just say they didn't take it lying down. Especially those Bell boys."

I was pretty sure I'd heard most of the stories before, but I didn't interrupt.

"Your father and some of his older brothers, they were scary. Not the sort of folks you wanted to cross. They didn't suffer fools, and they didn't suffer too many insults. I mean, they weren't like some of the crazy kids today. They wouldn't stab you or shoot you. But you might get the shit beat out of you if you looked at one of them funny. They were the real deal, and everybody knew it.

"Hell," Mort snorted. "I knew kids at school—if they saw your dad coming down the hall, they walked the other way. Or pretended they were the paint on their lockers until he passed."

"You're not the first person to tell me that."

"I'm not surprised. But there was more to it. I don't think you understand. Tommy *liked* to fight. He enjoyed it. He was hardly ever the biggest guy, but he was like a freckle-faced white Tyson. *Iron Mike*. He didn't run his head or exchange insults. He didn't give you a push and wait for one back like those candy-asses yonder. He was on you before you even had a chance to think about what you said or did that he didn't like. But, unlike Iron Mike—no offense—he was also the smartest guy in the room. Any room. Any room I ever been in anyway."

"He was pretty sharp."

"Shit," Mort shrugged. "I'd have rather fought him than argue with him any day. I was a year or two older and had twenty or thirty pounds on him, but I'd have been punching out of my weight class in either case. He was something. He was really something."

"So, what's up with the clipping?"

"Nothing. Nothing, really. But yeah. I thought you might like to read it. You should read it. It's hard for me to believe, but I haven't thought about it in a long time. It was also another life."

"How many have you had?"

"There ain't enough beer in this joint to explain all that."

"I don't doubt it. But what's this story about?"

Mort's smile faded a little.

"It's about me and your dad. It doesn't contain our names—that came later. But it's about us... and some others. And some twisting off we did back in the day."

"You want me to read it right now? Right here?"

"I surely do, TJ. Right here, right now."

Mort handed me the newspaper clipping, and I held it gingerly. I ordered another Amstel Light, and he ordered a coffee. I gave him a sideways look.

"Just a little pick me up," he mumbled. 'Fore we get too far off into this. I need to keep half my wits about me."

The newspaper clipping was faded yellow and fragile. Mort said it was from March of 1959, and it appeared in the *Fort Worth Star-Telegram*. The headline in large, bold-faced lettering said, "House Burglaries by Youths May Total 100." I glanced at Mort and he nodded.

My mom had shown me some newspaper clippings from back then, but not this one. Football and track coverage. They described my old man as a "lightning quick" running back, but I'd been told he didn't even start playing 'til his junior year. I was about to find out why.

I read the article. It described a theft ring operated by a bunch of teenagers who, over a period of a year or so, had burglarized dozens of houses in Fort Worth and *acquired* thousands of dollars' worth of stolen property. Some of the victims were quoted in the piece, but only one of the perpetrators. The theft ring was broken up when one of the boys' fathers found some stolen jewelry and turned him in. There were thirteen teenagers involved in the gang, but neither my father nor Mort's names were listed. It occurred to me that my father was a minor at the time. His name may not have been mentioned, but I recognized his description from the remarks made by one of his fellows, a quoted perpetrator whose name was Wally Parsons. Parsons "identified a

Paschal student, yet to be arrested, as the youth who started the burglary ring." Parsons said "this boy was a 'toughie' who would take loot away from other boys in the ring."

"Oh, shit," I said.

"Yep," Mort replied, sipping on his coffee.

"I guess I know who the 'toughie' was."

"Yep," Mort repeated with a laugh. But his laugh was drowned out by a dozen others by then. The Poop Deck was starting to get crowded. Mort and I grabbed our beers and moved to a corner in the back. We had a long talk.

I immediately learned two things. First, Mort's days in the navy were the result of his arrest after the break-up of the theft ring. He was a little older than my dad, so the sentencing judge offered him jail time or military service. Second, my 15-year-old father's punishment was reduced to probation by a prominent local attorney, who was retained by one of the victims of the theft ring.

"How does that work?" I asked.

"We—your dad—had taken something a local rich fella wanted back. Something he wanted back really bad. He was hoity-toity, from a family with deep pockets. Connected."

"What was it?"

"It was this necklace. It had an old silver amulet on it."

"Amulet?"

"Yeah."

I told him the story about my dad looking for an amulet in the couch right before he passed.

"You think we're talking about the same thing?"

"I don't know," I said. "Sounds like it."

"I'm pretty sure it's not possible," Mort squawked. "I mean, your dad... he gave it up. It was a strange deal, T.J. That's for sure. First, this guy met with your old man while he was in the juvie lock-up. And then the guy hired a top lawyer to defend your dad, get his sentence reduced. He had to go live with his oldest sister because his dad was already gone, and his mother couldn't control him. She suffered from serious bouts of depression and bipolar stuff. But I know him being able to lawyer up was all predicated on the return of the amulet."

"That's odd."

"Extremely. But your daddy was no dummy. He knew that was as good as it was gonna get, and I gotta say... he made the best of it. He went all Henry the Fifth on the gang. Transferred to Trimble Tech, became a straight "A" student, and started playing football. Had an offer or two and a tryout to play in college, but he didn't wanna' leave your mom."

"I heard he visited McMurray in Abilene and San Angelo State and wasn't impressed by the co-ed enrollment."

"It's a story he told, sure. But your mother was a looker. He wouldn't have found anyone like her out there."

"Who was this guy? Who was my father's benefactor? Do you remember his name?"

"That was a lotta' years ago, but it was foreign. Maybe Spanish. Enrique or Enrico Esteban or something like that. He got his amulet back, and we never heard from him again."

"Do you remember which house was his?"

"I'll never forget it. His place was decorated to the nines. It was just off the nice part of Hemphill back then, and it had a copper-dome roof feature." Mort ordered another beer. "The place is still there," he continued. "But I doubt he's still around." He was thirty or forty back then, I think."

"That's a helluva story."

"Your old man was a helluva character."

"I'll drink to that," I said.

I took a long slug off my Amstel. That's the thing about too many of us, I thought. We miss the forest for the trees. Here I was chasing down stories down all over the state, but somehow completely missing one in my own life. A big one, involving my old man.

When I left the Poop Deck, I thought about calling my mother, but found myself lost in reflection, and tracing the threads that connected my thoughts to specific and now very pertinent memories. I'd had my first run-in with the law when I was ten years old. My Uncle Dan lived right across from an elementary school in the Hallmark area of South Fort Worth. One weekend, while we were visiting, I'd stayed out playing on the playground and suddenly realized I was by myself, that it was getting late. I began walking back toward my uncle's house, but was disturbed by the dark windows of the school as I passed. I saw something or thought I saw something. I picked up a handful of rocks and began moving faster. I was suddenly and inexplicably spooked, and I began throwing rocks and smashing windows as I ran. By the time I was out of rocks, I had reached the edge of my Uncle Dan's front lawn. There was an older man standing out in the street with a shotgun, and I froze.

I didn't even try to run. I immediately started bawling.

The man with the shotgun was a member of the maintenance crew at the elementary, and he knew my uncle. He'd heard the smashing glass and left his house to investigate—and found me.

He never pointed the shotgun at me, he just followed me to my Uncle Dan's front door. My parents and my Uncle Dan and Aunt Ellen found out, and a Fort Worth Police "paddy wagon" showed up. I bring this all up because I didn't see the whole picture. The police officer didn't arrest me—he just gave me a good talking to. But what I remember the most was my Uncle Dan's response.

My mother and father viewed the entire matter grimly, but my Uncle Dan thought it was hilarious. He laughed and laughed and laughed, and I couldn't understand it. He even paid for all the damages at the school. I was mortified. I was convinced my father would clobber me. But what I got was worse, and it was followed by something far worse.

But I'm getting ahead of myself.

It made sense now. Neither my parents nor any other member of my family had ever mentioned that my father had a criminal record. They'd kept that from my brother and me. But sometimes DNA is destiny. Uncle Dan had guffawed over the irony of it. My folks keeping this from me, sheltering me... and he was tickled that my natural proclivities might make me a Bell boy of old, regardless of what my parents did differently, or right, to prevent it.

I understood his frivolity on that occasion now. I was almost smiling, but that incident reminded me of what came after.

It was late in the school year and my parents grounded me for an entire summer. We had a house and a couple of acres in a small, farm town suburb, lots of briar and bramble to clear and a decent size garden to tend. I worked hard all day, every day, in the garden or clearing brush or just tackling regular chores. My birthday was smack-dab in the middle of the summer, and I was shooting for a time-served, good behavior pardon. I was young, but I wasn't stupid. My folks belonged to a hickoid, backwater country club and golf course that had a large swimming pool with a diving board. I wanted to go. The thought of spending all summer without going to the pool roiled my preteen brain. I worked hard and kept my nose clean, with extra "yes, sirs" and "yes ma'ams" thrown in at every opportunity.

And it worked.

I can't remember now and neither can my mom. But I'm pretty sure I was unconditionally released from the grounding on my birthday—but definitely on or for my birthday—and we went to the country club that day. I was elated and having fun. I could already do front and back flips, and I was trying copy-dives with my friends. We were eyeing the girls our age with wonder and new interest and therefore showing off. And that's when it happened.

My friend Devin and I were engaged in a contest to see who could hold their breath the longest, the winner of which would not be declared by scientific results. No one wore watches in or around pools in those days, so our competition would be determined by the length we could swim underwater without coming up for air. It was really a determination of breath and stamina, but we didn't realize that then.

Usage of the pool's only diving board (which was over-springy for our small bodies) wasn't permitted in the contest, because we obviously couldn't have jumped off it at the same time. At least fairly, anyway. So we dove off different edges of the far side of the deep end of the pool and swam toward the shallow end. We also, obviously, had to swim with our eyes open to avoid other swimmers, waders, children, etc.

I usually won these contests, but I hadn't been in the pool that whole summer. I'm pretty sure Devin was beating me that day, but I never found out. He dove in on the right side of the diving board and I dove in simultaneously on the left side. I was excited and gleeful, breast-stroking underwater and kicking my legs fiercely. I didn't even look over at Devin.

Unfortunately, the drunken, sixteen-year-old son of a local construction company owner was in the middle of a clumsy prank on my side of the pool. He had his 3-wood out, practicing a stroke on an errant, multi-color (blue-orange-white) kiddie beach ball. He brought the club-head up to the beach ball twice before attempting to execute a drive. But after he exaggeratedly perfected his grip on the 3-wood and, then, swung the club, rearing back and attempting to impress anybody watching with a perfect drive on the unsuspecting beach ball, I came up for air directly beneath it, and the 3-wood struck me squarely just above and behind my left ear.

It was worse than a scene from *Jaws*.

<hr>

Impossibly weightless jets of bright red blood spewed from my head. Several pool patrons began screaming.

I felt dizzy and had problems standing up.

The other kids and their parents fled the water for dry concrete, quickly emptying the pool. The sixteen-year-old "golfer" dropped the 3-wood and began backing away, wetting his pants and beginning to sob.

My wails were less rhythmic than the blood, and a lifeguard dove in immediately and scooped me up. My parents wrapped a beach towel around my bleeding head, and I lost consciousness.

<hr>

I came to in the middle of the night, alone in a hospital.

Groggy, disoriented and unsure of where I was, I slid off the bed, taking sensors, an IV stand and a food tray with me. Two nurses were on the scene in a flash, resettling me in the bed, reconnecting the lines and tubes, checking me, calming me, and warning me to stay where I lay.

I didn't swim again that summer.

But now I understood.

Now I had kids of my own. None of my kids had ever vandalized a school or been hit over the head with a golf club. None of my kids had turned out anything like me or my old man, which was probably good. But it suddenly made me sad. As I mentioned before, my father and I had both been wrong. We were much more alike than we thought, and so much more than I realized or wanted to admit.

His life had changed in juvie. My life changed after a severe blow to the head. I wanted to find the man who helped my father, and my pool accident played no small part in a major reason why.

I was forced to take it easy the rest of that summer. And it's easy to forget that cable TV and the internet didn't exist back then. We had one TV and five TV channels, and Atari was still a few years away. My head injury might have turned out to be a cruel prescription for utter boredom, except that one whole wall of my bedroom was books.

My parents had recently added on to the house, and my brother and I had our own bedrooms. Mine had a bay window and my parents' small library. The shelves were homemade, consisting of 1" x 6" wood planks laying horizontally on evenly spaced bricks stacked floor to ceiling.

The shelves had all kinds of books, most of which I had very little interest in. But it was that summer that I stumbled onto Edgar Rice Burroughs's *A Princess of Mars*, *Tarzan*, Victor Hugo's *The Hunchback of Notre Dame* and Alexandre Dumas's *The Count of Monte Cristo*. Somewhere around that time, I also discovered *The Great Brain* series by John D. Fitzgerald. But it was also the 1970s, so I also stuck my head in *The Bermuda Triangle* by Charles Berlitz and *Chariots of the Gods* by Erich von Däniken. Other formative reading materials included dozens of issues of *National Geographic* (which I was later told my father purchased a subscription to the day I was born) and a number of comic books I was able to purchase with my allowance.

I couldn't go swimming or do a lot of working or playing—but I became an eager reader and probably decided then what I wanted to be when I grew up.

I wanted to be a writer.

I didn't know what I wanted to write about or anything really about learning how to do it, but it seemed like a worthwhile way to spend a life. And I remember something else I also discovered then.

About midway up the shelves on the far right-hand side, there was a decent selection of hardback books. I still have at least three of them in my personal library today. They are *The Astounding Science Fiction Anthology* (edited by John W. Campbell, Jr) with stories by Isaac Asimov, Robert Heinlein, A. E. van Vogt, L. Sprague de Camp, Theodore Sturgeon and others; *The Treasury of Science Fiction Classics* (edited by Harold W. Kuebler), with stories from Edgar Allan Poe, Jules Verne, H. G. Wells, Arthur Conan Doyle, Aldous Huxley, Ambrose Bierce, F. Scott Fitzgerald (!), E. M. Forster and others; and *The Best from Fantasy and Science Fiction, Sixth Series* (edited by Anthony Boucher), with stories from Ray Bradbury, C. S. Lewis, C. M. Kornbluth, Rachel Maddux and others. The reason I kept and mention them regards how they came to be on the shelves in the first place, and, specifically, how they came to be in my father's possession. They were all given to my father on his thirteenth birthday. They were gifts from his mother, and they each featured the same inscription: *Birthday Greetings to Tommy Bell from Mother, November 10, 1957.*

In my ten-year-old mind, the volumes struck me as strange gifts, perhaps even lame. But that was before I knew how poor my father's widowed mother and he, the youngest child, had been. A strange, precious gift bundle to my budding, juvenile delinquent father, ten years before I was born.

The books I read and the books I stumbled onto created an interest in reading and writing in me. It was years before I would exercise that interest, but that was the beginning.

My research on the 1953 bombings in Fort Worth was coming along fine, but my wife, Cassandra—Cassie—was weary. She was a laid back, West Indies woman who'd grown up playing in the waves—not making them.

She hadn't said anything when I mentioned the bombings; we'd had unpleasant discussions about the subjects I covered in my writing before. "People should know," I proffered tactfully.

"I agree," Cassie replied. "But why can't someone else write about it? Why does it have to be you?"

"I stumbled onto it," I said. "You think it's something I should ignore?"

"No, of course not. But you seem to stumble a lot," Cassie observed, concerned, but half smiling. "People don't like it. I can't say that I like it. I don't want another..."

She didn't finish.

She didn't have to.

***

About ten years back, I'd written an editorial that infuriated some local conservatives and I'd gotten death threats and hate mail. They'd mailed a 12" X 9" manilla envelope to our home. It was filled with sequential pages of MapQuest directions that led from the guarded gate of the plant of a certain local aerospace and defense contractor to our front door, and it included an anonymous threat. Cassie had opened it, and it scared her.

I imparted the same wisdom to Cassie that my father would have shared with me. "If somebody's really interested in hurting you," I said, "they hurt you. They don't talk about hurting you. Someone is just trying to scare us."

Cassie's light brown eyes held me squarely. She nodded slowly, placed her hands on her slim hips, and put me on the spot. "Well, they're doing a good job," she said. "Why can't you write something like *Harry Potter* or *Twilight*? Why does everything have to be a cause?"

"That's not fair," I replied. "Someone has to care, right? "

"Don't be melodramatic," Cassie said. "You know I agree with you, and you know I care. It's not about caring. It's about a world full of psychos—armed psychos—*armed psychos that you're just daring*. What if somebody shoots you? What if somebody shoots me or hurts one of our kids?"

It was a point I couldn't argue. But I knew that was why so few writers pursued these subjects. My default response was a banal platitude about speaking truth to power, but she'd heard it before. So I kept it to myself.

The face of the man in the bed was almost waxen over his skull, but his dark brown eyes had a mild glimmer. He was obviously dying and probably had been for a while. But there was no fear in his countenance, no doubt. His servant, who had introduced himself as "Primo" at the front door, led me to a position close to the old man.

We stood next to Enrique Esteban's bed. A life-size bronze bust of someone who looked vaguely familiar sat on a short, columnar stand on the opposite side of the bed, perpendicular with Enrique's resting left elbow.

"Mr. Ricky," the servant said. "A man is here to see you."

Ricky—short for Enrique—stirred.

"What?" Ricky said. "Who?" He turned to the bronze bust. "Oh, Siddy," Ricky continued groggily. "Look, we have a visitor."

I examined the bust again. The subject was handsomely dour, in a jowly, country club way. The pose it struck seemed mildly fierce, but sincere.

Primo leaned over. "Mr. Ricky, I tol' you already, this is Tomás Bell."

"Tomás," Ricky puzzled. "Tomás. Tommy? *Tommy Bell*?"

"Yes, sir," I replied. "Pleased to meet you, sir."

Ricky reached for his glasses on the bedstand closest to Primo and I, and the servant helped him put them on. "That's much better," Ricky said. "Yes." He studied me quizzically. "That's not young Tommy Bell, Siddy," Ricky said, without turning to the bronze bust. "Is it?"

Ricky looked me up and down.

"He hasn't aged a day, or he's a younger version of Tommy Bell. A son. He has to be. A son? A grandson?"

"Son," I said.

"Do you see the similarities, Siddy? I do." Ricky paused, as if listening to the bronze bust. "Broad-shouldered, yes. Just like his father. A certain reckless *joie de vivre*."

Ricky tilted his head toward the bust, again appearing to listen.

"Yes," he observed, finally. "Faded with age, perhaps. Quite right, quite right. But still there."

I was a little surprised. Ricky turned back to me.

"Where are my manners?" Ricky continued. "Come, come, Mr. Bell. Have a seat, please."

Primo smiled and pulled a chair over from the nearest wall and placed it at Ricky's bedside.

I sat, inspecting the bust. It faced me more than Ricky and, sitting upright, I was closer to eye level with it. I recognized the visage, but I wasn't sure why.

Ricky took a deep breath, and it made him cough, but just once. He turned toward me, his head never leaving the pillow. "I haven't thought about you in a long time, Mr. Bell." Ricky turned and leaned slightly closer toward me and whispered. "Siddy... he once called you a wily little guttersnipe."

Ricky laid back into his pillow. "It made me smile. I remember seeing you on the news. I remember the coverage of you—your father, that is—being led into the police station. "'*Surly Tommy Bell*,'" they said. "*Ha*. You were just fifteen or sixteen." He nodded. "But that report was what made me check."

Ricky had obviously been bedridden for a while, and I expected to smell stale piss, sterile pads or Pine-Sol. But all I detected was a faint hint of lavender. Ricky was mixing me up with my father. His confusion was off-putting, but navigable. "For what?" I asked. "Check for what, I mean?"

"The burglaries you boys were accused of had all occurred in this area. And the perpetrators had made away with things that the victims didn't even know were missing. I was even told the police had only known about a dozen of the houses that you burgled. That two detectives took your father out in a patrol car, and he actually pointed out most of the rest. Random, soft heists, with rarely any evidence of disturbance. It was so clever. It made me wonder."

Ricky looked away, and then turned slowly to the bronze bust. "I wasn't always with Siddy," he continued. "I was a young man, too, once, and I didn't come from landed gentry, money or title. In fact, quite the opposite." Ricky paused and shook his head. "No, Siddy. I want to tell him. It doesn't matter now."

I turned to the bust again. My host's discussion with the bronze figure was mildly unsettling, but almost comical. Cliché, even. But Ricky was profoundly engaged in whatever conversation was being held. The bronze bust remained stoic, and never haughty. But still. I decided the sculptor conceived it with Marcus Aurelius in mind.

"Don't be silly," Ricky addressed the bronze bust. "This is his son. Why shouldn't he know? *Do you realize how long it's been since I've had a visitor?* He could be my last visitor. Everyone's gone, dear. All I have left is you. Why do you have to spoil this for me?

"Sorry," Ricky said, returning his drowsy gaze to me. "And Siddy is sorry. You didn't come here for that. A lovers' quarrel. We have them now and again, even now. Siddy is still so protective of me—he can't help it. I so understand. I didn't at first, but..."

Ricky paused again. His eyes welled up, but he slowly recomposed himself.

"It was a short time after the arrest," he said. "Siddy had been unwell for a while. I lost him. We were down at his island. St. Joseph Island. But I digress. Ah, yes. *That's how I knew.* I had this sneaking suspicion. *Sneaking.* I was a sneaky boy myself, once. Before I met Siddy. I was never as clever as your father, but I was sneaky. I had to be. And then I didn't have to be. I'm sure this isn't making any sense at all."

"I don't know, yet," I replied. "I think I'm following you, but I'm not sure."

"It's a long story," Ricky said. "And so long ago. So far, so long. Can you come back tomorrow? It will give me a chance to gather my... to think about it, and how to share it with more focus."

"Are you sure?"

"Yes," Ricky replied. "Quite. This is exciting, and though excitement is something I've been told to avoid in my condition, I adore it. This far along, this late. A mystery, Siddy. Think of it. A riddle. And me and you at the center. Oh, Siddy."

On the way out, I asked Primo about the bronze bust. He didn't know much but said that Ricky had told him it was commissioned for an important man who had a museum named after him in Fort Worth.

I mulled them over. Amon G. Carter, the Kimbell, The Modern. Those were the main ones. And the Roberson—The Sid Roberson Museum. When I got home, I looked it up. The museum's website had a portrait of Roberson. The bronze bust was a younger version of oil tycoon Sid Roberson. It surprised me, but it shouldn't have. Roberson hadn't had any children, and he'd left a fortune to a niece, which filtered down to his grandnephews. I think they own part of Disney now.

There were rumors about Sid Roberson, but I'd never paid much attention. I'd come of age in the 1980s. If Roberson had been gay, so what? Ricky appears to have been his partner—again, so what? What did it have to do with the amulet?

I thought about calling Mort but didn't. Wouldn't have been any more his business than it was mine. But it was a strange scene there, today, Ricky talking to the bust of his former lover. Maybe his last lover. It was touching in a way.

I looked up "Enrique Esteban" on the internet. There was only one hit, and it was from a *Southern Living* article from 1969. That's where I saw the phrase "neo-rococo decor boudoir." I hadn't known anymore what it meant in 2019 than my dad knew in 1959. But I made a mental note to take note.

When I returned the next day, Primo seemed more upbeat. He told me Ricky was waiting for me. As we passed by it, I gave what was presumably still the neo-rococo boudoir a quick study. It didn't seem to have changed much since the photo shoot for *Southern Living*. When we entered the master bedroom, Enrique was sitting in a chair facing the one I had sat in the day before. It had been moved back a bit for extra room.

Ricky was dressed in a deep blue satin robe and gray flannel pajama pants. His left leg was crossed over his right, but I suspected Primo had helped him with that. His hands were freshly manicured, perhaps also by Primo.

"Siddy and I have been waiting for you, Mr. Bell," Ricky said, smiling. "It's good to see you again."

"And you as well, Ricky," I replied, with a nod toward Siddy. "You look like you feel better."

"It's pure subterfuge. But it's been a long time since I had visitors. Siddy's friends were my friends, and he was much older than me. Now they're all gone. But I have Primo and Siddy. And now I've met you. It's... what is the word? Ah, yes. Thanks, Siddy. It's fortuitous."

"Why do you say that?"

"Because it's the truth. I'm dying. Surely you suspected."

"I wasn't sure. And I didn't think it was the best thing to lead with."

Ricky grinned and then smiled broadly. "Siddy said you were clever. I wasn't sure, but I believe it now."

"It's been a while since someone told me I was clever," I said. "But I assure you. I came here with no designs or ill intent. I just—"

"You want to know about the amulet, and my arrangement with your father."

"Yes."

"There was nothing untoward about it, I assure you."

"I never thought there was. He got a second chance, and I think he made the best of it."

"I agree. And I was like him. I got a second chance with Siddy, and he changed my life."

Ricky turned and stared at the bronze bust. "It doesn't do him justice," Ricky sighed. "Obviously. But it's better than nothing. I commissioned it from an Italian artist in 1955. I was twenty-nine. Siddy was fifty-four. I was a hapless princess, and ours was a fairytale romance. But I know you didn't come here for that, a dying queen rambling on... *ha*. Siddy doesn't care for that sort of thing either. And I think Primo only tolerates it." Ricky smiled again. "Suffice it to say, I had a life. I had a great love. I had great adventures and excitement. And I had someone who looked after me always, even after he passed through the veil."

I didn't know what to say.

I admired that. Ricky was calm and satisfied. Who says those things? How many of us can really say those things? I thought of my mother. I think she could say those things. My wife was younger than me... would she say those things someday?

I hoped so.

"And that brings me to the amulet," Ricky said. "And your father."

I gave Ricky my full attention.

"The amulet was procured by Siddy long ago, in Egypt. In fact, Cairo. It was before I met Siddy. He was younger. His business acumen was uncanny, but he wasn't like the affluent today. He was not narrow-minded. He had a passion for many things, and not just western art. He had interests in antiquities as well, and other cultures. I think he knew he was different, and he sought out cultures and company where his differences would not be vilified. You understand, of course."

"I do," I said.

"Do you condone?"

"It's none of my business, really. And it's not my place to judge."

"I don't know what your father would have thought. Those were different times. I didn't bring it up. It wasn't germane to our transaction."

"Transaction?"

"Poor word choice, perhaps, but yes. He was in jail, fatherless and with no other means of support other than his brothers. And he had something I wanted... Ok, yes, Siddy. Something that *we* wanted."

"Right. The amulet."

"Yes."

"But why? Sid—Siddy, I mean—he was rich. He was very wealthy."

"Yes, he was. Incredibly wealthy. But the amulet was special, and not just to him. It offered something that all the money in the world wouldn't be enough to buy..."

I half nodded. "I'm just playing devil's advocate," I ventured, "but what exactly might that be?"

"Deliverance. Safety. Freedom. *Acceptance.*"

"Okay," I replied, a bit confused

"I know it sounds silly but hear me out. I'm not even a superstitious person. I know it all sounds fantastical."

"Yes, but I'm listening."

"Mr. Bell. There was a time when people did judge—our entire culture judged. There was a time when people believed that disease or misfortune were far from incidents of happenstance, random or unpredictable. For much of human history, inexorable suffering or calamity were believed to be wisht upon people, like spells. Like curses or punishing afflictions." Ricky suddenly raised the amulet by its chain in front of his face. "This crude piece of silver, Mr. Bell... it was forged millennia ago to ward off evil wishes, dangerous accusations and hypocritical, bigoted rabble. Forces that could assign people like Siddy and I to a wretched doom with a gesture, a word. A rumor could get us pilloried, quartered or burned at the stake. For most of human existence, it was a serious business, inhumane, scandalous. But the depravity only profited those miserable enough to wield it against others, and especially against marginalized parties... in any population."

"So, you're saying it protected people against evil and demonic forces?"

"In a manner of speaking, yes—that's what I thought at first. It makes sense, yes? Societies become fragmented... *ha*, yes, Siddy, denominational. Dangerous for those of us who go a different way. A single glare snidely cast or a suspicious glance at the man who was too nurturing, the woman who was too fierce. We could discuss dozens of examples—they run throughout history. A man or woman who is different, or a man or woman who isn't exactly what their biology suggests, for example. They called that an 'abomination.'

"Siddy did his homework and had help from a team of archeologists. He knew the truth."

"The truth," I replied, still unsure.

"Yes, as plain as my decrepit mousiness or the nose on your face."

"Well, I can feel and use my nose, but I can hardly see it without a mirror."

"That's funny. But what I mean to say is, it was obvious to Siddy all along, or for a long time. It didn't have anything to do with the devil or demons or evil spirits. It was simply symbolic. The amulets weren't crafted to save you from demons. They were made to protect their possessors from reprehensible religious zealots. Christians, Jews, Muslims, Mormons, whatever, whomever."

Ricky seemed pleased that I wasn't surprised; but I was.

I was surprised it hadn't occurred to me before.

"Christians may be the most judgmental lice in creation," Ricky said. "So, they were a danger to us and what we had. And Siddy knew they'd be a danger to me, especially after he was gone."

"And that's why it was so important to get the amulet back," I said. "That's why you stepped in."

"That's why Siddy stepped in. I was just the messenger. Your father didn't know what it was. And I didn't tell him. But I'm telling you now."

I was silent for a moment. "I appreciate that," I said, finally. "It makes sense."

"It does," Ricky agreed. "Is it magic? I don't know. Did it save me or keep Siddy and I safe? It seemed to. At least in his lifetime and the rest of mine so far. Now things are different. We actually even have rights. Our love wouldn't be as dangerous now as it was then. Back then, it could mean murder, character assassination, prison. Chemical castration, and so on."

"I know that. I understand."

"I think you do. And so does Siddy. I couldn't tell your father back then. I had no sense of how he might react. We wanted the amulet back, so I left the details out. I'm happy to be able to tell you the truth."

"I'm glad you did."

"And now I'm growing tired," Ricky sighed, looking uncomfortable in the chair. "Primo, will you lower this leg?"

Primo lowered Ricky's leg carefully.

"That's better," Ricky said. "Thank you. Mr. Bell?"

"Yes."

"One more thing, please. One request."

"Of course."

"I want you to have it."

"Have what?"

"The amulet."

"What? *Why?* I'm not—"

"I know you're not gay. It's not about that."

"What then? I couldn't..."

"You could. You can. *And you will*. That last part was from Siddy. And he almost always gets his way."

"Why?" I asked.

"Yes, you do," Ricky said to the bust. "Why what?" he continued, turning back to me.

"Why give it to me?"

"I'll be gone soon, and I no longer have any use for it. Siddy is waiting. At St. Joseph's. We had our own spot. I want my ashes spread with his."

"But the amulet... I don't even believe in that kind of thing."

"Neither did I."

"I don't need it."

"No? That's not what Siddy says."

"What?"

"What is your vocation?"

"I'm a consultant."

"That's what you do for a living. But what is your vocation? What is your calling?

I didn't reply.

"Aren't you that writer?" Ricky asked. "Aren't you the—"

"Yes," I said. "Yes. But I have no interest in writing about this."

"I'm not worried about that," Ricky said, smiling weakly. "Wait until I'm gone if you change your mind. But you are kidding yourself. I have been reading your stuff for years. I've even read it to Siddy. We knew who you were... *what's that Siddy?* Really?"

"What?"

"Mr. Bell, shame on you. You haven't been forthcoming."

"What do you mean?"

"You didn't mention your father. You know what we mean."

"I don't know what you mean. What are you referring to?"

"What was your father searching for, that night, right before he passed through the veil?"

"That was... that was years ago, that didn't..."

"Oh, but it did."

"What?"

"He knew."

"Knew what?"

"Your father knew that you wouldn't be safe. He must have sensed what the amulet was. I don't think I told him. He knew what you were working on, he knew what you were writing. In our day it was our door the menacing hordes I mentioned might show up at with torches and pitchforks. But, today, it's yours. It's your door, Mr. Bell. Your father was trying to find the amulet for you. Just before he died. He knew— but he was confused. He'd forgotten where it was.

"Now, you're here," Ricky continued. "And Siddy and I both agree. We want you to have it. Your father held up his end of the deal—he never said a word, not even to his own family."

"I can't."

"You can. I insist." Ricky nodded at the bust. "Okay. *We* insist."

It was a lot to take in. And even more to take the amulet.

Ricky insisted. Siddy, reportedly emphatic, commanded. Primo coaxed.

Ricky lowered the amulet into my open right palm by its chain and then sprinkled the chain links around it. Then he hugged me and kissed my cheek. "Don't stop," he said. "But keep the amulet close."

His eyes welled up, and he turned to the bronze bust, starting to cry. "I can't help it... Siddy. I'm so happy he came to see us. The circle is complete. It makes me happy, my love."

Primo led me to the front door. "Thank you for coming, Mr. Bell. He never expected something like this... it has meant so much to him. It made him proud. It made him stronger. It's magic. It's magic in the end."

"Maybe so," I said. "Thank you, Primo."

I stepped out into the sun and decided to visit my mother.
Closure.
Hope.
The Poop Deck, soon, with Mort.
But, most importantly, my wife, Cassie.
I had something special to give her.

six
the judge

I CAME TO WORK LATE. It had been a late night.

I had closed down another subpar pickup bar, my latest hobby. There were several pairs of fair-to-middling thirty-somethings dancing like it was still 1999, and the scene was sprinkled with copious heads of receding, colored and bleached hair, fake boobs, one bad toupee and at least one enhanced arse—which seemed to complicate the proud owner's stride.

I drank two beers, contemplating how much she may have spent on it. I wondered if the fake arse felt as hard and unwelcoming as fake boobs. It was the same sad crowd. There were no new prospects or intriguing old ones. Just straining bozos and bimbos, flirting and pawing, everybody feeling and looking better after each round of drinks. I viewed them with contempt, trying to avoid the full realization that I was one of them. No better, no worse. We had nothing else to do. It made me miss married life.

Before I could even get a decent cup of lukewarm coffee at the station, the Captain let me know I was up in the bullpen.

"Most of us knew this guy from the old days," Captain Gary said, handing me a file. "You're the hayseed, so he's yours."

"What was he bagged for?"

"Murder. He doesn't even deny it. But he doesn't exactly spell it out, either. He needs a once-over. Take his statement."

"Yes, sir."

As I followed the rear half-glass wall around to the bullpen door, I noticed the perp was elderly. His thinning white hair was matted and unwashed. When I opened the door and stepped in, it occurred to me that I might know him from somewhere. But I didn't know why. And even if we'd met, I didn't think he'd recognize me.

"Hello," I said.

"Hello, officer," he replied.

I sat down and opened the file. I *did* know him. I recognized the name. *Herman Mear.* According to the file, his wife, Carrie, had been asphyxiated. The working assumption was he had choked her to death.

Mear looked tired. One shirtsleeve was damp at the bicep and his eyes were red. He'd been crying.

"I need to talk to you about last night," I said.

"Last night?"

"Yes."

"I couldn't sleep," Mear said.

"Okay. Is that why you killed her?"

"Who?"

"Your wife."

"Carrie?"

"Yes."

"I don't... I don't. *Carrie.*"

"Yes. Your wife, Carrie."

"I don't expect you to understand."

"Understand what? That you killed her?"

"She... she broke my pillow."

"Your pillow."

"She broke my pillow. I couldn't sleep. *She broke my pillow.*"

Mear seemed discombobulated. Too unfocused for the discussion taking place. I decided to ease him back around. "Mr. Mear."

He looked up. "Yes, officer."

"You say your wife, Carrie, she broke your pillow."

"Carrie. Yes. *Poor girl.* I couldn't sleep. There was..."

Mear stared off. I waited.

"She broke my pillow," he continued. "I couldn't sleep. I couldn't rest. It was driving me crazy. She broke my pillow."

"Mr. Mear. How does one *break* a pillow?"

"I don't know. I have no idea. But it didn't work anymore. My pillow was broken."

I stared at the two-way mirror I knew the captain was standing behind. "How did you know?"

"I couldn't sleep."

"Did your wife remove the feathers?"

"Not that I'm aware of, no. Not to my knowledge." He twitched.

"Did she forget to put the pillowcase back on after she washed it? Were feathers poking through?"

"No. I don't... *No.* Nothing like that. She never forgot that." Mear looked at me as if I'd suggested something completely unreasonable.

"Well, Mr. Mear. How did she break your pillow?"

"I told you. I don't know. I just know it was broke. I just know that I loved her." He sucked in a heavy breath with a sound that could easily have turned into a sob.

"You loved Carrie, your wife?"

"Yes. Dearly."

"Then why'd you kill her?"

"She broke my pillow."

"Mr. Mear," I said, frustrated. A hangover was pounding in my head now. Like an aluminum bat. A hollow thudding. *Contact, contact, contact, contact.* All foul, like my mood. I massaged my temples with the thumb and index finger of my left hand.

I knew the guy.

My parents separated for about six months when I was around ten. My mom rented a small house out near Weatherford, a few miles from the lake. Our next-door neighbor had a big garden, a half-acre at least. He worked at the city hall in Fort Worth, I think. Every day after work, he came home and tended his garden, weeding, watering. One day he applied Sevin dust. It was yellow. A yellow powder.

His kids were grown, and it was just him and his wife. The Mears. I only knew them as that or Mr. and Mrs. Mear.

"Mr. Mear," I repeated, snapping out of the daydream.

"Yes, officer."

"The pillow."

"Yes, officer."

"You say... your wife, Carrie. She broke your pillow."

"Yes. But I fixed hers."

"Fixed?"

"Yes."

"What do you mean?" I knew the answer before I asked. Then it came to me exactly why I remembered him.

"I mean, I fixed it," he said. "She's sleeping now. She's asleep."

"Aslee..." I started but didn't finish. My head seemed to swim and his face, Mr. Mear's face—*it came back*. It *all* came back to me.

I couldn't have been more than eleven years old. We were coming home from a friend's house. My best friend Denny and I and two other friends. It was late, and we'd been playing whiffle-ball. It was one of those endless summer days and we played until we lost the ball. Damnedest thing. It landed in Mr. Mear's garden and we couldn't find it. In fact, it never turned back up at all.

It was humid, and just before dark. We startled a big toad out in front of the Mears' house. I was carrying the whiffle-ball bat in my right hand, swatting at lightning bugs. I spotted the toad first and grabbed it underneath its ribcage. I was trying to be funny.

"Gnarly," said Denny.

I held the frog out. "Pitch him to me," I said, waving the bat.

"No way," Denny replied. "I ain't touching that thing."

One of the others spoke up. "I'll do it," Tommy Gordon said. He was a year younger and eager to impress. "I'll pitch."

"I'll catch," said Ross Kensy. He was Tommy's age.

It was settled.

We stopped at a patch of St. Augustine grass on the line between the Mears' yard and my mom's. Tommy took the toad. I found a spot for home plate and tapped it with the whiffle-ball bat. Ross stood just behind me.

I leveled a practice swing, waiting on the pitch. Tommy pretended to check first and third base for baserunners.

"Oh, shit," Denny said.

Tommy sent the toad underhand, right down the middle. I swung and missed, and Ross dropped it.

"He's all wet," Ross said.

"He pissed himself," Denny cried. "That's his piss on your hand."

The toad jumped twice, and Tommy grabbed him. "Don't be a pussy," Tommy said. "*Strike one.*"

Tommy did a full wind up this time. I took a couple more practice swings, putting the bat exactly where I wanted the ball. Hitting a whiffle ball was much harder than hitting a frog.

Tommy sent another underhanded pitch at the right level and in the exact spot and *plupppppp!* The whiffle-ball bat slammed the toad sideways to my right. Something moist struck my cheek.

"Foul ball," Ross exclaimed. "*Strike two,*" Tommy said.

The frog landed in front of Denny. He froze and the frog, lying on its back, began extending one of its forelimbs as if it was reaching for something.

I wiped the moisture away from my cheek, but didn't look at my hand. The game was suddenly a lot less funny, but it had been my idea. I played along.

The toad had blood seeping from its mouth. "You busted his lip," Tommy said. "But I bet he's got enough left to strike you out."

"Batter up," said Ross.

I looked at Denny. "This is messed up," he said. "Let's go catch some lightning bugs."

"One more strike," Tommy said.

I had felt the toad's mass through the bat and between that and the moisture on my cheek; I was more than a little weirded out. But, again, it had been my idea. I couldn't afford to look like a wimp. "Bring it," I said, leveling a few practice swings again.

Tommy wound up, getting ready to send the toad. I didn't want any more of the toad's blood or piss on my face, but it was too late.

It was Mear who intervened.

"Hey!" he screamed, startling us with an abrupt entrance.

"What do you think you're doing?" Mear continued, jerking the whiffle-ball bat out of my hands and hitting me over the head with the handle end.

We were shocked. Everyone except Tommy stepped back.

"Give it to me," Mr. Mears demanded. Tommy complied.

"Uhhhh," Denny started.

"Shut up," Mr. Mear replied. "Game's over. You ought to be ashamed. *What's wrong with you?*"

I started to cry first.

"I'm sorry," Tommy said, his eyes welling up.

"It was his idea," Ross chirped, pointing at me.

"Does your mother know you're here," Mr. Mear said, addressing me. I considered running. "The rest of you boys get home," Mear continued.

I didn't answer. The other boys left.

"Why would you do such a thing?" Mr. Mear asked.

"I'm sorry," I said, between sobs.

"You should be. What did the toad ever do to you?"

"I don't know. Nothing."

"Exactly."

"Will he be okay?"

"I don't think so," Mr. Mear said. He held the toad up. Blood was still seeping from its mouth, but now its tongue was hanging out as well. And the forelimb it had extended had receded back to its side. "I'm sorry," Mr. Mear continued.

"Me, too."

"Get on home, now."

"Okay."

I ran straight to my front door and slipped inside. I never told my mom, and neither did Mr. Mear. I avoided him until we moved.

"Are you okay?" Mr. Mear asked, still seated at the table in the bullpen. He studied me for a moment and then continued. "Do I know you?"

"I don't think so," I answered.

"Did you ever come before the bench? In my courtroom?"

"I don't think so."

"You look familiar. I've seen you before."

"People say that. I get that a lot. You say you fixed your wife's pillow. Is that after she broke yours?"

"Yes. No. Yes. I don't know. But she's sleeping now."

"That's why you're here."

His eyes welled up. "I know. *I know.* And now I remember."

"What do you remember?"

"The toad."

"What?"

"The game."

"What game?" Mear gave me a long look. I couldn't hold his gaze. *"She's sleeping now?"* I continued.

"She is," Mear answered, without looking away. "I'd like to. I'd like to sleep now, too."

"Once you've answered my questions."

"I have answered your questions."

"No, you—"

"Hey!" Mear interrupted. "Yes. I gave you your answers. And now I want to sleep."

"Sleep?"

"Yes. I want you to fix my pillow. Carrie—she's asleep. I'm sleepy. I'm tired. *Please.*"

"I can't."

"You can."

"I can't."

"It's not fair. *You can.*"

"I'd like to help you—but..."

"*You.* You *owe* me. I remember."

"I don't know what you're talking about."

"You do. You most certainly do."

"I don't. *Please.*"

"You do. I'm begging you."

"I can't know—I don't know what you're talking about. I don't."

"I won't say anything to your mother. I promise. *I promise.*"

<hr>

The captain was concerned. "Why was he talking about your mother?"

"I think he was confused."

"He didn't know your mother?"

"No."

"He seemed to recognize you. You ever seen him before?"

"No. Like I said. I think he was confused."

The captain gave me the rest of the day off. I took the rest of the week.

Mr. Mear was transferred to a psych ward. He hadn't just worked for the city all those years back. He'd been a judge. I'd forgotten all about him.

A few days after our interview, Mr. Mear fixed his pillow by leaping headfirst out an unbarred second-floor window in the hallway leading to the psych facility he was being placed in.

Now, my pillow is broken.

I can't sleep. Not even with pills. No matter how much I drink at the bar, who I bring home or how late we stay up degrading each other.

I can't sleep. He broke it.

Mear broke my pillow.

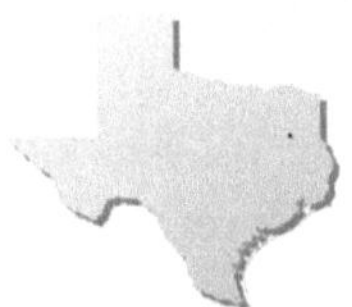

seven

a dark white postscript

THE FIGURE WAS as black as sackcloth, and it moved awkwardly in the dark. Tieg Bertram smelled it before he saw it.

It had an odor, like it was badly burnt. The reek was almost overpowering; but it was also familiar. Something that Bertram remembered from his past.

The figure moved closer.

Bertram lifted himself up on his elbows and looked around. An elderly man, his eyesight was bad in daylight, even with glasses. But at night, without them, he might as well have been blind. He didn't notice that only the form's lidless eyes and the front teeth of its lipless mouth caught light. The rest of its body was dark and indiscernible. Bertram could hear it, though. Its rough hide cracked as it moved.

"Hello," Bertram said. "Hello? Who's there?"

As Bertram sat up and fumbled for his glasses, the creature stopped.

Bertram retrieved his glasses from the nightstand and placed them over the bridge of his nose, securing the temple arms over his ears. Then he flipped on the bedside lamp.

When Bertram's bleary eyes finally adjusted to the light, they abruptly widened, and his jaw dropped. Before him stood a dark, twisted figure, solid black. His mind had problems processing it.

The creature stood motionless.

Bertram pushed the sheets and comforter away, swung his legs off the bed, and faced the dark form. Except for its eyes and teeth, the scorched figure was as black as the grave. And with no lips, its countenance was frozen in a hellish grin.

"Hello," Bertram repeated weakly. The creature remained mute.

In Bertram's mind's eye, he knew this spectre, this grim form in the shape of a man. Its blackened contour, which looked as if it had been hewn from coal, now glistened in places where secretions of pus, pink with blood, gathered at the cracks in its hide.

It was grotesque, but Bertram was not afraid. There was something recognizable about this figure.

Bertram's memory was dim, but his mind began reaching back, sifting through the sedimentary layers of a long life. The creature was a man, or it had been a man. Bertram was sure of that.

The shadow remained motionless, its hands at its sides. The pungent smell it arrived with lingered like gloom. Bertram continued to stare.

A speck of memory flickered in one of the far corners of his consciousness, an inkling at first, evolving slowly and quietly. He turned his head and saw his face in the mirror above a chest of drawers.

The reflection of Bertram in the mirror was young and lean. His eyes were bright, and his face was handsome and angular. His glasses were gone. It occurred to him that he couldn't have looked like that when he was any older than a teenager—and then it came to him.

He stared away for a moment and then turned back to the silent apparition. He looked it up and down slowly and his bottom lip quivered.

"That's not possible," Bertram said, as he looked back at the mirror, the face there now, his face, the face of an old man. "That's..."

Bertram's protestation trailed off. The apparition stood idle, an unstirring totem.

Bertram turned back to the figure and peered into its lidless eyes. They stared straight ahead, above him, beyond him, the orbs seemingly immobile. Bertram lowered his gaze to one of its legs, a thick vine of charred sinew. A tear ran down Bertram's left cheek. Then, he looked again at the creature's eyes.

"Petty," Bertram said. "Pettigrew Smith."

The apparition's eyeballs shifted then, directly observing Bertram for the first time. Its bloodshot orbs seemed the only thing alive against its blackened head and torso. The rest of its burned carcass remained motionless.

"Is it really you, Petty?"

Bertram knew the answer.

He removed his glasses and wiped his eyes. Then, before turning back to the creature, he sniffed and folded his glasses and placed them on the nightstand.

"Oh god, Petty. It wasn't..."

Bertram placed his hands on his knees and then clasped them and let them rest in his lap.

"I'm sorry, Petty."

The dark creature moved then, unsteadily stepping towards Bertram, but Bertram didn't flinch or cringe. He held out his hand. The creature came close and slowly lifted its rigid right arm.

"Sorry, Petty," Bertram repeated.

The apparition touched Bertram's white, wrinkly fingertips with the nubs of its shriveled, charcoal knuckles, and Bertram burst into blue flame. The blaze roared orange and then yellow as it encompassed Bertram's body immediately and en masse. Bertram grunted, but nothing more.

The dark apparition stood over Bertram as the flames raged. When the fire began to die down, the spectre turned and shuffled away.

Sheriff Dunphee got the call on the radio about seven o'clock the next morning, just as he was leaving his home in Harkin.

Edna Jenkins in Troup had phoned the sheriff's department and said something had happened to her granddad, Bertram. But she couldn't explain what. When the dispatch officer pressed her for details, she grew agitated.

A little strange, Dunphee thought. But he knew Edna was harmless and getting up there in years. Their families were both from Harkin and Dunphee had even met Bertram once or twice, in Daingerfield or Ore City; he couldn't remember. Bertram had known Dunphee's grandmother but had left Harkin when he was a young man. Dunphee had wound up back in Harkin after college, and Edna had moved to Troup ages ago when she married.

Troup was just southeast of Tyler and not far out of Dunphee's way. When he traveled through the town, he always drove by the Troup Boxing Gym. It had originally been named after a 16-year-old Black boxing phenom named Byron Payton, but the novelty and memory had worn off. Sheriff Dunphee had boxed against Payton in the late 1970s and lost in a decision; but only, he suspected, because Payton had gone easy on him.

Most of Dunphee's family and friends had been at the fight and assured him he was cheated, but he knew better. There was a way things were where they lived, and Payton's success simply rubbed white folks the wrong way.

Payton had been the complete package, a knockout punch (with either hand), a devastating jab and uncanny fist and foot speed. In retrospect, Dunphee knew that he was lucky he had even made it out of the ring alive and fairly sure he couldn't have beaten Payton even if there'd been an extra Billy Dunphee in the ring with him. Payton's talent and determination had been spectacular. Dunphee had just been a tough country boy who was pretty good at taking a punch.

Payton had won the Texas Golden Gloves State Championship twice and was on his way to making the U.S. Olympic team in 1980—the year the United States boycotted the summer Olympics. But Payton never got the chance to experience that disappointment. He and twenty-one U. S. boxers, trainers and coaches had perished in a plane crash on the outskirts of Poland a few months prior.

As Sheriff Dunphee drove through Troup, he wondered at it all over again. You never forget the first time you get laid out in a fight—especially in front of a large group of spectators.

It was what came to be known as a bolo punch. A hook combined with an uppercut. It dropped Dunphee immediately. He didn't even see it coming.

Dunphee was a plodder. It didn't hurt him, but it surprised him. When the bell rang and he got back to his corner, his trainer asked him if he was okay.

Dunphee nodded.

"Kid Galivan," his trainer said. "Sugar Ray Leonard. Scrunch up. Economize. And make him reach."

Dunphee didn't find out who Kid Galivan was 'til later. But he obviously knew who Sugar Ray was. Payton was shifty, but not showy. He was quick and punched with precision. He parried several of Dunphee's jabs and punches. He changed his lead foot a time or two. And his ducks, paws and feints were practically dizzying.

Dunphee caught Payton once and made him stumble. It was a counterpunch after he slipped a lead right. The mostly white crowd roared, but Payton was all business. If he smiled, it was only with his eyes. He didn't lose his temper. He just kept coming. He worked Dunphee over pretty good.

But it made Dunphee feel good, too.

Strike and parry. Absorb a blow, backpedal, reengage. Counterpunch. Body work. Dish it out and take it. Look for an opening. There was almost a rhythm to it. It was a good, honest contest. *Mano y mano.* No head butts. No silly point taps or fouling in the clinches. No razzle-dazzle. Dunphee had done his best.

Payton's invincibility in the ring had meant nothing in the end. All that was left was a statue dedicated to him and the others in Colorado Springs and an on-again, off-again annual boxing tourney held in his name at the Troup Boxing Gym. Dunphee sat ringside every year it was held.

When Dunphee had heard the news of Payton's death on the AM radio in his beat-up, old pickup truck in 1980, he hadn't believed it. It didn't seem possible.

Now, an officer of the law for over twenty years, he knew anything was possible and sometimes the worst things happened.

Dunphee realized that maybe the best thing he'd ever done, perhaps the closest he'd ever come to a brush with greatness, was the match he'd had with Byron Payton. And the fact that the young man was gone still haunted him.

The boxing gym was one of the only things of note left in Troup, but Troup was practically cosmopolitan compared to Harkin. Harkin had shown some life early in the 20th century, but it sputtered out in the mid-thirties. Harkin barely had a post office. Tyler was beginning to expand out past them both, and Dunphee was thinking about moving away when he retired.

The Jenkins place was on a couple dozen acres just off State Highway 135, heading to Arp. When Sheriff Dunphee turned off on the gravel drive and crossed the cattleguard, he drove slowly so as not to disturb the handful of cattle and two nags that had the run of the pasture. He parked under one of the big oak trees that sat out in front of the house, and Edna immediately appeared on the porch. She was nervous and fearful. Dunphee stepped out of the patrol car and took off his hat.

"Are you okay, Edna?" he asked.

"I don't know, Billy—*Sheriff Dunphee.*"

"You can call me Billy, Edna. You know that."

"Billy—I don't know what happened. I'm not sure what I'm seeing. I went in the spare bedroom I keep for my granddaughter when she visits, and he was..." Edna cupped a hand over her mouth and started to cry. Dunphee placed his hand on her shoulder and gave her a moment.

"Show me," he said.

Dunphee followed Edna into the house and recoiled when the stench hit his nostrils.

"It's bad, I know," Edna said. "But I didn't want to touch anything."

Dunphee put his hat back on and they took a left down a hall. Edna stopped at the last door on the right and held the doorknob. There was a towel at the base of the door, tucked there in an attempt to contain the odor.

"He's in here," Edna said. "I think. I didn't touch anything. I think it's him."

Edna opened the door and led Dunphee in. The smell got worse.

Noting the odor when he stood in Edna's entry, Dunphee had prepared himself for a spoiled cadaver, but there wasn't one. There was just a large pile of black and gray ash on the near side of the sheets on the queen bed, and a smaller collection on the floor in front of the bed, settled in, on and around a pair of fairly new, leather moccasins. The pile on the bed was still smoking.

"I think that's Bertram," Edna said, breaking into tears.

While Dunphee was staring at the ashes on the bed, he pulled a handkerchief out of his pocket and covered his nose. If that was Bertram, he thought, he'd lost a lot of weight or the fire that consumed him had gotten incredibly hot—so hot that it probably would've burned down the whole house. Dunphee glanced at the house shoes and then the shape of the ash piles. It looked like Bertram had probably burned to death, but to the point of cremation? It was a new one on Dunphee. He continued to scan the room for clues. When he turned back to Edna, she was still crying.

"Did Bertram smoke?" he ventured.

"No."

"If I didn't know any better," Dunphee continued, "I'd say someone poured gasoline on him and lit him on fire. That or jet fuel. But I don't see or smell any gasoline and jet fuel is tricky to handle. And if gasoline was poured on Bertram, what are the chances that someone could do that without spilling any... or cause him to burn up without burning anything else up?"

"So, you think it's him? I mean, there's hardly anything left."

Dunphee spotted something on the bed and took a ballpoint pen out of his shirt pocket. He stood next to the bed and picked at the ash pile that appeared to have been the head. He isolated a clump of cinder that contained a small, twisted bead of silver.

"Did Bertram have fillings?" Dunphee asked.

"I think so."

"This looks like part of a filling. And I assume those are Bertram's moccasins?"

"Yes."

"I guess this is Bertram. Is there anybody else it could be?"

"No."

Dunphee took her at her word, but there was still the job.

"Edna."

"Yes."

"I don't mean to be indelicate, but I have to ask. You didn't do this, did you?"

"No, Billy."

"I had to ask."

"I know."

Dunphee tried to lighten the moment. "Edna—this ain't some old cowpoke you hooked up with, and things went south?"

"Oh, goodness, no," she said, with a weak smile. "Since I lost Arthur, you know I never. I don't need another man to take care of."

"I hear you. I've felt the same way since Linda passed."

"Oh, I still can't believe it," Edna said. "She was so young."

"Yes, she was."

Dunphee nodded, and Edna managed another weak smile.

"What happened to Bertram, Sheriff?"

"I'm not real sure."

They stood there, quietly, considering what Dunphee assumed were Bertam's remains. He dialed the office and requested a couple of deputies and a Crime Scene Investigation unit. He led Edna out of the room, shut the door, and replaced the towel. Then they went out into the yard to wait in fresher air.

When the deputies and the CSI unit arrived, Dunphee headed to Tyler. Old man Bertram's odd remains had ruined his appetite, but he knew he should eat something. He got to Nat's Dine-In just after 10:00 a.m. and had the place to himself. Not many late-risers frequented Nat's.

He took a chair in a wall booth that featured a crooked, eight-by-ten snapshot of Nat (a tall Black man and the long-time, sole owner and proprietor of the Dine -In) standing next to Earl Campbell, Tyler's most revered native son. Nat's hair was black and full in the picture, but of late it had faded white and was receding. Nat appeared and poured Dunphee a cup of coffee.

"What'll it be, Sheriff?"

"One egg over medium," Dunphee said, adding "one piece of bacon —make that two—and a side of grits."

"Toast?"

"One piece of wheat toast."

"Coming right up, Sheriff."

Nat was close to Bertram's age, and also from Harkin, but he grew up in Kilgore. Dunphee had known him almost all his adult life.

Nat had served in the military and relocated to Tyler in the 1980s. He started the diner and made it into a local landmark, popular because it was folksy and Nat was the genuine article. When the occasional, uninitiated customer made or inquired about to-go orders, Nat was known to point at the sign out front and remind them he ran a *dine-in* establishment. If they wanted fast food, he'd add, they could take their business to the Whataburger down the street. Nat was Black and— excepting Earl Campbell—Black was underappreciated in Tyler. But Nat's Dine-In reminded folks middle-aged and older, Black and white, of what things used to be like in East Texas before everyone bent their knee to the hurry up and plunked down in front of cable TV after the daily race.

Dunphee sipped on his coffee. He had to see his grandmother later, and he didn't relish the thought of mentioning Bertram's passing. His grandmother and Bertram had known each other when they were young. She also knew Nat.

Nat appeared with Dunphee's breakfast momentarily. The bacon smelled good, perhaps especially after the olfactory trauma he'd experienced at Edna's.

"How things goin'?" Nat asked.

"Okay," Dunphee answered. "But it's early yet."

Dunphee finished his bacon.

"When you going to retire, Nat?"

"The day after never. How's yer grandmama doin?"

"She's alright. I'm going to see her at the home tonight."

"Please send my regards."

"I will. But I think she'd rather me bring her a piece of your pecan pie."

"Bring her by later. I'll have it made fresh."

Dunphee picked at his egg.

"How long you known my grandmother, Nat?"

"Since I was around six. She was older, I think eleven or twelve when we left."

"Did you know Tieg Bertram?"

Nat looked directly at Dunphee and then glanced out the front window. "Hmm. You could say that. I knew *of* him."

"I think my grandmother knew him."

"Probably so. It wasn't a big town back then."

"Still isn't."

"No. It isn't." Nat rolled up his sleeves. "Tieg Bertram left Harkin 'round same time my folks did, been gone since forever. Why you askin' about him?"

"I think he's dead. I just saw what I took to be his remains over at Edna Jenkins's place."

"Here?" Nat asked abruptly. "In Smith County?"

"Yep. I just found him in a pile of ashes."

Nat's face changed, and he tried to conceal whatever he was thinking by staring at the egg left on Dunphee's plate.

"You okay, Nat?" Dunphee asked.

Nat continued to stare.

"That's sad to hear," Nat said, seeming dazed.

"Nat?"

"Yes, sir?"

"What's wrong?"

"Nothing, Sheriff. Nothing. There's just some water under that bridge. Bertram and some others caused some trouble for us back in the day."

"I never heard that."

"We don't talk about it. Nobody talks about it."

"Can you tell me about it?"

"Rather not, Sheriff."

Dunphee leaned back and stared at Nat, surprised. Nat stared back.

"It was a long time ago, Bill Dunphee," Nat said pointedly. "I think we'd all be better off if we left it there."

Dunphee was shocked, but he didn't show it. Nat had always been oak solid, and here he was, rattled. Harkin wasn't big enough for secrets. Hell, neither was Tyler.

Nat noticed the crooked eight-by-ten of him standing next to Earl Campbell and straightened it.

"I gotta' get back to the kitchen," he said nonchalantly. "Anything else I can get you, Sheriff?"

"No, thanks."

"Thanks for coming by!"

"Thank you."

Dunphee set a ten-dollar bill under his coffee cup and left.

When he got into his patrol car, Dunphee turned on the ignition and sat for a moment. He was mildly stunned. *What just happened in there?*

Dunphee phoned the Department and told his secretary to hold his calls, except for those regarding the investigation into Tieg Bertram's death. He sat for several moments, thinking, and then turned off the car's ignition and went back inside. Nat was still in the kitchen.

Dunphee sat down in a wall booth closer to the kitchen and waited. After a few moments, Nat returned to bus Dunphee's dishes. He was carrying a dishrag and a plastic bus bin.

"We need to talk," Dunphee said.

"That right, Billy?" Nat replied coolly. "You askin' as a friend? Or you tellin' me in an official capacity?"

"You know me better than that."

"Do I? I know—*as a friend*—I just asked you to leave this alone."

"I'm aware. But I'm trying to find out what happened to Bertram."

"Doesn't matter."

"What does that mean?"

"Maybe he got what was comin' to him." Nat regretted the statement as soon as he made it.

Dunphee's eyes narrowed, and he considered what Nat said carefully. He doubted Nat was involved in Bertram's death, but the way he initially responded to the news was peculiar.

"I see them wagon wheels spinnin' in your head," Nat continued. "Don't let this thing get stuck in yer craw. Won't do you no good. Won't do any of us any good." Nat started gathering Dunphee's dishes. "I know you got a job to do," Nat added over his shoulder. "But this one—it's ancient history. Let the dead bury the dead."

Dunphee switched seats in the booth. He was now staring at Nat's back. "You have any idea how crazy you're sounding?"

"Yes, Billy. I do." Nat turned to head toward the kitchen with the dishes and then stopped at Dunphee's table. "I'm an old man, Billy. You oughta' let me alone. I slipped up. That's all."

"This just gets worse and worse," Dunphee groaned.

Nat laid the bus bin aside and sat back down across from Dunphee. He was quiet for a minute, thinking, staring into nothing. Finally, he spoke.

"Remember the 'slaughter rule?'" Nat said. "In Little League Baseball... when you were a kid?"

"Yes."

"This is like that, Billy. For a long time, white folks around here ran up the score, but there was no rule against it. There were no rules against killing Black people. Or raping Black women. And the game went on and on. White folks just kept on going, running up the score—and Black folks just kept on dyin'. And suffering. It was before your time, most of it. But I'm gonna say this, and you need to hear me, Billy. We're friends and you need to really hear me."

Dunphee nodded.

"What happened to Bertram ain't got nothin' to do with anything goin' on today. It's a game that started a long time ago... and was bound to finish. Your grandmamma obviously didn't tell you about it... she had her reasons. I can't tell you about it now. It ain't my place.

"No one told you and no one told anyone, because they were scared or ashamed. And it's been like that here since Johnny Reb came limping home after the war. My family left Harkin 'cause of it. And our hometown is still a nothing little smudge on the map 'cause of it."

"What are you saying?" Dunphee asked.

"I'm sayin' what happened to Bertram may have been a long time coming, probably because he stayed away."

"Stayed away. Stayed away from what?"

"What he did, Billy. *What he did.*"

Dunphee sat in the booth dumbfounded. He had no idea what Nat was talking about. And he suddenly felt like he had no idea where he was from or who the people he grew up with were. "Nat," he said. "I can't let this stand. I feel... I feel undermined."

"Sorry," Nat replied. "But that's a fine word for it. That's exactly how I might've put it."

"You know I gotta' know," Dunphee added.

Nat looked Dunphee directly in the eyes. They stared at each other for a long moment, and then Nat nodded.

Nat told Dunphee he had to get ready for the lunch crowd, but that he would meet with him later. At the library, at 3:00 p.m. Dunphee hadn't been to a library in years, and he regretted it. He decided to move up his date with his grandmother. As he got up to leave, a familiar face in a frame caught his eye. This image wasn't crooked. It was a newspaper clipping of Byron Payton.

Dunphee had seen it a thousand times. Payton's head was slightly cocked to the right and his hands were gloved. He was hugging a heavy bag, probably during or after a workout, and he was smiling.

Dunphee's grandmother's nursing home was not too shabby and had been her idea. He had protested, but Alta Jean, as his grandmother preferred to be called (by everyone except her grandson), usually got her way. When he entered her room, she was sitting on the side of her bed, staring out the window.

"Alta Jean," he said.

She turned her head slowly. "Hello."

"Hello. How are you?"

"I'm alright. What about you?"

"Doing okay."

"How are my great-grandbabies?"

"Still off at school, one at A & M and one at UT."

"That'll make for uh..." Alta Jean trailed off.

"An interesting Thanksgiving," Dunphee said, finishing her sentence. "Yes."

"Thanksgiving? *Already?*"

"No, Mee-Maw. Not yet."

"Seemed awful soon."

"Yep. We've got awhile."

Dunphee looked around the room at all of Alta Jean's old pictures. The TV was on but the sound was turned down.

"I saw Nat," Dunphee added.

"How's he doing?"

"He's doing well. He sends his regards."

"Oh, I miss him. He's a sweet man."

"He's a good guy. Always was."

"Yes."

Dunphee walked over and sat in a chair next to Alta Jean's small couch. Then he stared at her. She kept her white hair neat, and her nails filed, but she was visibly frail. She tried to carry herself well, but her advancing age was really starting to show. Alta Jean noticed that he was staring.

"Can I talk to you about something?" Dunphee asked.

"I suppose... so."

"Okay. But you may have to put on your thinking cap."

"Okay. I can do that."

"Do you remember Tieg Bertram?"

Alta Jean glanced downward and was slow to answer. "Bertram. Yes. He moved away."

"Yes," Dunphee said. "What do you remember about him?"

"Oh. He was a bully."

"He was?"

"Yes."

Dunphee waited for her to elaborate, but she didn't.

"Yes," she repeated. "Why do you ask?"

"Well, he came back over the weekend."

"Back..." Alta Jean said. "*Here?*" She turned to face Dunphee. "Bertram is here?!"

"Yes."

"Is he okay?"

"No."

Alta Jean clasped her hands and brought them to her face, her knuckles just under her nose. She appeared to be praying, but Dunphee knew she wasn't. It wasn't her way. Or his.

Alta Jean's hands were clasped tightly, and they started to shake. She unclasped them and placed them at her sides. She held them there for a moment and started to sob. Dunphee came over and placed his arm around her shoulders.

"Are you okay Alta Jean?"

"No, Billy," she said, between sniffs. "I'm very tired." Alta Jean wiped her eyes. "Sorry," she continued. "I'm just so tired."

"You need a nap?" Dunphee inquired, perplexed.

"I don't know. Just let me lie down. I'll be better in a minute."

Dunphee hugged his grandmother and then helped her lay back in the bed. She closed her eyes, and he stood over her, wondering what the hell was going on. When she fell asleep, he left.

Dunphee walked out to his patrol car and put the department on the horn. The CSI unit had wrapped up and Bertram's presumed remains had been transferred to the coroner's office. There was no official word yet.

Dunphee was frustrated, and it was still early.

Alta Jean had finished raising Dunphee after his parents were killed in a car wreck. A head-on collision in Seagoville, south of Dallas. Drunk driver.

Dunphee was eleven at the time, about to turn twelve. He spent the rest of his adolescence on his grandparents' farm, milking cows, driving tractors and hauling hay. He hunted and fished and canoed the Nueces and Sabine Rivers. And he played sports.

Dunphee's grandfather passed not long after he graduated high school. His name was Roscoe, and he was from Valdosta, Georgia. He was a tall, quiet man, patient and witty. Dunphee had loved him and his grandmother dearly, and now Alta Jean was all he had left. His aunts and uncles still all lived close, but he didn't see much of them. Especially after he came back from Sam Houston State University and joined the Sheriff's department.

They had all been there on the night he fought Payton, like he was Harkin's own Great White Hope. His grandparents had remained composed after he lost, Alta Jean giving him a tight, loving hug, and his grandfather winking at him and nodding, realizing how hard he had worked to even put things in the hands of the judges. There had been no doubt in Dunphee's mind who won, but at least he went the distance. His aunts and uncles raised redneck hell.

That nigger cheated.

Goddamn spear-chucker!

Dunphee knew Payton had heard them, because Payton had looked at him the way Black people you know and like look at you when a racist antagonist interrupts the moment you've shared. And the Black person knows the circumstances will force you to agree with the antagonist or hold your tongue, a betrayal either way. But the way things were and sometimes still are.

Dunphee had lowered his head then, soundly defeated. And ashamed.

Twenty years removed, Dunphee sat in his patrol car hoping Payton had understood that. That he had been ashamed.

The dead don't bury the dead, he thought. *The living do.* To make things easier. To make it easier to betray them.

To Dunphee's way of thinking, the best way to bury the dead was to live right by them, and he figured that's why Byron Payton had remained a friendly presence in his mind all these years. Like his parents, his granddad and, more recently, his wife. They weren't meant to be disposed of. They were supposed to stay with you, in memory and spirit, guides as much as reminders. And they still made Dunphee as much of who he was as anything else.

Nat's advice had done no good at all.

What happened to Bertram and whatever it was he may or may not have done to deserve it stuck in Dunphee's craw and vexed him something fierce.

The cryptic talk, the warnings; he knew Nat was being straight. But the missing pieces, which seemed to indict Bertram and the entire town of Harkin, disturbed and frustrated him.

Alta Jean slept fitfully.

She kept mumbling a name under her breath, inaudible at first, but finally plain.

"Petty," she moaned.

She was back at her parent's place, early in the Depression. Up in her bedroom.

Her parents were out front, watching a group of Harkin citizens leave on horseback. They were followed by a one-horse wagon. A Black boy was lying unconscious on the worn planks in the bottom of the wagon. It was Petty. His lips were smashed, and he was bleeding from his side and his head above one eye. His hands were tied behind his back.

Alta Jean moaned again, barely audible.

She had been forced to do something that day.

Not by the Black boy lying in the wagon, but by her parents and their neighbors and their friends. By the community.

When they brought Alta Jean out and she saw Petty in the wagon, she thought he was dead. *There was so much blood.*

When her parents asked her to do what she did, she thought it wouldn't matter because Petty looked like he was already gone. And her parents had told her to do it. Told her that if she didn't do it, they could lose the farm. Told her that if she didn't do it, their neighbors might turn against them and run them off.

Did she realize they could lose everything? Did she realize they might have to move away to make a living?

Alta Jean had done what her parents asked. Alta Jean had done what she was told, and they had kept the farm and their friends and stayed in Harkin.

From that day forward, however, there were unintended consequences. Alta Jean suddenly enjoyed small town celebrity, importance, and pity—as a victim.

It was all a lie. And Alta Jean resented the lie.

Petty had been her friend. Petty had taught her how to catch crawdads and trap fireflies in jars. And she was trying to teach Petty his letters.

Alta Jean remembered hearing her parents argue that night after they carried Petty away in the wagon.

It's our fault... what they done to that boy.

How could we have known?

She shoulda' known better.

We shoulda' known better.

Petty wuz just a boy, a good boy.

Don't matter a lick. You know what the talk woulda' been.

Alta Jean hadn't seen what happened. She was told later by a neighbor's bragging son. It had turned her blood cold, and she didn't think it would ever thaw.

And it didn't for a long time.

What happened to Petty was never forgotten; it was just never spoken of. Alta Jean was not inclined to forget, but it was an ugly thing to bear. She busied herself with chores and schoolwork. It had a lot to do with why she was late to marry.

Alta Jean had plenty of callers, but they were all from the Harkin area. One by one, she politely turned them away. Her mother began to worry she would be an old maid. Her father wondered if she was simply doing it out of spite. Alta Jean didn't believe the cold in her would ever subside, but it did. Life went on.

She met Billy's grandfather, and she grew to love him. Their courtship was prolonged, because she had grown comfortable in the cold. She may have felt she owed it to Petty. But Roscoe was persistent and when he proposed, she told him about it, tested him with the truth, the shame of it, her long sadness and her soul laid bare. And a curious thing happened.

Roscoe didn't comfort her or try to help her rationalize it. Roscoe understood.

There had been a similar incident, maybe even worse, outside Roscoe's hometown. He had some experience with the same kind of guilt and revulsion. He was afflicted with some of the same pain and doubt and sadness. They were both disfigured on the inside, and she realized they could shelter one another. And they did. When Roscoe passed, Alta Jean had Billy. Her surviving sons and daughters had become little more than East Texas detritus, subject to the same ebbs and flows of the communal neuroses that had seized the citizenry of Harkin when she was young. But Billy was different. Billy was like her and Roscoe, capable of empathy. Conscience. And he, too, was alienated by his own decency in the midst of dimwitted hayseeds and slack-souled buffoons. They were everywhere and all at once, the products of a dangerous mob mentality that seemed to thrive in the environs of red dirt and piney wood forest.

Idiots like Tieg Bertram and his kind had fed off frenzy and reveled in it. Men like Billy usually stood back and away, and tried to keep some perspective.

In Alta Jean's dream, Petty was awake and being drug by a rope tied around his chest and arms. He hadn't been dead in the back of the wagon and this disturbed her.

Petty was being led to a tall tree stump by a dozen white men. He was crying and calling out to the ones he recognized, to the ones he had worked for or grew up around—but they all ignored him. Disassociation was necessary. It made what they were about to do easier.

"Petty," Alta Jean repeated weakly.

Her eyebrows furrowed, and she began to turn.

Though distracted, Nat worked the lunchtime crowd with his typical, imperturbable contrarianism. And customers still managed to spill coffee, forget to tip the waitpersons and asininely inquire about catering or "to go" orders.

When the lunch traffic began to fritter out, Nat thought on Dunphee's line of inquiry while he bussed tables.

It had never occurred to him that the lynching of Petty Smith would ever come up again—especially in a conversation with a white man. White folks were great at forgetting history that presented them less than favorably and even better at portraying folks who viewed them unfavorably, well, unfavorably. It was a crippling one-two punch and Nat had heard it all.

Jim Crow was a long time ago.

Reverse discrimination is the real problem.

If you people will just quit belly-aching about race.

He marveled at the simplicity of white avoidance and almost admired the sheer and utter gall of it. It was as if white folk really believed that Black folk were incapable of keeping track of what had been done to them. It had been less than a year since James Byrd, Jr., was beaten severely and then dragged to death behind a pickup truck carrying three young white men, and the first reporting on the crime had focused on Byrd's past issues with alcoholism. And once white folks at large got their head around the actual facts concerning the murder, they acted like it was the first time anything like that had ever happened in Texas.

Nat shook his head and checked the time. It was 1:45 p.m.

Nat was also dumbfounded that Bertram had come back. Nat was a young man in the early 1950s when the last incident occurred, and it had happened the exact same way. Lester Grissem had returned home for a funeral and one funeral became two. Lester was cremated before cremation was even a thing. And they had all known damn well, or at least suspected the truth of it then. But everyone had just gone on about their business. Black folks and white.

Could Bertram have forgotten?

Nat found that hard to believe, but Bertram was getting old. Maybe he had gotten old enough he didn't care. Maybe he thought something had changed.

Nat thought on what it had meant to his own family. They had had some hard years after, forced to start again in a new town. Grissem's death had absolved them all. But too little, too late.

Nat finished cleaning a section of tables and carried his bus bin to the kitchen. Then, he abruptly told the girl behind the register he was taking off for the rest of the day.

Nat decided to go to the library early. He had started participating in a local Black genealogical research group on the weekends. He'd quickly learned his way around the library and was well-familiar with the microfilm machine. He figured he'd go on down and locate some of the articles he wanted to show Dunphee.

Dunphee was in trouble.

Bertram's death was inexplicable, his grandmother's reaction to it was puzzling, and Nat's insinuated secrets about them both were unsettling. And when Dunphee remembered the phrase that seemed to describe what happened to Bertram, he immediately wished he hadn't.

Spontaneous human combustion.

It was straight out of *Night Gallery* when he was a kid. Or maybe it was *Kolchak: The Nightstalker*.

Oh well, he thought. He was up for retirement soon. Maybe he could buy the old Troup Boxing Gym and start a boxing club.

When Dunphee arrived at the library, Nat was waiting for him. There was a short row of three microfilm machines in the back corner, and Nat had them all to himself. He had microfilm spools installed in all three.

Nat smiled, stood up, and shook Dunphee's hand. "You ready for this?" he asked.

"I don't know," Dunphee answered. "It doesn't matter. I need to know."

"Okay," Nat said. "First, let me give you some background. Last week you were on the news for that memorial the city put in on the west side of the courthouse square. The one for the fallen law officers."

"'Fallen Heroes.' Yes. Fire department and law enforcement personnel who died in the line of duty."

"And the ceremony was moving," Nat said, "and the water fountain was pretty, and you had a good turnout."

"Yes."

"Have you ever noticed how you don't see a lot of Black folks down there? Except to report to the courthouse across the street?"

"Not a lot, but some."

"Probably only a few. Nice memorial dedication, right? The courthouse, the monuments? You like it down there?"

"It's alright, I guess."

"*Only 'cause you don't know any better.*"

"Well, tell me then."

Nat nodded. "And the same thing is true of Harkin. But I ain't ready to talk about Harkin. Or Bertram. Tyler first. We'll take a look at Tyler first."

"Okay."

"You sure?"

"Sure."

Nat sat down at the middle microfilm machine and had Dunphee sit at the one on his left. He gave him brief instructions on how to scroll the microfilm forward and back and how to focus in and enlarge. Then, he enlarged a story on a page that he had already pulled up for Dunphee. It was from the October 30, 1895, edition of the *Dallas Morning News*. The title read "Roasted to Death."

Nat had Billy glance at it and then lean over and examine the article pulled up on his machine. It was from the October 31, 1895, edition of the *Wills Point Chronicle*. The title read "Burned at the Stake."

"Is this the same guy?" Dunphee said.

"Yep."

"He was burned at the stake?"

"Yep."

"Where?"

Nat nodded at the microfilm machines. "Take your time," he said.

Dunphee began reading.

He learned that in late October 1895, a Black man named Robert Henson Hillard had been the only suspect in the alleged sexual assault and murder of a young white woman. And the victim, the only eyewitness, was dead. But Hillard hadn't faced a judge or jury. Dunphee learned that one of his predecessors, Wig Slerrit, had discovered Hillard asleep in a cotton pen near Kilgore. On Slerrit's's way back to Tyler, a large white mob surrounded him and relieved him of his suspect. Then the mob finished Hillard's transport, planted a steel rail in the middle of the present-day memorial section of the public square and burned him alive in front of a crowd of thousands.

Dunphee learned that Hillard's lynching party had taken its time, starting, extinguishing and restarting the fire over and over—letting it rise a little higher and burn a little longer each time—so Hillard would cook as slowly and painfully as possible.

"Oh... *my*..." Dunphee sighed.

Dunphee also learned that halfway through the ghastly proceedings, Hillard had begun smashing his head back against the rail he was bound to, attempting to bash his own brains in to escape the prolonged, horrendous suffering. But his agony elicited hoots and snickers from his tormentors.

"Is this for real, Nat?" Dunphee asked.

"Real as you and me sitting here."

Dunphee finished.

"The same part of the square where we erected the Fallen Heroes Memorial?"

"Yep."

"Damn."

"Damn is right. Now look at the story on the last machine."

Dunphee moved to the last microfilm machine in the short row. It displayed an article from the May 26, 1912, edition of the *Dallas Morning News*. The title read "Negro Meets Death at Stake in Tyler." The Black victim was Dan Davis. Like Hillard, Davis was accused of attacking a white woman, denied a trial and due process and burned at the stake on the west side of the courthouse square in front of a mob of thousands. When the flames had begun to consume him, he begged his executioners to slit his throat, but they ignored his pleas.

Dunphee finished reading again. His gaze met Nat's momentarily, and then he averted his eyes. "You think you know a place," he said. "There are bad things, but you assume the good outweighs the bad. But this... How could folks not know about this?"

"Some do," Nat replied. "But not many. And they're almost all Black and old-timers, like me. No one talks about it. People don't want to hear it."

Nat and Dunphee remained silent for a minute or two, and then Nat sat down at the first machine and began rewinding the microfilm.

"Those are just the ones they burned in town," he continued. "They burned more out at Camp Ford during the Civil War. It was the largest Confederate prisoner of war camp west of the Mississippi. They burned several Black men there; Black men enlisted in the Union army or Union sympathizers amongst the slave population."

Dunphee turned back to the machine he was sitting at and mimicked Nat. They rewound the rolls of microfilm and reinserted them in the small boxes they came from.

"Someone should do something," Dunphee said. "Is there anything we could do? Davis and Hillard ought to have memorials themselves."

"That's all well and good, sure. But if you ever suggest it you'll lose your job or they'll bury you under the damn thing if it's ever erected. This is just what went on. It started during the war and continued after Reconstruction. There was no slaughter rule. There were no rules at all where Blacks were concerned. Remember those three boys that dragged 'ol James Byrd to death in Jasper last year? That one that received the death penalty? He'll be the first white man that ever received a death sentence for killing a Black man in Texas. Think about that."

Dunphee shrugged. It was a lot to take in. "What can we do?" he asked.

"Nothin'," Nat replied. "But we know. You know—I know. We can know. And maybe later we can tell more people. Right now, no good'll come of it. People don't wanna' know and wouldn't believe you if you told 'em. Let's talk about Harkin."

Nat told Dunphee what he knew. The Tyler atrocities were a primer, but as bad as they were, they were tame compared to what happened in Harkin.

Pettigrew Smith, a thirteen-year-old Black boy, had simply been accused of being sweet on Dunphee's grandmother, nothing more. Petty's mother had worked in the fields with and for Alta Jean's folks, and it was natural that Alta Jean and Petty started playing together, running the pastures and exploring the creeks. But the townsfolk took note and were not unfamiliar with how their neighbors in Tyler handled their "negro problems."

The town of Harkin was the proud hometown of two Confederate war heroes, both deceased, and the youngest son of one was still insanely bitter about the "War of Northern Aggression" and Lincoln's attempt to turn Dixie into "Nigger York." This yokel, whose name escaped Nat, had been the instigator; seven Harkin boys, including Lester Grissem and Tieg Bertram, had done the deed.

With the son of one of the dead Confederate heroes coaching, Petty was accused of making eyes at Alta Jean and beaten. Then, "making eyes" became "making advances." More young men beat on Petty and by the time he was brought unconscious before the town elders, his guilt was a foregone conclusion. All that was missing was a semblance of proof.

Petty was taken out to Alta Jean's home, and she was coerced to give it. Then Grissem, Bertram, Tom Huff, Jack Walls, the son of the Confederate hero, and three others took Petty to a clearing heading out of town (toward New Summerfield), and bound him to a tall, broad tree stump with rope. Then they cut his tongue out, castrated him and bullwhipped him 'til he was unconscious.

The soaking, antiseptic sting of kerosene revived Petty, just in time for Tom Huff to apply the torch. Huff ridiculed him first, asking him if he had any last words. Blood poured from Petty's mouth and tears streamed down his cheeks. As the others laughed, Huff set Petty aflame.

"Even without his tongue, they say he wailed for several terrible minutes," Nat said. "Eventually, the flames burned through the ropes holding Petty up. He fell over. And even after the fire had burned him chimney chute black, something inside held on. Right as Huff walked over to poke Petty's charred body with a stick, Petty suddenly writhed and contorted, twisting away from the coals."

"Oh, god," Dunphee said.

"It scared the hell out of the lynching party. Bertram supposedly yelped out loud, and Huff threw up. The son of the Confederate hero dropped to his knees. But Jack Walls and one of the others started stomping on what was left of Petty and kicked him back into the fire. Huff gathered some more brush and struck Petty's head with a chunk of it, revealing his white skull plain through his charred scalp. And then they just piled the rest of the wood on top. When Petty had burned down to cinder, they left. And that's when things got really scary."

"When did my grandmother find out?" Dunphee asked.

"I'm not sure. Once her folks got wind of what happened, I think they kept her locked in for days."

Dunphee's phone rang, and he answered it. He nodded a few times and said "yes" and "thanks" and hung up. Then he turned back to Nat.

"That was the lab," Dunphee said. "Those are Bertram's ashes."

Nat and Sheriff Dunphee left the library and went to the courthouse square. Dunphee gave Nat a ride, and they parked on the west side. Then, Dunphee went over and stood in front of the Fallen Heroes Memorial. Nat joined him.

"It's a nice monument," Nat said.

"It is," Dunphee replied. "I certainly prefer it to the one dedicated to the Confederacy back towards the courthouse—but you didn't hear me say that out loud."

"I understand," Nat said. "I do."

Dunphee sat down on a park bench and Nat joined him. "It doesn't seem like a bad place, does it?" Dunphee asked.

"No," Nat replied. "It's not too bad. It's a lot better than it was."

Dunphee laughed out loud. "Sorry," he said.

"No," Nat said. "I understand. It's crazy. Sometimes I feel like we're still living without slaughter rules... Here at home and overseas. Other times, I think we've come a little way."

"So, what you told me so far wasn't scary?"

"It was scary, but not real scary. Not hide-under-your-bed, tooth-rattling-scary. White people had burned plenty of Black boys at the stake in Texas before Petty."

"Shit."

"Yep." Nat looked around to make sure no one was within earshot. "The thing is, the next morning Petty's remains were gone."

"Yeah?"

"Yep. The tree stump was burned all to hell, but Petty's ashes were gone."

"Holy crap."

"It frightened the lynching party at first, but then they decided it was some kinda' prank or Black folk just tending to their dead. Members of the small lynch-mob told some folks and later, after some time had passed and they were no longer afraid, they did some bragging. Word got around. Nothing was ever done about it. Petty's mom moved away. Dallas, I think."

Dunphee took off his hat and placed it on his knee.

"About a year later," Nat continued, "Tommy Huff disappeared. Got up early one morning to milk cows, and all they found was three or four piles of ashes under a cow. Sound familiar?

"Human remains?" Dunphee asked.

"They didn't have high technology in those days, Billy. Whadda' you think? They suspected, but they didn't know for sure. Didn't even singe the bone-dry hay around the ashes. But Huff was gone and no one ever heard from him again. Then, Jack Walls and two of the others disappeared the following week. All the same way—out in the dark, missing, a pile of ashes in one of the places they were supposed to have been. And that's when we had to leave."

"Leave?"

"Yep."

Dunphee chewed on it for a moment. "They couldn't explain what was happening," he deduced. "But they started to think they knew."

"Yep. A Black boy had been burned at the stake and now white folks were disappearing."

"They thought someone in the Black community might be responsible."

"Exactly," Nat said. "They thought we were retaliating somehow."

"Wow."

"Yep. But we weren't. We weren't stupid. In that day and age, angry white folks could run Black folks out of entire cities, even counties. My family fled and so did the rest. Gave up our land and homes, whatever we couldn't carry. We started over.

"The son of the Confederate hero hung himself a few months later and the 'disappearances' seemed to stop. But what really happened—"

"*Bertram and Lester moved away*," Dunphee said.

"Bingo," Nat replied. "And you know most of the rest. Grissem came back for a visit in 1951 and got burned to a crisp. They called it a freak accident. I think any of the old-timers who'd convinced themselves that it'd been us behind the disappearances finally considered otherwise. And, of course, Bertram stayed away almost for good."

"Was there anybody else involved? I mean—not that I'm buying a charbroiled Pettigrew Smith still walking around like some kind of vengeful ghost—but was there anybody else Petty could be targeting?"

"No one else still alive was directly or even indirectly involved, Billy. Except maybe your grandmother."

"Oh, shit."

———

Dunphee dropped Nat off at the restaurant and headed back over to the nursing home. Alta Jean was waiting.

When he saw her, he hugged her as if he hadn't seen her in years.

"Take it easy, kiddo," she said, smiling.

"Just glad to see you, Mee-Maw."

"Glad to see you, too, Billy. But it's only been a few hours."

Billy smiled. She was feeling better.

Alta Jean turned off the silent TV, and they sat in the chairs in front of it.

"It's a little before your time, Billy," Alta Jean said. "But do you remember those old cathedral-looking radios?"

"Maybe. I think so. I know I've seen pictures."

"We used to have one when I was younger. A Philco 90. It was a tired old thing. It would lose the signals. You could set it on and leave it on your favorite channel, and then, when you turned it on again, the signal would be gone or it wouldn't be there all the way. We'd turn it off and when we turned it back on a few hours later, the channel would be working fine. Never could tell when the signal would be all there."

"You want one of those old radios, Alta Jean?" Dunphee asked.

"Oh, honey," Alta Jean replied, laughing. "*I am one of those old radios.*"

"Alta Jean."

"No, William Taggert Dunphee, I'm dead serious."

"Okay."

"I'm not always around—and I know that—I wasn't completely around earlier when you came by. But I'm here now."

Alta Jean took one of Dunphee's hands and squeezed it. He squeezed hers back.

"I'm glad," Dunphee said.

"Me, too. But I need you to do something for me."

"What?"

"I need you to take me somewhere."

"Sure. Let's go do something. You want to go out to eat? You want to see a movie?"

"No, no. Nothing like that. Thanks, though. For offering. You're such a good boy, and a strong man." Tears filled Alta Jean's eyes. "I'm so proud of you."

Dunphee's eyes welled up. "Thanks, Mee-Maw. You know how much I love you."

"You know how much I love you, too, boy." Alta Jean got up and hugged him. He hugged her tightly again, and she laughed. "I wish I would remember to say things like that more often."

Dunphee released her from his embrace. She walked over to her closet and took a light jacket off a hanger. "I need you to take me back to Harkin, Billy."

"What?" Dunphee said, standing up. "No, Alta Jean. Why?"

"You don't *know* why?"

"No, ma'am."

"I called Nat's Dine-In inquiring after you a little while ago. I guess you were on your way."

"Oh, Alta Jean."

"It's okay. I know you know. But I'm glad you know. I sure miss Nat. You forget my piece of pecan pie?"

"We can go there right now. I'll buy you the whole pie so you can bring it back here. And we'll get some vanilla ice cream to go with it."

"Maybe later, Billy. Maybe later. Please take me back home to Harkin."

"Why Mee-Maw? *Why?*

"They did keep me locked up for a spell," Alta Jean said. "But eventually things went back closer to normal—except Petty was gone. My best friend. I didn't know everything that had happened until later. I hadn't even been aware of some of the boys disappearing, or what they said were disappearances. But there were rumors."

Alta Jean walked to the center of the room and continued.

"They said on the days those young men disappeared, there was a Black boy playing, just off a clearing on the road to New Summerfield."

"There's no clearing there now, Alta Jean. It's thick woods. Through and through."

"I don't doubt you, but I have to try."

"Try? Try and do what?"

"I'd like to see him again, Billy. You don't know what it's like. All these years. What happened. I'd just like to see him one more time."

"I doubt he's out there if he ever was. And if he is out there, he may not be the same."

"Maybe not. But I can try. Tieg came back, and he's gone. Petty is here. I know it."

"What if he's looking for you?"

"Then there's no sense in hiding. Please, Billy. I'm ready. I been ready. I'm old. I'm not even myself some days."

"But I don't want you to go. I don't want to lose you."

"You'll never lose me, Billy. You never lost your granddad. You never lost your parents. I see all of them in you... when the dial on the radio is working.

"I never lost your granddad. I never lost your mama or your daddy. And I never lost Petty. And now he's back. What would you give to see Linda again? Or Papa Roscoe? Or your mama and daddy?

"Please help me, Billy. *Please.*"

Dunphee took a deep breath as he approached Harkin. His place was located down a turn-off opposite of the old county road to New Summerfield, and he thought about just driving his grandmother there. But she wasn't having it.

Alta Jean was light and anxious. She talked about Dunphee's granddad and his parents. She talked about his baseball games. Dunphee wished she could stay like this, suddenly full of vigor and familiarity. But he knew she was right about that part. The channel would come and go. And eventually it would fade away.

They took the county road toward New Summerfield just as it was starting to get dark. Dunphee was having second thoughts about the whole crazy narrative and still wasn't sure they'd see anything—but that's when they did. If they hadn't been looking for him, they wouldn't have seen him at all. And he wished they hadn't.

Dunphee started to speed up, pretend like he didn't notice; but his grandmother grabbed his arm.

"There he is," she said.

The figure was off to Dunphee's left, right at the edge of the thick woods. It was a curious sight and Dunphee felt his stomach drop.

He slowed down, pulling over about thirty yards in front of it on its side of the road. When Dunphee opened his car door, the smell stung his nostrils, and he drew his gun. His grandmother was already out on her side of the car and spryly walking around it toward the figure.

It didn't seem to notice either of them until Alta Jean said its name. Then it stopped.

"Petty," Alta Jean repeated. "*Petty, it's me.*"

The apparition turned to Alta Jean and then stepped in her direction.

Dunphee screamed "Stop!" and ran toward the dark form.

The figure turned back to Dunphee and limped stiffly forward. Dunphee yelled stop again, but it kept coming.

"Billy," Alta Jean said. "Please. *Please.*"

The dark figure approached Billy, its roasted hide cracking, its eyes bright red, and its ghastly smile offering a profound image of menace. Dunphee stopped, watched the figure disbelievingly, and then took aim.

As Alta Jean approached, the creature stopped and stood stock still, approximately fifteen yards from Dunphee.

Dunphee stared at it, a blackened human ligament. Twisted, repulsive. He could hardly believe what he was seeing—but he couldn't look away. He held his aim steady.

"Stay back, Alta Jean," Dunphee said.

She stopped, but Petty turned toward her and took an awkward step. Dunphee began firing and emptied his clip.

The dark figure was rocked backwards and sideways, tripping and then stumbling, every bullet producing a flash of yellow-orange flame as it penetrated or passed through the creature's blackened form. But it never collapsed.

As Dunphee reached for his spare clip, it slowly steadied itself and began coming at him. Alta Jean began screaming.

"No, Petty, no! STOP, PETTY. STOP!"

The apparition froze in its tracks, its lidless eyes still aimed forward in the direction of Dunphee. Alta Jean stepped closer.

"No, Alta Jean," Dunphee cried.

But it was too late.

The creature turned its head slowly, almost mechanically. Its grotesque face and teeth were expressionless.

Alta Jean beamed.

Dunphee raised his gun again, but he couldn't fire. He screamed "Mee-Maw" but Alta Jean didn't hear. He aimed his gun, but his grandmother took another step toward the creature and extended her left arm. The creature turned its body slowly and stood awkwardly, raising its right.

Dunphee watched helplessly.

Alta Jean's fingertips touched the creature's charred knuckles and there was a brilliant flash of blue flame.

In the glowing light, Dunphee saw Petty, a young Black boy, at the edge of the woods. He was dressed in well-worn britches with suspenders slung over his over-sized, yellowing, hand-me-down long-johns. And facing him stood a young Alta Jean in a light, cotton dress, with more life in her than he thought he had ever seen before. Both of them were bright and happy, and so young. And they were smiling.

Smiling.

Dunphee started to cry.

Then, Alta Jean and Petty were laughing and Dunphee was no longer there.

As Alta Jean and Petty turned to run, the blue glow flashed yellow and orange and became flame. And then they were no longer there.

Finally taking a breath, Dunphee wiped his eyes with the sleeve of his gun hand, and then re-holstered his weapon.

He walked over to where they had stood last and saw two separate sets of ashes. Two sets of ashes touching just above the mid-sections, as if they were holding hands.

Dunphee began crying again, but this time he didn't stop. He dropped to his knees and let everything out.

Dunphee sat next to the two sets of ashes for half an hour, crying like a child, for everything that had gone on and for everything that had gone wrong. Then he drove home.

At the house, he parked the patrol car and went inside and changed. He came back out with two empty five-gallon plastic buckets and a shovel. He drove back out to the spot where he'd left Alta Jean and Petty. He shoveled them into separate buckets, put them in his truck, and then transported them to his house.

The next day, he drove out to the old, overgrown Harkin cemetery in a sorrowful daze. He buried Petty and Alta Jean in two separate sections of his grandmother's reserved plot, next to his grandfather's.

As he finished tamping down the dirt with his boots, his eyes welled up again; but he wiped the tears away quickly. Then he shook his head and smiled.

He couldn't help it.

Tieg Bertram's bizarre death was described as "possible spontaneous human combustion."

Local and state media outlets had a field day with it, but Dunphee refused to comment. He even turned down a call from the *National Enquirer*.

Alta Jean's remaining children filed a "Missing Persons" report after she had been gone for a week. They wouldn't have known, but the nursing home called.

Dunphee's aunt and uncles pushed for the county to issue a death certificate after six months, and he stayed out of it. When the certificate was filed, they fought over what was left of Alta Jean's bank accounts, but it wasn't much. And they never concerned themselves with purchasing a headstone for their mother's presumably empty grave.

Dunphee eventually bought one that matched his grandfather's and placed it at his grandmother's plot himself. He had the initials "P. S." etched into the center of the back of Alta Jean's marker in four-inch letters and didn't think anyone would notice.

For a long time, no one did.

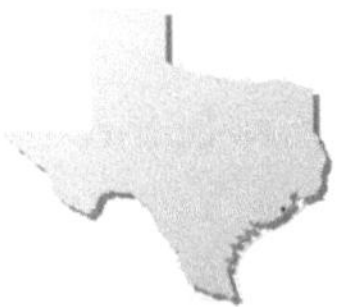

eight
pendulum grim

"Pendulum Grim" riffs on the oft-cited legendary disappearance of author Ambrose Bierce with astute imagination, and delivers a creation that flows with the smooth energy of a Grover Washington sax solo.

*--**Bret McCormick**, legendary Indy Horror filmmaker and author of* Texas Schlock: B-Movie Sci-Fi and Horror from the Lone Star State.

EMMA FOUND the book at an estate sale in the 2100 block of Bissonnet.

A stout, white-haired patriarch informed her it had belonged to his eldest son, and that the son had died young. Emma turned the volume over in her hands and inspected it.

In excellent condition, it was an early copy of *The Standard Diary*. Though copyrighted in 1874, the trademark year—1889—was indicated prominently in the center of the first page, framed by a circular astrological calendar. The graphics were fabulous, and the top margin of each leaf featured a chronological date. Emma flipped through it and realized only a fraction of the volume had been used.

The first entry was dated December 28, 1913. It was a couple of lines of verse recorded in heavy cursive that tilted right:

Late, perhaps, and with diminished vim,
I confront at last, the pendulum grim.

The rest of the page was blank.

The diary must have sat in the poet's possession for years before he or she decided to utilize it. Maybe it had been a gift.

The following page began with an entry from what appeared to be a subsequent owner. The handwriting was much less florid, and the ink was slightly watered down.

My name is Hester Villon. I finded this diary on the El Paso run. I decided to make it my own. I want to give tell of my life and I will lay it all down here. I reckon I'll have plenty of time.

Emma asked the patriarch how much he wanted for it.

"Twenty bucks."

It was a bit high, Emma thought, but she forked it over. She was intrigued.

That night Emma made a nice dinner, after which she and her partner, Lauren, watched TV. Emma forgot about the diary until the following day. She cracked it open while Lauren was at work.

Villon had been a Black train porter who learned to read late in life. In short entries, he chronicled his thoughts regarding the railroad service back and forth from El Paso to "San Antone," his home. He described the passengers on the train and the weather he witnessed through the windows of the railroad cars in which he worked. He mentioned trips by local and state dignitaries. He described his wife and kids in various settings, and with warm detail. It was all fairly basic stuff for several pages. But then, he mentioned a strange occurrence.

Villon was sitting on a stool, staring out a window on the other side of a railroad car. He saw a stray buffalo in the distance. It seemed to be running parallel to the train, but Villon decided it was not. He surmised that either the "buff" was pursuing a point of convergence farther down the track or he was trying to outrun the train and get around it. Then it occurred to Villon that the "buff" was taking an angle that would put it on a collision course. He described it in the diary as peculiar. "I say I never seen the like," he wrote.

Emma looked up from her reading. The condo was suddenly very quiet.

She glanced out the condo's immense bay window. The Houston skyline towered against an impossibly blue sky.

Villon watched the buffalo come closer and closer. The angle it was traveling seemed to place it ahead of the train, but it abruptly turned in. Fairly stupefied, Villon "leaped" up and grabbed the exterior bar of an overhead rack just before the beast struck the train. The collision was recorded by a dull thud and a slight jostling of the car—but hardly any of the passengers noticed. Villon subsequently stepped over, opened a window and put his head out to survey the remains of the animal, but it was just a pile of bloody fur. And the train was none the worse for wear.

It was a strange episode, and Villon had clearly been disturbed by it. But he was understandably hesitant to inquire as to why the other passengers in the car—all white—hadn't noticed.

Emma decided to skip ahead.

In the March 1889 section of the diary, a new owner, Jebediah "Jeb" Dickson, described finding the diary in a swap shop on the outskirts of San Angelo. His entries began May 6, 1953, in Waco.

Since coming back from WWII, Dickson had enjoyed a well-paying job at a Woodmen of the World insurance affiliate, but he hated the work. His days were long and boring, and he frequently doodled on the pages of the diary. On May 9, the entry noted massive thunderstorms followed by "air like molasses." And then, Dickson was almost run down by a Studebaker while walking across the street near his office.

Though Dickson admitted cursing the driver, he recorded an "insane" aside. He suggested that—had he been questioned—he would have sworn the Studebaker had no driver. Or at least not one "as far as he could ascertain." He even drew a profile view of the driver's side of the Studebaker, depicting an empty driver's seat.

Dickson's entries ended on May 11 with an unfinished note. He said the clouds that day were "oppressive" and that he was feeling "pusillanimous, if that was the right term." And he thought it was.

Emma wasn't so sure.

She quickly looked it up on her phone. *Showing a lack of courage or determination; timid; fearful; faint-hearted.* "I bet he meant fearful or faint-hearted," Emma said to herself.

She shook her head.

Before TV, she thought. When people still read newspapers. *When people still read.* "Before people were 'pusillanimous.'"

When Emma first met Lauren, she was an accomplished local stage presence. But Hollywood never came calling. Now, Emma was an adjunct professor at the University of Houston. She was working on a PhD in English Literature and did an incredible amount of reading. She loved it.

Lauren was a Senior Counsel for Hegel Barker, a TK company, energy division. She hardly had time to read herself, except for contracts and briefs. Dispute resolution. She was also the Honorary Consul-General for the small island nation of Tonga. TK was involved in a budding offshore drilling project in the Pacific, and Lauren took Emma for a working holiday there twice a year. Homosexuality was against the law in Tonga, so they stayed in separate rooms; Emma was listed as Lauren's "assistant." Lauren's job was the reason they could afford to live in an eleventh-floor corner condo on the edge of downtown Houston. Lauren's job was also the reason Emma could afford to work as an adjunct professor and pursue a doctorate. The week before, they had enjoyed a staycation, just lying around the house. But now Lauren was back at work.

Emma got up from the couch with the diary and started for the bay window. She had read Lauren a poem not long after they moved in. Emma recalled the last lines:

> Sunlight through glass,
> The air, blue and deep, proves
> We are endless, and nowhere, and nothing.

Emma smiled and looked out. Then she went back to the couch and grabbed a pen off the coffee table. When she returned to the bay window, she thumbed through the diary to the last entry and placed the open volume near the center of the glass, holding it up with her free hand. Then, on a leaf dated June 4, 1889, she wrote the last three lines of the poem. And she remembered the name. It was called "High Windows."

The next day, while Lauren was at work, Emma examined the entries from the other diarists. There were two more in the volume. There was Eliza Deering of Lufkin and the stout patriarch's son, Jake Frankel. She didn't read all their entries, but she thought it peculiar that a diary might pass through so many hands.

Emma read one of Frankel's entries. He seemed agitated.

> *Lisa doesn't understand. I'm not sure I do. And I don't know how to tell her.*
>
> *I'm very taken with her, and that's what stops me. I can't give her the attention she'd deserve. There are things I need to accomplish, things I need to commit to. That commitment would be a half-measure if I let Lisa in even a little. If she even got close to a hold on my heart, I'd be finished. Happily so, to be sure, but I wouldn't be able to get done what I—it sounds melodramatic, silly even—but what I think I was meant to do. She's not someone I could stay away from.*

Emma smiled faintly. She contemplated Frankel's efforts to remain devoted to something, perhaps a craft. Efforts that reminded her of being young and focused. Had Frankel been naïve? Had she?

Emma wondered what had happened to him. Was that morose?

She grabbed her laptop and took a seat in a large leather chair that faced the bay window. Lauren called it the "porno" chair. Their lovemaking often began there. Sometimes it concluded there as well.

Emma opened up her laptop, accessed a search engine and typed in "Jake Frankel." Before she initiated the search, she changed the "Jake" to "Jacob" and added "death." In the brief moment the laptop was processing, Emma glanced out the window. A bird—a blackbird—slowly flew into her line of vision.

Emma looked at the search results and was shocked at the first heading. Frankel was one of the teachers who had been shot down by a student at Santa Trevizo High School a couple of years earlier. His first book had just been published. Emma recalled his name and remembered hearing about the incident. Seven students were killed as well.

A loud, dull *thwump* startled Emma, and she looked up just in time to see a blackbird crumpling in the center of the glass pane of the bay window, immediately sliding downward. There was dab of bright red blood at the point of impact. "What the hell?" she said, standing up with the laptop in her hands.

Emma stepped closer to the glass and scanned the high-rise neighborhood. Nothing grabbed her attention. "That was strange," she continued.

She sat back down with the laptop and glanced at the bay window one more time. *Was the bird's blood in the same spot she had placed the diary to write in?*

On a lark, Emma looked up Hester Villon. She thought it was probably a long shot, but the name wasn't terribly common. She accessed an online newspaper archive. It popped right up. Like Jake Frankel's.

Casualties in the employ of the El Paso and Southwestern Railroad include John Treble, aged 22, and Hester Villon, aged 45...

According to the October 13, 1914 edition of the *Austin Statesman*

Villon and two dozen others perished in a train derailment near Comstock. Emma's curiosity was piqued. She couldn't stop there.

Emma looked up Jebediah Dickson and, again, the pertinent results appeared immediately.

"Fuck's sake," she said.

Dickson died in the massive tornado that demolished Waco on May 11, 1953.

Eliza Deering's arms, legs and torso were discovered cut up and stacked neatly in the freezer of her pink, Imperial Frost-Proof Frigidaire refrigerator on November 1, 1962. One of her sons discovered her remains when he dropped by to check on her and discuss plans for Thanksgiving.

Deering's head was never found, and the police had no suspects. The killer was never apprehended, and Deering's murder was still one of the longest unsolved cold cases in Harris County.

Emma realized she was sweating. She stood up and sat back down.

This wasn't a little strange. Actually, it was exceedingly strange. Emma closed her laptop and decided to start dinner.

She glanced at the bay window, and the bird's blood was gone.

Emma whipped up a salad and blackened some fresh salmon. She and Lauren were trying to eat healthier.

Emma decided she was getting excited for no reason. She didn't have a superstitious bone in her body. She didn't believe in curses or *Final Destination* plotlines. It was pure happenstance, period.

It had to be.

Happenstance or not, however, Emma was unsettled. When dinner was ready, she had a few minutes before Lauren arrived. Maybe longer if the elevators were busy. She placed her laptop on the kitchen counter and thought for a moment. "First entry," she mumbled.

She cleared the search engine and typed in "poet in El Paso." Lots of names came up and she recognized a few, mostly Texan; but the time-lines didn't fit. She revised her search: "writer in El Paso in 1913."

A timeline of El Paso came up. And a link to Florida J. Wolfe—a

Black woman who was a "consort and common-law wife to Irish Lord Delaval James Beresford." She died of tuberculosis in May of 1913.

Then, below, but still on the first page of results, a 2013 article from the *San Francisco Chronicle*. It was titled "Stranger Than Fiction: The Disappearance of Ambrose Bierce." It discussed the 100th anniversary of the mystery. Bierce vanished in December of 1913. His last known correspondence was a letter written to a friend on December 26, 1913. Bierce concluded the letter ominously: "As to me, I leave here tomorrow for an unknown destination." And no one ever heard from him again.

Emma remembered Bierce's name, but she was fairly sure he wasn't a poet. She heard Lauren at the door and closed her laptop.

They had a wonderful dinner, and Emma listened to Lauren talk about her day. Sipping a glass of wine, they worked on the dishes together. Then they sprawled out on the couch in front of the flat screen TV and watched *Seinfeld* reruns. Lauren held Emma tightly and Emma considered mentioning the diary. But she didn't want to spoil the moment.

Later, in bed, Emma made love to Lauren with passionate abandon. She was afraid, but unsure of what. Lauren fell asleep with Emma in her arms, and, after a while, Emma slid away gently and returned to the kitchen.

It was silly to obsess over this, she thought. There probably wasn't anything to it. But now the academic in her was interested.

"*Devil's Dictionary*," Emma said.

That's what Bierce wrote, among other things. Emma remembered that he wasn't religious. And she remembered Lauren once quoting him. It was part of his definition of a Christian: "One who follows the teachings of Christ insofar as they are not inconsistent with a life of sin."

Emma was certain that Bierce didn't write poetry, but she decided to look it up. She simply typed in "Ambrose Bierce poetry"—and links to Bierce's verse appeared. He'd written over four hundred poems.

Emma read the first stanza of "The Gates Ajar."

> The Day of Judgment spread its glare
> O'er continents and seas.
> The graves cracked open everywhere,

Like pods of early peas.

"Hmmm," she said. Then, she read "An Inscription."

> A famous conqueror, in battle brave,
> Who robbed the cradle to supply the grave.
> His reign laid quantities of human dust:
> He fell upon the just and the unjust.

Emma re-examined the first entry in the diary. She read it out loud. "Late, perhaps, and with diminished vim, I confront at last the pendulum grim."

She looked at one more Bierce poem, titled "An Unmerry Christmas."

> Christmas, you tell me, comes but once a year.
> One place it never comes, and that is here.
> Here, in these pages no good wishes spring,
> No well-worn greetings tediously ring
> For Christmas greetings are like pots of ore:
> The hollower they are they ring the more.

"This might be him," Emma concluded.

She examined the diary entry again. The cursive handwriting was heavy and tilted right. She was still a bit unsettled, but she was also curious. What had she stumbled onto? She typed "Ambrose Bierce handwriting sample" into her search engine and then stopped and deleted "handwriting sample," adding "letter" in its place. Then, instead of utilizing the search engine "All" filter, she clicked on "Images." The query provided several original Ambrose Bierce letter images. She opened one and covered her mouth with her right hand. The cursive handwriting was heavy and tilted right. She was no expert, but it looked like an exact match.

Had Bierce been the diary's original owner?

His verified verse wasn't great, and certainly no better than the couplet in the diary. But that didn't mean it wasn't him. *Had she discovered the last thing Bierce wrote?*

And those were secondary considerations. As excited as she was about the discovery, she couldn't ignore the implications.

It now appeared that all the identified diarists in the volume were deceased—and not too long after their entries started. *Did being in possession of the diary or having written in it portend her demise?*

Insane. Stark raving.

Crazy, yes.

But.

The next morning, Emma got up and fixed Lauren a big breakfast. Emma decided she would leave with Lauren and go to a library to do more research. A decent night's sleep hadn't settled her.

They had breakfast and then showered and dressed. At the elevators, Emma realized she had forgotten the diary and told Lauren to go on, that she'd meet her in the lobby.

Emma returned to the room, grabbed the diary, and then circled back to the elevators. When she pushed the "Down" button, she heard a loud *boooom!* and the entire building shook.

Beside herself, Emma rushed to the stairwell and ran down the stairs two and sometimes three at a time. She got to the bottom without stopping and rushed into the lobby. It was sheer pandemonium, and Lauren was lying unconscious and bloody. A building security officer was attending to her.

Emma was at Lauren's side in an instant.

The elevator had stopped twice, first on floor seven and again on floor four. Then, the elevator cable snapped, and the car plummeted four stories to the lobby. Three tenants died, but Lauren was still alive. She had a shattered ankle, a broken femur and a separated shoulder. An ambulance transferred her to the St. Joseph Medical Center, and a specialist performed surgery. Lauren was placed on a tranquilizer and painkiller regimen, but Emma waited at her side until she regained consciousness.

When Lauren tried to speak, Emma realized she also had a broken tooth or two. Emma kissed Lauren's face all over.

"Oh, my dear," Emma whispered. "Oh, my girl. Are you alright?"

Lauren tried to smile. "A little sore," she managed, with as much of a grin as her bruised face would allow. "What about the others?"

"Mrs. Kessler and Mr. Baker... oh, Lauren dear. They... I'm afraid they... *they're gone.*"

"Shame," Lauren said, her blackened eyes tearing up.

"It's terrible. I'm absolutely mortified."

"How long the croakers say it's going to take me to... to recover?"

"They're waiting to see how your body responds to the surgery. You've got titanium pins in your ankle and femur. Some serious damage."

"Who's going to take care of me?" Lauren joked, trying to smile.

"You know the answer to that."

"I do. I do."

"I'm just glad..." Emma began to sob. "I'm just so glad... I'm just so glad you're here with me. I mean, not here, but *here.*"

"I know what you mean, babe. I'm not going anywhere."

Emma covered Lauren's bruised face in light kisses again and then leaned in cheek-to-cheek. "I love you," she whispered.

"I love you," Lauren replied.

Emma spent the whole day and night at the hospital. She was afraid to let Lauren out of her sight. She was spooked. The diary hadn't said anything about close calls or misfortunes befalling loved ones or friends. Was the elevator accident a coincidence? Or was a "pendulum grim" at work, activated, inevitable, counting down?

It sounded preposterous.

But Emma couldn't be sure.

Deep down, she harbored little doubt that the plummeting elevator was meant for her and that Lauren would just have been collateral damage if she'd been in the elevator herself.

What would be next? A flood? Some kind of bus or taxi crash?

Emma was afraid to leave the hospital. *If she went to the condo, should she take the stairs? What if she slipped and fell in their walk-in shower?*

"How do you prepare for fate?" she asked herself.

The following day, Emma only returned to the condo to clean up and change her clothes. It couldn't have taken more than an hour.

But another bird crashed into the bay window.

A shallow *thunk*.

Emma almost jumped out of her skin, but it was followed by two more, both smaller.

Whhappp. Fwhhip!

Emma hastily grabbed a change of clothes, stuffed a few more things in her backpack, and then bolted to the nearest stairwell. She would shower at her gym. But was her gym safe?

Emma was a nervous wreck. She was convinced something was waiting to befall her. Something that had already missed and almost killed Lauren in her stead. It was waiting now. That's all.

Down the next flight of stairs.

Around the next corner.

Out on the street.

And denied her it had crippled Lauren.

Could this really be taking place? And what would occur next?

Emma was concerned about what might happen to her; but she was petrified to think that something else might happen to Lauren.

"Late, perhaps, and with diminished vim," Emma said. "I face at last the pendulum grim."

Face? That wasn't right.

"Confront. *I confront at last the pendulum grim.*"

Pendulum grim.

Fate? Destiny?

Mortality? Death?

Everyone who had written in the diary had apparently died shortly after. Or in Bierce's case—if it was Bierce—disappeared. Disappeared, perhaps, because he died. What did it mean? Was it—had it—become a curse?

Was there anything she could do?

Back at Lauren's bedside, it occurred to Emma that all that mattered was Lauren. Protecting her.

Emma had bought the diary. Emma had opened this fucked up can of worms that seemed to be hellbent on making her worm's food. But what exactly could be done about a giant tornado? How could you predict or stop a train derailment?

Lauren woke to the sound of Emma's scream. A large gull had smashed into and cracked one of the panes in her hospital window. A flabbergasted nurse came running and started trying to calm Emma, who, in turn, apologized to Lauren over and over.

"It was just a seagull," Lauren said woozily. "It happens sometimes."

Emma bit her tongue. She was nervous. It dawned on her that she was kidding herself. She couldn't protect Lauren. She couldn't save Lauren or anyone else.

But maybe she could stop it.

Writing in the diary had activated some sort of pendulum. Some kind of countdown. She was sure of it. Villon, Dickson—all of them— they must all have experienced scares before they died. Close calls. One after another, they had picked up where Bierce left off. In their minds, there may not have been any rhyme or reason—or perhaps they died before they noticed or suspected it. But that didn't seem to be the case with Bierce. "As to me," he'd written, "I leave here tomorrow for an unknown destination."

Had Bierce known he was going to die? Was his destination death?

Something was at play here, but Emma didn't know what. She was simply certain that Lauren hadn't been the real target.

Lauren went back to sleep, and Emma was glad. It allowed her to concentrate.

Perhaps it was a calculation of some kind. A metaphysical logarithm.

Could she extricate them from it?

Could she change a variable?

No, Emma thought, answering her own question. She had unknowingly removed herself as a variable before. And Lauren had taken her place.

If Emma couldn't change the calculation, maybe she could answer it. Or maybe she could finish the equation. Maybe she could destroy the calculator.

But what if the whole thing was some bizarre, inexplicable coincidence?

What if Bierce had ventured into Mexico and joined Pancho Villa and died later?

Bierce's contemporary, Mark Twain, had been born shortly after an appearance of Halley's Comet and famously predicted that he would "go out with it," and did. On April 21, 1910. Not to be outdone, what if Bierce had simply dramatically composed his "unknown destination" last words, tied himself to a rock and hurled himself into the Rio Grande?

The next time Emma returned to the condo; two more birds smashed into the glass. One right after the other.

Thoook. Whammp.

Emma didn't even look over. She made sure she had the diary in her backpack and grabbed a sixteen-ounce container of Grill King Charcoal Odorless Lighter Fluid, which she and Lauren used when they grilled steaks on their hibachi in a local park.

Emma had already been by to see Lauren, and she was doing better. Emma kissed her full on the mouth several times, nervous but doting. Lauren would recover. She was going to have to go through extensive rehab, but she would be okay. And be "hell on metal detectors at the airport." It amused Lauren. And Emma loved seeing her smile. It was enough.

Emma could stop this. Emma *would* stop this.

Lauren's car was in storage, and Emma didn't want to destroy it anyway. She needed a contained space. Preferably without windows. If someone saw what she was doing, they might try to stop her. That wouldn't do.

She remembered that there were two dumpsters behind the next building over from theirs. She'd seen them in the alley from the bay window. A dumpster would work. She was certain.

Emma took the stairs down ten flights. Going down was definitely easier than coming up. And she wasn't sure that she couldn't just use the elevator. What were the chances lightning would strike twice in the same place?

She exited her building and made her way down to the alley. It was dingy but not overly cluttered. The dumpsters sat on the far end. As she proceeded toward them, a brick from the building on her left shattered on the patchy asphalt right in front of her.

She looked up but couldn't tell where it came from.

She kept going.

Just as she walked up on a heavy metal manhole cover in the alley, she paused cautiously, and it exploded upward with a nauseating swoosh of sewer tunnel-filtered air. She stepped back and watched the cover rise and then start to fall. It seemed to career over her, and she jumped aside as it began to come down. It slammed into the alley's asphalt with a muffled clang. There was no doubt about the pendulum in Emma's mind now. It was bearing down on her. She had to keep going.

She stepped up her pace. Then she began to run.

As she reached the side door of the first dumpster, she heard a loud, deafening *crack* and turned to see an exterior beam in the adjacent building begin to crumble.

She ignored it and slid the side door to the container open. It was full.

As she reached the second dumpster, clumps of concrete began falling all around her. She slid the side door open and climbed into the container with her backpack.

The dumpster was half full and stuffed with cardboard and paper goods. She opened her pack and took out the diary and the lighter fluid.

Emma heard more cracking noises and steel beams groaning as they lurched. She squeezed the lighter fluid container and doused the pages of the diary. The ink in some of the entries began to run. She doused herself, hair first, then her blouse, and then all over everything else around her. A small stack of refuse rose and fell away in front of her, and she watched the mild commotion holding the lighter fluid over her head with both hands. A large rat suddenly emerged, and Emma squirted it with the fluid. It made a hasty retreat.

Emma heard the hydraulic brakes of a garbage truck. It was pulling up and stopping.

She experienced a frantic moment of abject terror, contemplating the prospect of being crushed—but that was ludicrous. She had already resigned herself to burning.

She almost began to laugh.

Emma was smiling when the garbage truck picked up the dumpster. She knew she only had a few seconds before the container would be turned upside down. She retrieved the lighter from her backpack and took a deep breath. Then she lit herself. She thought of Lauren as she clung to the diary. She was instantaneously engulfed in purple flame. The flames yellowed as they spread to the paper goods.

When the bin tipper inverted the dumpster, Emma did not scream. Her goal was to hang on to the diary. She tumbled end over end into the truck's hydraulic crusher compartment. For an instant she was afraid that the refuse poured over her would extinguish the conflagration, but the entire contents of the container were now ablaze. The fire just rose, and Emma welcomed it. She wanted the flames to swallow her and the book whole, the whole curse, the entire malignance. It was the only way.

Emma inhaled the smoke and flame deeply as her flesh was seared, her tongue and gums boiled, and her limbs withered. Her lungs blistered, and she began to choke.

Emma was going to do it. She was going to pull it off. She was going to thwart the grim pendulum.

The garbage truck operator was shocked by the fire in the truck's master compartment and decided crushing the combustibles might limit the flames. He engaged the hydraulic crusher and stepped away from the vehicle. He almost tripped over the misplaced manhole cover.

Most of Emma was turning to the ember already, and she could no longer see. The last instance of her consciousness focused on one thing. Making love to Lauren.

Death was like a high window.

A richness of intensity.
An unflinching vastness.

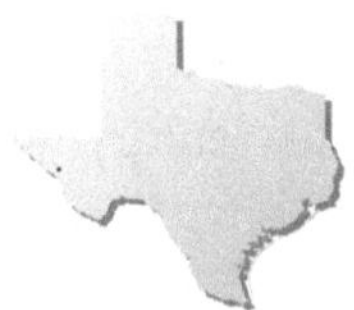

nine
nature calls

Solid--like old-school 80s era John Shirley or Bloch. Great characteriza-tion through dialogue, excellent pacing--and likable, empathetic charac-ters, too. Their dread fate at the end was affecting--and the denouement with the "Clock of the Long Now"? Chilling. When Paco first mentioned it to Rios, I wondered how, like Chekhov's famed rifle on the mantle-piece, will it go off? And then it did, and not with a bang.
— **James Pepe**, horror writer and IT professional at Portland Community College

RAUL NAJERA WAS a serious young man. He had lived in the Kermit area of West Texas all his life, and the only reason he took a job at the Andrews County Nuclear Waste Authority was to leak the goings on behind the storage facility's heavily fortified walls. The Nuclear Waste Authority (NWA) had applied for another permit to dump radioactive materials near Kent, and Najera had family in nearby Van Horn. The NWA had promised to pay for a new school and a state-of-the-art football stadium and track in Van Horn if the dwindling community signed off on the project. So far, Van Horn had balked.

On this particular nightshift, Najera and another employee, Doogie Ross, were walking the perimeter of the facility, taking a long smoke break. They strolled away from the front gate, toward the first corner to the south.

"You ever been over here in the daytime?" Ross asked, zig-zagging his flashlight along the ground.

"No," Najera replied. "Not since I applied."

Ross smoked and dipped. Najera didn't even drink coffee. Their walks outside the NWA walls were just a break from the stultifying routine. Najera felt like a prison guard on the midnight shift. Except nothing in the "penitentiary" was alive, much less penitent. The term radioactive, though. Was an active ingredient really dead?

"Well," Ross said, lighting up. "I've lived all over Texas and one thing every place in Texas definitely has, is fire ants. Fucking fire ants everywhere." Ross spat, using his flashlight hand to track the gob's landing, and then, took a long drag. "Not here, though," he continued, gesturing expansively with his cigarette hand. "And that's weird, right? It's like they sense what's here. It's like they know."

"They may be smarter than we think," Najera replied. "It makes you wonder."

"It does. But it's damn good money. Hell, I was working fast food at Taco Vato's before I landed this gravy train. Now, I'm drivin' a King Ranch."

Something moved in the darkness beyond the perimeter lighting that wilted outside the facility walls. Ross swung his flashlight in its direction. "Did you hear that?" he rasped.

"No," Najera replied. "What was it?"

But they both heard it now, out past a clump of stubborn desert shrub. Ross flicked his cigarette away. It bounced and rolled in the uneven sand.

A low clicking and scuttling sound filled the air, and it was getting louder.

"What the hell is that?" Ross said. "I—"

By the time Ross trained his flashlight on the approaching creature, it was too late. It caught him in an instant, and Najera ran. The light from Ross' fallen flashlight lit Najera's path.

The thing looked like something from those Pokemon cards Najera collected as a kid, a *Venipede* or a *Whirlipede*—but he didn't stick around to see how accurately it compared to his childhood memories.

This was his first full sprint since junior college, but he was long-striding now, trying to remind himself to breathe. For a moment, he thought he might make it, but the clicking, like the sound of his heart, grew loud. Right when he thought his chest might burst from the pressure, the thing was upon him.

Treat Kearny's friends called him "Tree," because he was tall and rangy, crowding most doorways and an imposing figure in the hall outside his classroom. He taught Latin at L.D. Bell High School in Hurst, Texas, and was as amicable as he was huge.

Sitting cross-legged in his eight-man tent (a two-man tent was much too small and a four-man tent was still something of a squeeze), grading papers by lantern light, he lamented getting such a late start.

A few years back, a group of Germans had purchased the abandoned ghost town of Lobo sixteen miles south of Van Horn on US-90. Every other summer they staged the Desert Dust Film Festival at a converted gas station and abandoned hotel. This year they were holding the event in late fall, over Thanksgiving break, the long weekend after the holiday. The Germans held a similar harvest celebration in early October. They called it *Erntedankfest*.

Treat had met one of the Germans at a hostel in Prague several years before, and this would be his second festival attendance. He was eager to see his European friends, but slow to get away after a Thanksgiving visit with his family in Dallas. His delayed departure put him in Odessa around 11 p.m. and, just after 12:20 a.m., he decided to stop in Kent. Kent was also a ghost town, located about an hour-and-a-half east of Van Horn. He decided to pitch his tent there by headlight, behind the shell of the abandoned schoolhouse on State Hwy 118, just south of I-10. He liked the windowless façade of the old rust-brick schoolhouse in daylight. It was picturesque, a mark of civilization against indomitable, frontier desolation—what Latin used to be in the old days. The tent smelled vaguely of Deep Woods Off, but there were no mosquitoes in that part of Texas in late fall.

At around 2 a.m. he put his red pen down and decided to call it a night. First, however, nature called. He unzipped the tent entrance and slipped outside. He stepped off about twenty paces to relieve himself and stared into the cloudless night sky. He could see millions of stars and the low, glowing curve of the Milky Way perpendicular to the far horizon.

As he unbuttoned and unzipped his cargo shorts, he heard something. A clicking, and then a scuttling. He spotted something moving low and fast about fifty yards out. The clicking and scuttling got louder as he turned, holding up his shorts, and ran. But it was too late.

He only screamed once.

Annette Carden was finally getting used to Texas.

Originally from Colorado, Carden attended college at Oregon State. Neither locale was especially useful in terms of her degree, entomology —the study of insects. But her specialty was centipedes and millipedes, and, broken down further, the phylum Myriapoda. Carden was on a tenure track at Texas Tech University, West Texas being one of the best places to study Myriapods and the perfect habitat for her favorite, millipede diplopods known as *Orthoporus ornatus*. They looked like thick earthworms, except they had legs. Hundreds of them. And, after a heavy rain in far West Texas, thousands attempted to cross state roads and highways in search of new places to burrow.

Carden spent her summers in the Big Bend area and, this year, her Thanksgiving break. After a rough semester, a trip home to Colorado held little appeal. More than family time, she needed to decompress. To Carden, Texas was becoming startlingly medieval for women and education, and especially science. Perhaps, after receiving tenure, she might move on. For now, however, she was going to relax at her place near the Christmas Mountains.

That was where the deputy sheriff found her.

Carden kept a decent little getaway cabin on a sandy, five-acre lot in the Terlingua Ranch Estates. Very few Ranch residents had power, because the waspish inhabitants refused to agree on or mutually concede to power company easements in their dusty refuge from cellphone reception, traffic and on-the-grid accoutrements. Carden had water delivered to her 1,000-gallon, ground-mounted water tank during her summer residency, and the cottage's metal roof was neatly corralled by a gutter that emptied into a separate, 500-gallon rain storage tank. She got her power from a combination of solar panels, a wind turbine and, as a last resort, a diesel generator, slab-mounted, protected from the elements by a ventilated shed-like structure. She also had propane gas delivered for cooking and some heating. She took solar showers in summer, but relied on the trailer's tankless, 120V insta-hot water heater in the cooler months. The locals kept to themselves and she didn't get many visitors. So, when she spotted a vehicle stirring up dust on her long gravel drive, she was slightly alarmed. Then she saw the red and blue flashers.

The cruiser pulled up, and the dust settled. A Culberson County sheriff's deputy, with mirror-lensed sunglasses, stepped out. He was tall and wiry and looked to be about Carden's age.

"Hello, ma'am," he said.

"Morning, deputy. What can I do for you?"

"Are you Dr. Annette Carden?"

"I'm Assistant Professor Carden."

"Well, ma'am. I'm a county or so over from my jurisdiction, but we need your help."

"My help? I don't know how I could be of any help—"

"I—Dr. Carden, ma'am—it won't make any sense. We have a problem. I can try to explain it on the way over."

"Over where?"

"Kent, ma'am. North-northeast of Van Horn."

"That's a long way. I'm sorry, I don't think... I don't know what I could help you with."

"Can the sheriff speak with you?"

"I suppose so."

The deputy removed his sunglasses and placed them in a shirt pocket. Then he used his cell phone to call the sheriff. Carden noticed that the deputy's eyes were a light, bright blue.

"Sheriff," the deputy said, "I found her."

The deputy handed Annette the phone. The sheriff was direct and brief. They had a strange death on their hands, and they needed additional information—an expert opinion. They believed an insect may have been involved. The sheriff assured Annette that she would be compensated for her time. The deputy waited for her to get ready.

Carden wanted to take her own vehicle, but the deputy—whose last name was Therber—noted that it was best that they both took the cruiser. He could turn on the flashers and they would make better time. Traveling at speeds upwards of 90 mph, the drive would still take a while.

When they were on the road, Carden eyed the steel mesh barrier that separated the front and back seats of the cruiser. She'd never been in a police car before. Or a sheriff's department cruiser.

"What made you decide to become an "ickyologist?" Deputy Therber inquired.

"*Ickyologist?* Where'd you hear that?"

"I heard it in an Elvis movie once."

"About an Egyptian mummy at a rest home?"

"Something like that."

"*Bubba Ho-Tep?*"

"Actually, yeah. I think that was it."

"That wasn't Elvis, deputy. That was Bruce Campbell playing Elvis."

"The guy from *Evil Dead*? The original?"

"Yes, sir."

"Oh, wow. That's embarrassing. I knew I heard it somewhere. What were the bugs called?"

"Scarab beetles. They were big in Ancient Egypt, but hardly flesh-eating monsters. Scarab beetles usually subsist on dung, decaying plant material, or carrion—the flesh of dead things."

"From what I've heard about the crime scene, I'd say it was something along the lines of a scarab that dispatched our vic."

"That seems unlikely," Carden replied, shaking her head.

Deputy Therber shrugged. "If not, I guess it was something like it," he maintained.

"I can take a look," Carden said, "but my specialty is centipedes and millipedes. They're more related to Crustaceans—crabs and lobsters—than most insects. 'Bugs' aren't really part of my wheelhouse. But I might be useful in a pinch... pardon the pun."

"What?"

"Nothing. It's not important."

"What made you want to study that stuff?"

"Do you really want to know? Or are you just making conversation?"

"We still have a ways to go before we get to Kent. I'm interested, yes."

"Do you subscribe to evolutionary theory?"

"Evolution? I think so. From what I know about it."

"Good. That's a start."

"Oh, well. Thanks. I guess."

"I just mean that plenty of people these days still don't. It's a little scary."

"Why's that?"

"I mostly try to stay out of these discussions—but you did rouse me from the hustle and bustle of Dune Ranch."

"Is that what they call it now?"

"That's what I call it," Carden answered. "May I speak frankly?"

"I'm a fan of straight-shooters."

"Well, the fact of the matter is... most things in our society—our very way of life—are propped up by science... advanced computer technology, medical technology, transportation, mobile phones, etc. They all spring from the scientific method, which involves the formulation, applicable testing, and refinement of theory and the research and development of practical applications. Criticism is the foundation of the scientific method. Every hypothesis is open to questions and testing. If a theory doesn't hold water, it's discarded for a better one. Does it explain everything? No. But it's usually an honest attempt, and challenges are hardly forbidden—in fact, they're invited." Carden was quiet for a moment.

"The truth is," she continued, "we cling to way too many ideas that institutions refuse to allow to be challenged or questioned. Our educational system is authoritarian but helmed by no real authorities. Just political operatives. And our political system is selectively forthcoming, and helmed by no real leaders. Just promulgators of obfuscation." Carden considered her mild harangue. It didn't seem appropriate in the cruiser, so far from the easy, predictable impudence of the faculty lounge. Maybe she belonged with all the eccentric cranks at Terlingua Ranch.

"Those opinions are chock full of ten-dollar college words I barely understand."

"Do you disagree?"

"I don't know if I know enough to disagree," Therber answered, smiling.

"That's honest."

"Well, it isn't a theory."

Carden grinned. Was he being flirtatious?

"To conclude my original point," she continued, "millipedes and centipedes are different than most insects, and actually pre-date them. My primary focus is on millipedes of the subphylum Myriapoda, but their cousins, predatory centipedes of the class Chilopoda, were the first land-based predators. We're driving through an area that used to be covered by ocean. Chilopods could have evolved here 430 million years ago. Their first steps from the sea could have been taken right here."

"I think anything is possible."

"I agree. But concepts that stretch back 430 million years ago aggravate certain sensibilities, religious dogma, and cherished faith directives."

"Directives?"

"Well, we are instructed what to believe, right?"

"A fair point. I suppose I am religious," Deputy Therber said. "Religious with a dash of doubt. It seems to me that Adam and Eve weren't all that, and they certainly didn't stick the landing. And if the Big Man is all He's cracked up to be, why didn't they? It hardly made sense to me when I was younger. Now, religious faith is something I allow myself on Christmas and some holidays." Deputy Therber put his sunglasses back on. "So, you really dig this stuff?"

"I do," Carden replied. "Myriapods and chilopods have been around as long as sharks. And coral reefs. And they'll probably be here long after we're gone."

"I don't exactly find that comforting."

"I'm not sure it thrills me, either. But it's where we find ourselves."

"It is the way you tell it. I bet you're a good teacher."

"I try. What's your first name, deputy?"

"Rodney, ma'am."

"How much farther, Rodney?"

———

When Deputy Therber and Assistant Professor Carden arrived at the ruins of the schoolhouse, the Sheriff and a dark-skinned DPS officer were standing out front.

As Carden stepped out of the cruiser, introductions were made. Then the sheriff, Axil Rafferty, held forth. "I don't like this at all," he said. "Miss Carden—we wouldn't have called you out here if it wasn't absolutely necessary. I'm at a loss."

"I hope I can help, sheriff."

"Me, too, ma'am. Me, too. We have a body over there... or at least parts of one. And we think—well, we don't know what to think. I'm not even sure I know what to say."

"Is it that bad?" Deputy Therber asked.

"It's pretty bad," said Rafferty. "The body is still out behind the schoolhouse... what's left of it, anyway. And the smell. But the victim—he had something in his right hand. I wasn't sure what it was at first, but... well. I don't even want to think it, much less say it out loud. You should see for yourself."

The sheriff stepped around to his trunk and opened it. "I've lived out here all my life. I had an idea what this was, but I just... I just couldn't believe it. Who would? I couldn't process it. I needed an expert." The sheriff removed an object wrapped longways in a black contractor's trash bag. It was the shape of a slightly bent human arm, but when the sheriff unwrapped it, it was clearly not human. It was about three feet long, dull yellow, segmented and curved, and tapered at the end, almost to a frightening point.

Carden swallowed hard.

"It almost looks like a stubby tentacle," Therber observed. "Except it's rigid."

"It feels like a giant, reinforced celery stalk," Rafferty observed. "As I said, I've lived out here forever and I think I saw something like this in a cave once. But it wasn't near this big. It was—"

"*Scolopendra Heros*," Carden suggested abruptly. "Perhaps even *Scolopendra Heros castanerceps*. With a red head. You saw it in a cave?"

"Yep," Rafferty confirmed. "Leaned over on a rock and almost placed my hand right on it."

"The head was red, the sections of the body were black, and the legs were yellowish?"

"Yes, ma'am."

"*Scolopendra Heros*. You call it the Texas redheaded centipede, the giant desert centipede, or the Devil Head centipede. It's a Chilopod."

"Like what you were talking about on the way over?" said Therber. Carden nodded without taking her eyes off the appendage.

"But these things usually don't get over six or eight inches long," Sheriff Rafferty replied. "We did find a dead one, over eighteen inches long, a year or so back. It killed a cat and then a neighbor's dog killed it. You thinking this is a leg?"

"I am. I don't like thinking it—I would need to run some tests first. I think I'm kind of in shock."

"We all are."

"You saying this came from one of those Devil's Head centipedes?" Therber asked. "The one with all the legs?"

"Devil Head. Again, it would require testing, but... yeah. It looks like."

"But that would mean... How long would that make it?"

"Forty feet," answered the DPS officer, Mateo Rios. "Give or take." Rios' eyes were dark and sharp, and wide set over a hawkish nose. He was slight, clean cut, and astute. Carden wondered if someday he wouldn't be the sheriff.

"That would make its antennae taller than me," Rafferty replied.

"Around four stories on its hind legs," Carden said.

"But that's impossible, right?" Rafferty asked.

"It was," Carden conceded.

"Hind legs?" Therber blurted.

"Yes. In South America, they've been known to stand on their hind legs and snatch bats in midair. And I agree, sheriff. I'd guess about six feet on the antennae. Which is what they use to identify their prey. Their eyes are useless."

"I bet that's what has been getting after the hogs," Rios replied.

"Feral hogs?"

"Yes, ma'am," Officer Rios said. "We thought it might be a big mountain lion, the granddaddy of all mountain lions. Or maybe a mating pair of mountain lions come down to feed. We been finding pieces of hog carcass all over and just made the logical assumption. But this changes things."

"I'll say," Rafferty agreed.

"That would explain how mangled the hog carcasses have been," Rios added, "and the smell."

"The *Heros* is venomous, and the venom is neurotoxic. The toxin it injects is pretty potent, and possibly deadly for any small mammal out here. And for a *Heros* that size, it would include feral hogs and mammals of the human variety. And, yes, it would rot the remains in a different way. Accelerated necrosis. Nasty stuff."

"That's what was weird," Rios replied. "Finding pieces of hog with no buzzards around."

"We found the leg of this thing in the hand of the man it attacked," said Rafferty. "He was a big dude."

"He never had a chance," replied Carden. "Devil Head centipedes are aggressive and fast. They usually attack other invertebrates or small vertebrates, including small mammals, reptiles, and amphibians. But one that big…"

Sheriff Rafferty had been right. There wasn't much left of Treat Kearny, especially intact. Blood, entrails, shit, strips of skin and shards of bone.

But they found his wallet in the tent. Besides that, a striated length of Kearney's leg, a strip of red-haired sideburn (or pubic hair), the right hand that had grabbed and held onto the creature's leg, and his entire left arm, which featured a tattoo of the Orion constellation on the interior wrist. Officer Rios held up a pair of bloody cargo shorts with a short stick.

It was difficult for Carden to micro-extrapolate the macro evidence, but she tried and took another look at the *Heros* appendage. Therber stood alongside, and Sheriff Rafferty nodded into his flip phone. "Yep," he said. "Uh-huh. What time you think? Okay. I'll get back to you." Rafferty's face seemed to lose its color.

There was an unreality to the entire crime scene, which made Carden wonder if it could even be called a crime scene. Could anything in the natural world, besides man or humankind, be considered criminal? She didn't get to reflect on the point very long.

"I think there's another one," Rafferty said. "At the Texas-New Mexico border, near the NWA facility."

"But that's a hundred miles away," Officer Rios replied.

"Where?" Carden inquired.

"Near a nuclear waste storage facility out there in Andrews County. Two more victims. Sounds like the same MO."

"North of Kermit," Deputy Therber added.

"Kermit, Wink, Mentone..." Carden mumbled.

"What did you tell them?" Rios asked.

"Nothing," Rafferty barked. "What do we really know?"

"That place was originally restricted to the monitored storage of low-grade, radioactive material," Therber said. "But I heard they fast-tracked a broader application to accept more hazardous stuff."

"I heard that, too," said Rios. "Nuclear waste with half-lives lasting thousands of years."

"That's why the citizens of Van Horn were fighting plans for a second facility," Rafferty replied. "We didn't want that crap in our backyard."

"What if it's led..." Carden hesitated. "That might explain..." Carden's entire person straightened.

"What?" Deputy Therber said. "What is it?"

Carden mulled it over and finally said it. "What if this giant Devil Head Chilopod is the result of an NWA leak or ground exposure?"

"That's a hundred miles away," Rios repeated. "Could something like whatever that thing is move that far in a night?"

"It's not impossible," Carden answered.

"Wait," Therber said, taking a step. "Dr. Carden, wait a minute. Do you really expect us to believe the goddamn King Kong of centipedes is hot-rodding around West Texas, mowing people down?"

"I wouldn't put it quite like that, Rodney," Carden said. "But, yes. It's possible. You saw the appendage in the sheriff's trunk." The sheriff noted Carden's use of Therber's first name.

"I did," Therber replied. "I know. But this is B-movie science-fiction stuff. *Ickyology*. You know that, right?"

Carden pointed at the dull yellow appendage and answered Therber with raised eyebrows.

Rafferty turned to Officer Rios. "You have a good map of this area?"

"I do."

"Could you grab it for me and bring it over to the hood of my cruiser?"

"I can, Sheriff. I will."

Carden spelled it out slowly.

"They've found record-breaking, giant millipede fossils that were six feet long and probably weighed over a hundred pounds. As I told Deputy Therber on the ride over, millipedes and centipedes were some of the first creatures to ply dry, solid ground; they were the first land predators and hunters. And that isn't the stuff of 50s B-movie sci-fi. Those are the facts. But speaking of the 50s, has anyone ever heard of the Bikini Atoll?"

"Girls skinny-dipping at Balmorhea in the old days," Therber joked, trying to be clever. "With no bikini at all."

Carden ignored him. "The Bikini Atoll in the Pacific Ocean is where the United States conducted multiple early nuclear tests. We detonated over two dozen nuclear bombs there, all told, and today, even after almost seventy years, dangerous levels of radiation still permeate every biological property in the area. Strontium 19. Genetic mutations. Decreased longevity. Sharks with strange fin configurations, invertebrates that are growing larger. And growing larger faster."

"Sweet Jesus," Sheriff Rafferty said.

"Yes," Carden replied. "I'm not stating anything for the record. But a Chilopod exposed to radiation? It could produce a mutation like this. I know it sounds like 'Godzilla' stuff. Except in Mr. Kearney's case, if this was a giant chilopod, sorry—he was Japan."

Officer Rios walked back up with the maps. They spread one out on the hood of the sheriff's cruiser, and Rafferty studied it. "A hundred miles in a night," he said.

"It's not impossible," Therber replied. "The Comanche could do three hundred a night on horseback."

"It would be feasible, for sure," Carden said. "*Heros* are nocturnal, so it'd probably stay away from the highway and travel in remote areas, away from light. But we're getting ahead of ourselves. How long has that nuclear waste facility been there? This may not be some spontaneous anomaly. It may be the accelerated evolution of an organism over a period of years."

"That doesn't help," Rafferty complained. "In fact, that makes my asshole pucker. Where do you think it'd go next?"

"I couldn't answer that with any real certainty," Carden conceded. "But where's the next big town? Especially one that might be approached in the dark?"

"Van Horn," Therber replied. "Population right at or just under two thousand, but the biggest place for practically a hundred miles in any direction."

"Are there any goat or horse ranches in the area?" Rafferty inquired. "Where are you finding the hog remains?"

"The outskirts of Van Horn," Officer Rios replied. "And there are seven or eight goat ranches."

"That might be a good place to start," Carden said. "It's finding food near light, or on the edge of lighted areas. Van Horn might be a good spot to check, especially before it gets dark."

"Should we call in the cavalry?" Therber asked.

The sheriff grabbed the map and started rolling it up.

"Maybe a chopper?" suggested Rios.

"The professor said they were nocturnal," Rafferty replied. "A chopper wouldn't do us much good at night, would it?"

"Probably not."

"And besides, what would you tell the chopper crew we were looking for?"

Rios smiled grimly. "Roger that."

"It's a guessing game," Rafferty said. "And I like the professor's instincts."

"You think it's heading west?"

"So far, it has."

"What about the highway?"

"It had to cross it to get here. And there are probably sixteen bridges and underpasses between here and Van Horn."

"That's right," Rios observed. "Should we release the information to the public?"

"I don't think so," said Rafferty. "I think it's a bad idea."

"Afraid people will panic?"

"Not at all," Rafferty replied. "People out here don't panic easy. But if the people know, the government might know. Or find out."

"And? What are you saying?" Therber asked.

"I'm talking out of turn," Rafferty replied. "But the government's patrons are making billions of dollars dumping radioactive garbage from all over North America at NWA—shitting where we eat, so-to-speak. Hell, there may be more money in that than there is in oil and gas. And definitely easier money. I think they'd swoop in and cover this up. Change the narrative. People might even disappear. Money talks, and obscene money—the kind of money we're talking about—stalks, always on the lookout for threats. I'd like to avoid finding myself in their crosshairs. And this little chilidog jailbreak would give them the perfect excuse to cover all this shit up."

"*Chilopod*," Carden corrected.

"Yes," Rafferty said. "Chilopod. I meant chilopod."

"Well," Carden wryly observed, "It seems counterintuitive, but I think Sheriff Rafferty is right. That's exactly how it might play out."

"So, what do we do?" Therber asked.

"Reach out to whoever you know you can trust and really count on," Rafferty advised. "Contact anybody you'd take a bullet for. Bring them in on the down-low, and on a need-to-know basis, only. We'll try to corner this thing and kill it. Be done with it."

"Kill it with what?" Rios inquired.

"M4 rifles," Therber suggested.

"We have some back at the office and even more at Van Horn PD," Rafferty said. "And some at the local gun shops. Buy 'em out, guns and ammo."

"But what do we tell them?"

"I don't give a shit," Rafferty replied. "Tell 'em it's for a raffle. Say it's to help protect the border."

Rios rolled his eyes.

Rios grabbed the M4s and some ammo and picked up an off-duty Border Security officer he was old friends with. Rafferty enlisted his son, who was home for the weekend from Angelo State. Carden stuck with Deputy Therber. They headed to Fort Davis, Rafferty to Van Horn, and Rios, eventually, due north on State Highway 54, toward the Guadalupe Mountains.

Rafferty was possessed of an increasing sense of dread, but he kept things as light as he could with his son, Harwood.

"Sounds pretty farfetched to me, Sheriff," Harwood said with a playful smirk. "You guys must really be getting bored."

"I hope you're right, meathead. Believe me, nothing would make me happier. I hope it's a wild goose chase."

"I'm kidding. Nothing surprises me anymore. The crap these days," Harwood said. "You think it can't get any weirder, but it does. Nothing seems set in stone anymore, like it's real or the only thing that's real."

"I hear ya—I really do. It's the truth. It seems like it's coming from all sides, even out here. But we can't curl up in a little ball. We gotta keep our shoulder to it and keep going."

"I know, I know. Hell or high water. I don't need a lecture."

"I know that, son. I'm well aware. I don't mean to… I wish you'd have picked another weekend to come home. Your mom and I are always happy to see you, but what's happening today—of all days—it's *Twilight Zone* stuff. It worries me. I hope it's a lark."

"Meadowlark Lemon," Harwood replied.

"*Meadowlark Lemon*," Rafferty repeated. "I can't believe you remember him, kiddo. That slays me. I haven't thought of him since—sheesh, I can't remember when. I'm impressed." Rafferty's sudden enthusiasm waned. "Thing is, we may need some of Meadowlark's moves if we run into this thing. I really just brought you along to man the radio. If things get out of hand, I want you to stay in the cruiser."

"I'm a decent shot. You know that."

"I do know that. But I don't know what we're looking at here. And we'll have plenty of guns. But if things get cattywampus, get on the radio. Stay put and call in reinforcements. Your mama would skin me alive if something happened to you."

Rios liked the drive to the Guads. The Delaware Mountains to the east and the Sierra Diablos Range to the west. His buddy Paco was a fan as well. Paco's father, who left him and his mother early on, was a full-blood Apache, and he talked about how his great-great-grandfather had snuck off to the Guads for ceremonies even after they settled on the reservations. The Guadalupe Mountains were sacred to them.

Paco was younger than Rios, but solid in the ways that counted. He was tough, practical, and kept things in perspective. Rios liked him. Family ties were important, but bonds of reliance mattered, too. Especially under fire. Under a microscope. Under extreme duress. A lot of Rios' law enforcement colleagues didn't have that kind of commitment. Paco was reliable. And he didn't make a habit of being up to things he shouldn't. Neither of them bought into the "Back the Badge" bullshit, or "Blue Lives Matter." If you did your job and did it right, and did it honest, you were the badge. And you didn't need to win any popularity contests or become political pawns. That's how Rios saw it, anyway.

"I'd love to have me a little hacienda out here someday," Paco said, "but I'll never be able to afford it. Bezos is a *pendejo*. Fucking 10,000-year clock, my ass."

"They say he owns half the Diablos," Rios replied.

"I know. To build a clock that ticks once a year."

"The 'Clock of the Long Now.'"

"Is that what they call it?"

"It is. They have two small prototypes, one in California and one in Europe. But the big one ought to come online in the next few years."

"What's the point of it? Why put it out here?"

"I have no idea why they decided to do it out here, outside of the fact that there's nothing out here and maybe it was cheaper to buy half a mountain range here."

"Again, though. Why?"

"They say they're doing it to make us think differently about time, to think more long-term."

"That's funny," Paco said. "They took this land from people that thought seven generations ahead, and they didn't need a fancy clock built in a mountain to do it."

Rios nodded. "I hear the hour or 'century' hand will advance every one hundred years. And they say a cuckoo will come out when the clock strikes a new millennium."

"Ain't that some shit," Paco sighed. "*Pinches gringos.*"

"*Pinches gringos,*" Rios repeated.

"So. You think we'll find this... this whatever-it-is thing?"

"I'm not so sure," Rios replied. "It may not be that simple, anyway. This whole thing is crazy, a precautionary measure at best. Which is probably smart. But we're not exactly sure what it is or if we'll be able to find it."

"Is it just us greasers?" Paco inquired, with a playful grin. "Or will Raff and Ponyboy be packing?"

"Rafferty has been around," Rios replied. Don't underestimate him. And Therber is no slouch. He's got some cactus to him when it counts."

"Good. Then, I guess we're set," Paco remarked. "Been awhile since I carried an M4 carbine. Seems heavy. And it can do some heavy damage." Paco grinned. "It wouldn't hurt to come home a hero, though. I hear your sister is graduating from New Mexico State soon."

"It'd be hard to call on her with an M4 stuck up your ass," Rios said.

"I'll keep that in mind," Paco replied. "It would definitely make it harder to aim."

Rios laughed, and Paco flashed another big grin. "You always were too uptight, bro."

"Just be ready," Rios said. "We may not see anything. We probably won't see anything."

———

Carden and Therber shot west across State Highway 166, took the jog on CR 505, and headed north toward Van Horn on US-90.

Biological imperative, Carden thought.

Not in terms of the *Scolopendra Heros*, but Deputy Therber. He was lithe and handsome, not exactly Pinot Grigio, but what they said in the movies about handsome men in this part of the world: a long, cool glass of water. And she was feeling thirsty.

Was it the abrupt, wild, surreal quality of the entire day, or the crazy, half-baked plan they were now engaged in? *Was danger an aphrodisiac?*

"Peso for your thoughts," Therber said.

"What?" Carden said. "Oh. Thanks. I was just thinking."

"That's what I said."

"Oh, yeah. Right."

"About what?"

Carden lied. "About how this wasn't how I planned to spend my day."

Therber smiled. "Yeah, I thought about dropping you off in Fort Davis and trying to arrange for someone else to take you home. I mean... if you wanted to sit this one out. For the record, though, I'm glad you came."

It was Carden's turn to smile.

"Now, don't get me wrong," Therber continued. "I truly, really do hope you're wrong. About all of it. Because, well, if you're not... hell, then I don't know when or how this all ends."

"I hope I'm wrong, too," Carden said. "But you saw that appendage."

"You ever seen anything like that before?"

"No. Nothing even close."

Therber drove for a while in silence, clearly chewing on something in his mind. "If it is what we think it might be, could this thing be a one-off? How do they... Do they lay eggs?"

"Yes," Carden said.

"Shit."

"But there's a good chance it's a one-off," Carden added. "A Frankenstein, of sorts. A sterile mutation. The kiss of extinction."

"Beg your pardon?"

"A dominant sterile or dominant lethal mutation," Carden explained. "They're often short-lived, so they wouldn't qualify for natural selection."

"The losing-est lottery ticket in the world," Therber said. "One and done."

"Exactly. And that would work in our favor."

"We'd just have to stop the one."

After they passed through Valentine, they soon saw the participants of the Desert Dust Film Festival on their left.

"What are they doing?" asked Carden.

"Some kind of desert hipster concert or carnival or something."

"Do you think they're in danger?"

"I don't know what to think," Therber admitted.

"Where are you from?"

"Juno."

"*Juno*. Like the movie?"

"Movie?"

"J-U-N-O."

"Well, it's spelled the same. But Juno is a ghost town now, southeast of here, in Val Verde County. Not too far from the Devil's River."

Carden shook her head. "Is there anything out here that isn't named after something ominous?"

"It's not like that freaky beetle of yours, professor," Therber replied, grinning. "In what we refer to out here, in ten-dollar college words, it's a misnomer. The Devil's River may be the prettiest place in Texas. It's just really hard to get to."

"Well," Carden said, raising her eyebrows. "Once we get done with this monster hunt, maybe you could take your professor friend out there one day."

"Maybe."

"I'd like that, I think."

"Me, too. I think. It would beat chasing a 100-legged freak all over creation."

Carden grew pensive for a moment. "That must be strange, coming from a place that no longer exists. A ghost town."

Therber grinned. "It's a lot like coming from a small town—that died."

"I'm serious."

"Well, Professor Carden. Since you asked. Life out here... it appears and disappears, and sometimes reappears. The places are like lightning bugs. They blink in and out. Communities pop up, collapse and vanish. There are places on current maps where no one even lives now. People always come to build a future for themselves, but sometimes they don't last. You look away for a minute, and they're gone. They're somewhere else. But never for very long."

"Is that what the sheriff meant earlier, about the people who live out here?"

"Close enough, I suppose. There are easier places to be, for sure."

"Why do you stay?"

Therber gave her a funny glance. "I like chasing fireflies." He grinned again. "I keep an empty jar in the trunk."

"With holes in the lid?"

"Of course."

They were both enjoying this, and they knew it.

Then they got the call.

<hr>

When they arrived, Rios' cruiser was upside down on the north side of US-180, about fifteen yards into the salt basin that sat on the western edge of the base of El Capitan, the southernmost tip of the Guadalupe Mountains. The cruiser's air bags had deployed and Rios and Paco suffered only minor injuries, which Harwood was treating with a standard first aid kit from Rafferty's vehicle.

Rios was heading west on 180 when the creature attempted to cross the asphalt in a hurry just ahead of him. Going about 70 mph, the cruiser T-boned the Devil Head and flipped, rolling twice. The Devil Head survived, but only long enough to drag its near-severed midsection over to the south side of the road and down into a dry gully.

It probably wouldn't have mattered, but Rios hadn't exactly been watching the road. Just east of the site of the collision, there was an old, abandoned adobe brick motel on the north side of US-180. Rios remembered staying there when he was young, but now it was just a collapsing ruin, filled with trash and pocked with tourist graffiti. He always checked it out when he passed by.

Paco was sitting off the shoulder, on the north side of 180. Except for some wicked contusions, he seemed to be in a surprised daze. Rios had a cut over his right eye and a sprained wrist. The creature had gotten the worst of it.

"I guess an exoskeleton is no match for Detroit steel," Sheriff Rafferty said. "Y'all were lucky." The sheriff already had a semi with a trailer and a backhoe on the way, and he was putting on a good face. But he was troubled. This is how it's going to start, he thought. Rafferty didn't know what the story was, or how it would end, but he knew this was how it would start. And he suddenly wanted to be someplace else, maybe Abilene or Fort Worth. Maybe San Angelo, closer to Harwood.

Sheriff Rafferty had a bone-deep suspicion that he didn't understand anything and that he would never understand anything. The unreality of the creature, the sections of what he considered its elongated abdomen torn, and guts splashed and stinking. It was freakish and hardly seemed earthly.

Did insects even have hearts?

Did they have brains?

He'd never thought about it before. And he'd always heard they would be here long after humans were gone.

Was that why?

Carden stood stock still, dumbfounded. Deputy Therber checked on Officer Rios and helped Paco to his feet.

"Is it dead?" Paco asked. "It's not still alive, is it?"

"No, it's not," said Therber. "It's gone. Are you okay?"

"I'm okay. I... I just can't believe... *What the fuck is that thing?* I've never seen anything like it."

"Me, neither, amigo. Me, neither."

Deputy Therber and Sheriff Rafferty walked over to Carden.

"We should bury it," Rafferty said. "I got a truck and a backhoe on the way."

"You don't think," Carden trailed off, "we should tell someone?"

"No. Absolutely not. If we do, there'll be men in black here tomorrow. You think they'll let this be? What was it Winston Churchill said? Never waste a disaster. This will open the door. They'll come in under the pretense of cleaning this up, but they'll stay to clean up... in terms of their pocketbooks. That other nuclear waste dump will be a done deal. They'll cover all this up. And they may cover us up, too."

Carden crossed her arms. "I'd like to say I could argue that point with serious conviction. But I can't."

"I say we don't give them the chance," Rafferty said. "I think it's our only chance."

Carden turned to Rodney. "What do you think, Deputy Therber?"

"I think this is a big fucking Devil Head kiddie train," Therber said. "With several cars and a caboose. And if it becomes a thing, it really will be the insects' turn."

"And we'll have brought it on ourselves," Carden stated unequivocally. "What if we got a television station out here? What if we got it to the press?"

"The nearest station is in El Paso... or Fort Stockton..."

"How long you think it would take them to get out here, sheriff?"

"A while, but they might beat the truck. What do we tell them to get them out here?"

"Tell them it's a cartel massacre," Therber suggested. "On US soil.

Bodies everywhere, kids, puppy dogs... they'll come runnin'. Offer them the scoop but tell them to keep it hush-hush."

The three hiked up the sandy incline to 180. Rios and Paco were leaning on the sheriff's cruiser.

"Where's Harwood?" Rafferty asked.

"He went to take a leak," Rios answered.

Rafferty got on the phone and called KASO, in El Paso. It was just starting to get dark.

It didn't even look real, Harwood thought. Almost like a bad CGI effect. But alien. If there'd been any cellphone reception out there, he'd have sent a picture.

Just as he finished relieving himself and started to button up his Levis, Harwood felt the earth move under his feet and stumbled backward. The walls of the old adobe motel shook and began collapsing.

Harwood heard a loud clicking, and then a rumble. He backed up two or three steps and then turned and started to run. "Dad!" he screamed, "Dad!"

Rafferty turned and dropped his phone.

He didn't have time to react.

An enormous, 747-sized centipede with a dragon-red head and a thousand dull, yellow legs smashed through the ruins of the adobe motel and suddenly dwarfed Harwood, front pincers scissoring him to bits without even slowing down.

The sheriff howled gutturally, drew his pistol and started firing into the ghastly scarlet hellspawn's approaching, beaky face. The creature's impossibly long antennae cut telephone lines as it surmounted US-180 and immediately began wreaking havoc on the cruisers and their defenders. Paco reacted first, spraying the creature with an M4, and everyone else except Carden emptied their weapons.

But to no avail.

The gigantic, seemingly horned Devil Head centipede slashed and gnashed, allowing none of its human antagonists to escape.

Bisected at the waist, Carden blinked in amazement until her gaze froze.

It was over in a matter of moments.

————

When the news crew from KASO arrived, there was nothing alive in sight and it looked like a string of railroad cars were laying on their side along US-180. But when the chopper lowered and hovered, the producer looked closer and said, "There's no railroad tracks out here." Then his eyes widened. The railroad cars rose up, and the giant centipede seized one of the copter's landing skids and began pulling it down.

The chopper tipped sideways. The copter blades sliced through the centipede's black, pus-filled abdominal sections and the Devil Head fell, dragging the copter down with it. The resulting explosion, expanded by the chopper fuel, ignited the cruisers as well. Everything was aflame in seconds. The flames licked at the *Scolopendra Heros'* massive carcass, and almost reduced everything to ash.

The Guadalupe Mountains National Park ranger who reported the strange sights at the scene of the incident the next day was never seen or heard from again. Federal authorities were at the site almost simultaneously and had the bizarre "shoot-out" solved in a matter of hours.

Cartel violence.

Multiple casualties, including an El Paso news crew and a female college professor who was taken as a hostage, all deceased.

The men in black cleaned it up, and plans for a second low-level nuclear waste dump near Kent were finalized within months.

Van Horn did, however, get a new football field.

————

On the absolute clockwork instant of the commencement of the year 3023, two doors opened at one of the northernmost peaks of the Sierra Diablo Mountain Range, and the metallic cuckoo of the Clock of the Long Now appeared to announce the occasion. No human beings were around to witness it, but there were some *Scolopendra Heros* specimens. With food sources scarce, they had grown much smaller in the long interim.

On the absolute, clockwork instant of the commencement of the year 12023, two doors opened at one of the northernmost peaks of the Sierra Diablo Mountain Range, and the squeaky metallic cuckoo of the Clock of the Long Now appeared one last time to announce the occasion. By then, there were fewer *Scolopendra Heros* specimens around, but a smattering of diminutive mammals, including small humanoid primates.

The strange magical event was noted by only a few, but it would reverberate in their collective consciousness for hundreds of generations to come.

ten
fandango

I've known E.R. for eight years, and his imagination continues to amaze me. His writing has just as much personality as he does, booming and forthright and magnetic. "Fandango" is a great example of just how haunting his stories can be. Full of quiet suspense and heartfelt human drama.

—**Russell C. Connor**, author of *Good Neighbors*

"SUMMMMMMMM."

The old man was on a gurney in the Reeves County Hospital. His buddies had rushed there when they heard a fracking fluid hauler was bringing him in.

"Dexter," said Tommy, one of the old man's closest friends. "Are you with us? Can you hear me?"

Dexter's eyes didn't open. They were full of sand. His ears, mouth, and beard were full of sand as well. His eyelashes were caked with blood.

Tommy, a tall septuagenarian with a full head of white hair, leaned over his friend. "Dex? It's Tommy. Can you hear me?"

"Sssuhhhh-muh," Dexter groaned. "Summmmuhhh. Muhhhhh-hhh-moooom."

Another close buddy, Doug, chimed in. "The moon? What about the moon, Dex?"

Tommy stared down the hospital's long, single corridor and shook his head. "Moon. You think that's what he's saying?"

"Dunno," said Doug, a bald fifty-something with a slight paunch that was always shaded by a ten-gallon straw hat. "Sounds like it. You hear that hauler? He said Dex's ol' dually was in awful shape. He said he must've rolled it three times by the look of it. And he claims there was two foot of sand in the cab."

"Sssssssssuhmoon. *Mmmmuhhhhmoom.*" Blood began to pool in Dexter's eye sockets. "*Suhuhuhmoom.*"

"What the hell?" Tommy exclaimed. Blood was now seeping from Dexter's ears and trickling out his nose.

"Dexter?" Doug cried. "Nurse! *Nurse!*"

A nurse appeared and Tommy and Doug gave her space. "What happened?" she asked.

"He started bleeding just now," Tommy answered. "He was fine, and then blood just started filling his eyes."

"*Suhmoom.*"

"What's he saying?"

"He keeps saying something about the moon."

"*Tulllll...*"

"Dexter?"

"Teh... Telll... *Heck...*"

"Dexter, hold on, now. We called Heck. Hector is coming. The nurse—"

"*Smmuhmoom!*"

Dexter gasped, shook and then sunk into the gurney. The nurse called for a defibrillator and started CPR.

Tommy's eyes welled up and Doug removed his hat and took a step back.

"Dexter? *Dexter?!*"

Dexter's grandson, Heck, showed up five minutes later. He was taller than Tommy and sported a Sul Ross University ballcap. He played quarterback there in the late 1980s. Doug was still holding his ten-gallon hat in his hands.

"What happened?" Heck inquired.

"He rolled his dually. A fluid hauler came across him just south of McIlvain Draw off County Road 232. He was crawling up to the road."

"The hauler brought him straight here," Doug added.

"He snuck off to Red Bluff, again," Heck said. "He's been spending lots of time up there, took one of those abandoned cottages for a cabin."

"Red Bluff Reservoir hasn't been diddly-squat for years," Tommy observed.

"He knew that," Heck said. "It didn't bother him none. He hated what it did to the fishing, but he liked how the red algae bloom cleared the place out. I kept telling him he was getting too old to go out there. But he wasn't going to sit idle. He and his Pa were some of the first folks to fish the reservoir after it was formed in '36. And he and my grandmother snuck out there regularly when they were young. He had some fond memories. How is he?"

Doug and Tommy exchanged weary glances. "He's gone," Doug said. "He went on."

"Awww, shit," Heck mumbled. "*Awww, shit*, old man. Awww, hell."

Heck cut between them and went into the ER. The nurses had already raised the sheet. Heck pulled it back and swallowed hard. The blood was already drying at the corners of his grandfather's eyes, his ears and below his nostrils. Heck sobbed once and then covered his mouth with his free hand. It was a while before he returned to the hall. His eyes were red.

"He looked like he got caught in a sandstorm," Heck observed. "But there wasn't one up that way was there?"

"Not that we heard tell of," Doug said. "Calm as far as the eye can see. It's mighty queer, I say."

Doug and me was thinking about driving out to take a look at Dexter's truck," Tommy added. "Waiting on you, of course. Wanna come?"

"Yes, sir. Definitely."

Tommy drove his old cherry red, King cab Ford, and Heck rode shotgun. Doug sat in the center of the back seat leaning forward.

"I still can't believe it," Tommy said. "It don't seem real. Why just yesterday Dexter and I..." His voice trailed off and there was a long silence.

"He seemed invincible to me," Heck replied. "I thought he might live forever. But he lived a good, full life. I'm sorry to see him go, but he would agree. He counted himself lucky."

"I know," Tommy said. "Just sudden is all. And not the way I..."

Doug placed his left hand on Tommy's shoulder and gave it a pat.

When Tommy, Heck, and Doug got out to Dexter's truck, they were immediately perplexed. It sat right-side up about fifty yards off CR-232. The front passenger side window was the only one that wasn't busted out or spider-webbed. The dually's cab and long bed were twisted and crumpled from the front bumper to the back. But there were no skid marks on the road that indicated Dexter had lost control or that a loss of control had facilitated a rollover.

"How'd he manage that?" Tommy wondered, staring back at CR-232.

"Hard to say," Doug replied. Heck remained silent.

"Try impossible to say," Tommy ventured. "How do you flip a dually without turning your wheel or at least leaving a half-ass rubber stripe?"

"What was it, you think?"

"I have no earthly idea."

"What about the wind?"

"You know how powerful and fast-trackin' the wind'd have to be to toss a dually like a Cheeto? It would've blown off my grand-auntie's panties in Midland. And she's been dead and buried for ten years."

"Yeah, but the sand?"

The three men walked over to the vehicle.

The fluid hauler was right. The cab of the truck was full of sand.

Heck opened the front seat, passenger side door, and two buckets of desert poured out, followed by a folded foil pouch of Levi Garrett chewing tobacco.

"Dexter's chaw," Doug observed. "Looks like he had half a plug left."

Heck leaned in and took the keys out of the ignition.

"You thinkin' what I'm thinking?" Doug continued.

"What are you thinking?" Tommy answered.

"I'm thinkin' where's the hurricane? It don't look like sand's been thrown up anywhere else 'round here."

"No, it don't."

"I don't understand," Heck said, finally. "You believe the truck was picked up and *thrown*?"

"I don't believe anything," Tommy replied. "Believing's a bad habit. I'm just wondering out loud."

"Give it a rest, Tommy. What do you think happened to my granddad?"

"I don't know, Heck. I'm sorry. I'm stumped."

"It's some kind of spooky," Doug added.

"It is," Tommy agreed. "It sure is."

"Could a twister have done it?" Heck inquired.

"We don't get 'em out here that often," Tommy replied. "Just the dust devils."

"What about that one in Saragosa in '87?" Doug asked.

"It picked up a boy I played ball against," Heck said.

"Oh, hell," Tommy remembered. "Stoved his head in. He's still a vegetable. Lives in a Houston nursing home. I forgot about that one. But there's no other damage around, Heck."

"I see that," Heck replied.

Hector stared out at the surrounding Chihuahuan desert. The silence and the endless, sprawling nothingness of it still occasionally surprised him.

Heat waves blurred the horizon, but nothing else stuck out. Tommy and Doug gave Heck another moment.

"It's a God-awful place," Heck continued. "But he loved it."

"We all do," Doug said.

"Yep," Heck replied. "Somebody has to."

"Let's head back," Tommy suggested. "I'll get a tow truck out of Pecos or Wink here in the morning."

The ride back was mostly a quiet one. Heck took the back seat and simply stared out the windows of Tommy's King cab. Tommy and Doug exchanged a glance or two, but, for the most part, did the same.

Later, they sat around a rickety table full of empty Lone Star bottles near the rear of Pecos Billy's Saloon. They had skipped dinner and were hitting the Beer Nuts hard. "Did he say anything?" Heck inquired. "At the hospital, I mean? Before he…"

"He was delirious," Doug answered. "Wasn't making much sense."

"He kept mumbling something about the moon," Tommy said.

"The moon?"

"Yep, The moon. A moon. The moon. Some kinda' moon."

"*The moon?*"

"What it sounded like. He was pretty weak, though. Hard to make out exactly."

"He said 'the moon?'"

"Yep. 'The moon, his moon.' Something like that or close to it. 'Tha' moon…'"

"Tha' moon," Heck clarified. "Something about 'tha' moon…'"

"Yeah," Tommy said, slapping some sand out of his jeans. "You got home fries in your ears? He kept saying something about the moon."

"*Tha' moon?*"

"Tha' moon. Does that mean something to you?"

"Maybe. I'm not sure. You both know Dexter was part of a tank regiment in North Africa during dubya-dubya-two. He told me a story about it years ago. About a deadly sandstorm. Or some kinda' evil wind. I think he said they called it a 'simoom.'"

"A simoom."

"Do you think that's what he was trying to say?"

"Could be," Tommy replied. "Like I said, it was hard to make out."

"Suhmoon. Is that some kinda' Al-Qaeda thing?"

Heck shook his head once. "From World War II, Doug? Really?"

"Those folks was doin' algebra when we was still countin' beans with Roman numerals," Doug replied. "I saw it on the History Channel a while back."

"That may be the case," Heck said. But I don't think anybody's after us out here. They have their own desert to reckon with. I think we're safe."

"It could've been 'simoom,'" Tommy said. "Or 'lagoon' for all I know. Dex was in the grip of it. But he mentioned you and said we should tell you."

Dexter Chaney's funeral was held the following Saturday at the Lara Cemetery just south of Mentone. Nine of the Mentone community's nineteen residents showed up and Larry Spotnitz, one of Dexter's old war buddies, came in from Santa Fe. Dexter hadn't been a religious man, so the brief graveside service was basically a few words from his family and friends.

"He was a good man," Tommy said. "True to his buddies and never a cruel word, even for his enemies."

"He was my friend," Doug said, his face cracking. "He was my best friend."

When it came Larry's turn, his eyes welled up, but he held it together. "All in all, he was a brother to me," Larry said. "And a real hero. He saved me. I'll never forget him."

Dexter looked like a wax figure in his Sunday best. The sand around the cemetery seemed to kick up a bit, but the ceremony went off well.

An hour later, they were back at the same rickety table at Pecos Billy's. There were no Beer Nuts left, but plenty of Lone Star. "Those Panzers had us dead to rights," Larry said. "Couldn't hide, couldn't run. And the heat was bearing down on us like a furnace." He tilted his beer toward the ceiling, and then took a long sip. "Then, it all changed," he continued. "A wild wind blew up and sand filled the air. We hunkered down and held on. Stuffed towels and rags into every nook and cranny of our battered Sheman. We rode it out in a tin can. But them Germans, they weren't so lucky. The sandstorm buried half a division. We could hear their muffled screams. Even underground."

Larry sat silent for two minutes and then shuddered. "Sheesh," he said, trying to sound nonchalant. "What they got the A/C on in here?"

Heck looked at Tommy. Tommy shrugged his shoulders. Like Dexter before he passed, Larry was showing his age, and maybe he couldn't take a winter or a cold A/C like he used to.

But Heck wondered.

Larry waved a waitress over. "They say it's not nice to speak ill of the dead," Larry continued. "I understand that. But this isn't that. I have nothing ill to say. But saying anything at all always felt wrong. Having nothing good to say doesn't mean you're speaking ill. It just...It just means we didn't know what to say. So, we didn't say anything."

Larry got quiet again. Heck studied him over his beer. Every wrinkle in Larry's face seemed to lengthen.

Larry shot Heck a glance and then finished off his Lone Star.

"It was a long time before any of us stopped hearing them," Larry continued. "It seemed like a long time. It must've been. It never sat well with your granddad. It was a terrible way to go, and Dex... Well, it's almost like he felt like we shoulda' done more. To help those damn Nazis, I mean. If that makes any sense. But that sandstorm probably saved our lives."

"Dexter didn't share much about the war," Heck said. "But he did talk about what you're talking about once or twice. When I was younger."

"What did he say?"

"He said 'Sometimes the bill just comes due.' He talked about the Germans a little."

"It was quite a thing," Larry replied.

"My granddad wasn't very philosophical. But he could sound that way about those Panzers. 'Dodge one bullet,' he said '...and you catch the next. Or you meet one down the road. So, you kick every minute—but you help where you can.'"

"That was Dex," Larry said. "'Death always doubles back.' That's how he used to phrase it. And he was right. It doesn't miss any of us, does it? He had a good run. But it doubles back for all of us in the end."

"Yep," Tommy said. "That's the long and the short of it."

Larry smiled. "Your granddad ever show you his battlefield collection?"

"You mean his *dirt* collection? In those beat up red tins?"

"I think so. Prince Albert was the brand. Crimp cut, cigarette and pipe tobacco. Or maybe pipe and cigarette. He didn't smoke, but he collected them tins from guys who did."

Heck smiled. "No Lugers or Nazi helmets for him. Just a couple of handfuls of dirt from every country he went through or fracas he survived."

"Ha, that's right. That's what he called every battle. A *fracas*. Did he have a tin for Algeria, too?"

"Yes, but not dirt. That one was different. Just sand, I think. Desert sand."

"Did Dex ever talk about the last shot?"

"Last shot?"

"That day."

"No, I guess not."

"That's what sticks with me."

"Yeah?"

"Yes, sir. That last shot."

A young, Chicana waitress placed another beer in front of Larry, but he didn't seem to notice at first. Then, slowly, he regarded it intensely, almost in a daze.

As a bead of condensation swelled and began to run down the side of the bottle, Larry started again. "It was a long while after the screaming started. They were suffocating. I'm sure of that. But then, I guess, one desperate Panzer commander got an idea. A notion that maybe a shot from their 75-millimeter would blast away some sand. They couldn't breathe and it had to be 120 degrees in the shade—except there wasn't any shade. So, then we heard this loud pop muffled by the sand, like the desert swallowing a burp. And then the screaming started again, but this time it was horrible. *Ghastly.* Hearing men suffocate is terrible, sure, but this was worse. It was like their howls and wails were coming from the depths of Hell. The heat. The splattering slag. I can't imagine it. It must've been like a pistol back-firing, except they were actually in the barrel of the gun. It took the starch right outta' my kit. I'll never forget it."

"Is that what you meant? You said Dexter saved you."

"He *did* save me. From myself. That was part of it, sure. But not all of it. That's for another conversation some other time, Hector. But your granddad, he was something else. He... He wanted to help those Germans. He wanted to get out and try to dig holes down, so they could at least breathe. But our tank commander, he wasn't having it. When Dex grabbed a GI-issue foxhole spade and headed for the hatch, the commander threatened to shoot him."

"Damn," Tommy said.

"Yeah," Doug coughed. "*Damn.*"

"Yep," Larry replied. "But it was war, right? It was *war.*"

Heck nodded vacantly.

"Lines were drawn." Larry continued. "Who were we to..."

Heck waited and then cut in. "Dex use to say something. Or maybe he said it once. I don't know, but I remember it. He said, 'the desert has very few answers, but they're always obvious.'"

"Nothing was obvious to me," Larry replied. "Nothing at all."

Larry didn't hang around for the get-together after. His eyes weren't what they used to be, and he wanted to make it back to Santa Fe before dark. He'd driven down early that morning in his Honda Civic. He'd taken Pecos Highway, US-285, and the country was different in broad daylight. He got a better look at the Horsehead and Threemile Draws, and they appeared to have been bone dry for a thousand years. And Orla was just a dusty crossroads that looked like it had never been anywhere at all. Larry was tempted to turn off and have a look at Red Bluff Reservoir, but thought better of it. He would keep on trucking in his Civic. No sense in taking any chances.

Larry was making good time til he got to the state line. Just before he reached the town of Red Bluff proper, he began to taste sand in the air. It came on fast, and the sky darkened. He rolled up his window.

"Shit," Larry said.

In a matter of seconds, the sand was a blinding swirl. Larry turned on his headlights and then his brights, but they were useless. He slowed down and was soon barely inching forward. It was like driving into quicksand.

Dry quicksand, Larry thought.

Then, for the first time in a long time, Larry found himself experiencing déjà vu.

"No," he blurted. "Hell, no. It's not possible." But then he noticed sand grains drifting through the A/C vents. He pressed the gas pedal slowly and started picking up speed. His visibility was almost zero, but he didn't care. It was better than the alternative. "No, sir," Larry continued. "It aint' happening. I ain't going out like those Nazis."

When the Civic left the ground, it was flying through the storm at almost eighty miles an hour. The last thing Larry said was Dexter's name.

Heck hadn't been keen on attending the get-together at Pecos Billy's after his granddad's funeral, but he did anyway. Dexter would have wanted him to. It was all the usual faces, and Heck drank too much. He was more than a smidgen hungover when he heard from Doug the next morning.

"Larry's done now, too, Heck."

"What?" Dexter asked, from his bed. "What do you mean?"

"They found his car south of Loving, New Mexico. Off Highway 285."

"What?"

"Yep. It was upside down."

"What happened?"

"They don't know. They say he got caught in a sand shaker and lost control."

"You're shittin' me."

"No, Heck. There was a bad crash and fire. And lots of sand. And some glass. Green glass."

"Green glass?"

"They say the fire got so hot that it melted some of the sand into glass."

"Are they sure it's him?"

"No question. Beats all."

Heck's mind drifted for a moment. Doug kept on. "End of an era," he continued. "They were the last two."

Heck wasn't listening.

The only thing worse than the hangover that was suddenly pinballing around his skull was the sinking feeling Heck felt in the pit of his stomach. His granddad was dead and his granddad's friend was dead. And both had somehow gone out something like those Germans had seventy years back. Larry's account of his and Dexter's time in Algeria stuck with Heck. It was a dark yarn.

As far as he knew, his granddad never picked at it. Maybe because he had acted in good conscience, even in war. Larry sounded like he was still trying to convince himself they'd done the right thing, even up to the day he died.

Was it a coincidence?

Heck sat up and swung his legs off the side of his bed. He coughed and massaged his eyeballs with the middle finger and thumb of his right hand. "What's happening here, Dexter? What happened to you? Green fucking glass?! Are you getting me into something I can't handle?"

After Dexter's truck was towed to Heck's place in Pecos, he found his granddad's .38 revolver under some sand on the floorboard behind the driver's seat. It had been fired three times. Heck knew that the pistol sat in Dexter's glove compartment and couldn't remember the last time he had heard about it being removed, even to clean—much less shoot.

Someone he knew was a Sheriff's deputy for Reeves County and she gave the dually a good once-over. What she said surprised him.

"He fired it recently," Deputy Rivas said. "Maybe on the day of the wreck."

"What makes you think that?"

Heck and Syliva Rivas had been a thing in college, and she was still a looker. But now they were just good friends.

Sylvia leaned into the front driver seat of the dually and pointed to a small, half-moon crater in the remaining glass of the windshield. "See this, Heck?"

"Yes, ma'am."

"I think this is what's left of a bullet hole. An exit hole. It looks like he shot at something."

"Another vehicle?"

"I can't tell. But from the trajectory, I would say he was shooting up. But he may have fired that round after he lost control."

"Dadgum," Heck said.

"I'm sorry about your granddad," Sylvia replied. "I liked him."

"Everybody did. I can't imagine why he would shoot at anybody."

Heck showered and dressed and headed for the reservoir.

Had his granddad fired at someone? Is that why he had lost control of the dually? Why hadn't there been any skid marks?

Dexter's cabin wasn't much. The peeling, lime-colored linoleum flooring and peach-colored drapes were probably both original. The only thing from the current decade was a burnt-orange camp chair Dexter must've brought from his place in Pecos. That and two unopened cans of RC Cola.

There was a broom in the corner of the living room and the floor appeared to have been swept recently. No electricity or running water, but the fireplace still had the remains of a fire in it. So much of West Texas was like this, Heck thought. Penwell, for example. Right off I-10. Right down the road. Toyah was fading, too. Kent was a ghost town. And Orla was gone. Pyote was going. Penwell was just a rusting oil field scrapyard. His granddad had commented on it just the other day.

"Big O"—that's what they collectively called the oil and gas outfits in the region—"Big O would sell you the whole town for a C-note," Dexter had said, "But then the state would stick you with a million-dollar bill for cleaning it up."

Heck took a seat in the burnt-orange camp chair and spotted a couple of faded red tins next to a green duffle bag on the floor of an adjacent bedroom. Dexter had brought his battlefield dirt with him.

What was the name of that Kevin Costner film that they shot the parachute scene near Pyote? The hangar they used was gone, now, of course. The wedding sequence was filmed in Marfa. Heck smiled. His granddad had been an extra.

Heck cracked open a warm RC and took a sip. "Fireworks in a cemetery," he said. "It was a war story in its own right." Heck had seen the movie in Fort Stockton with his granddad.

Heck was born in 1969 and had been a teenager in the eighties. The first Gulf War hadn't started until 1991, while Heck was still in college. It occurred to him that the 1980s were the only decade since the 1930s where a war hadn't defined a generation of young American men like his granddad and Larry. And, for the first time, really, Heck realized that the movies were as close as he had ever been to a war.

***

Heck finished off the warm RC and crushed the can in his hands. Then, he stood up and noticed something he'd missed before. One of the tins from his granddad's dirt collection was lying on its side, and the lid had come loose. Some of its contents had spilt.

Heck heard a creak in the back of the house. He looked in that direction and heard something outside.

The wind had picked up and the air in the abandoned cottage was growing thick. Heck couldn't process it at first. But then he glanced out a cracked window facing west and saw the earth begin to rise. It was a wall of sand building and climbing. It was like a tidal wave.

The darkening swell outside the cottage was approaching a full-scale sandstorm. It would be upon him soon and the clatter of the house was almost deafening. He couldn't understand it.

Then, Heck turned back to the spilt tin.

And there it was.

It wasn't dirt.

It was sand. And it was beginning to move.

As the frame of the abandoned house began to groan and another window cracked, Heck rushed over to the tins. A single word was scratched into the faded red paint of the loose lid.

ALGERIA

Heck dropped down to his knees and began scooping up the spilt sand. He scooped frantically and clumsily dumped half-palm fulls into the tin as fast as he could. He began to feel lightheaded. As the walls began to shake, the air pressure inside the cottage became intense and everything began to darken.

After just a few quick scoops, Heck replaced the lid and gasped for air. His heart was pounding.

When Heck was a little boy, his favorite toy was a cheap, dime-store army man attached to a plastic parachute by strings. It only ever worked once or twice, because once the parachute opened, it was almost impossible to fold back up right. But the time it did work, you just threw it up in the air and watched the soldier float back down to the earth. It was so simple and so much fun. Heck always imagined his army man was Dexter, parachuting in to fight Nazis. It was only later he found out his granddad was a tank loader and had never jumped out of a plane with a parachute. And now, according to Larry, he had never even seen the Germans as Nazis. It put that image in Heck's mind, an army man attached to a cheap plastic parachute, being tossed around in a sandstorm.

It was a weird thing to think of before he died, he thought.

But suddenly the din outside weakened and the air inside the cabin thinned.

As Heck crouched holding the lid of the Algeria tin firmly in place, the sandstorm dissipated and Heck realized Sylvia was right.

Dexter had discharged his pistol, but not at another car. He had fired on an old enemy.

Heck remembered the name of the movie.

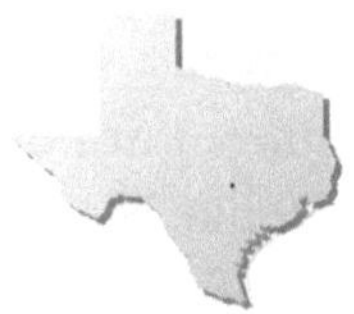

eleven
nia

While there has been an indulgence of post apocalyptic works in recent years, "Nia" delivers a breath of fresh air to the genre by addressing race-relations in the Lone Star State. Like the best work of Richard Matheson or Ray Bradbury, "Nia" uses the genre's conventions to address serious issues in ways that realism cannot.
    --**Shaula Schneik Edwards**, *Texas Books in Review* Spring 2020

NIA, *Terry, Shen, Rudy, Mrs. Burgess.*

Those were the names.

Those were their names.

I kicked up ash and watched it settle. The feather-like flakes folded and drifted, testing gravity. I walked through the drift, holding my breath.

The fallout was still everywhere, forming a loose grit in the eviscerated buildings and rubble-filled streets. Patrolling Austin was like sifting through the remains of a shattered urn.

We only returned to the urban areas to scare up supplies or flush out renegade Klanners. For the most part, resistance had been reduced to scattered acts of terrorism; but the Klanners were still a problem. You could tell who most of them were by the swastikas crudely branded on their foreheads. They used coat hangers fired by red-hot coals to make the marks.

World War III had been exclusively pushbutton. No one knew exactly who pressed what first or why, but after the election in late 2024, nations with nuclear capabilities suddenly launched everything they had at us. We retaliated and won (maybe survived is a better word for it) because we had more than the rest of the world put together. I'm not sure there's anything left of Europe, and Africa and Asia are like North America—wastelands.

The final, conventional phase of the war here was civil—civil war, I mean. All the boots-on-ground, blood-and-guts fighting was between neighbors.

After the radioactive clouds lifted and the looting began, what remained of the Trump Nation fled to the relative security of Neo-Nazi and White Supremacist survival camps and shelters. Neo-Nazi and Klanner types had been prepping for doomsday scenarios for decades, and when the bombs fell, they went underground. When they re-emerged, they came back on top.

For years they had stockpiled provisions and arms in subterranean bunkers, and, after the radioactive dust settled, they were sitting on what amounted to the largest store of uncontaminated food and water in the country and no small arsenal of munitions.

In no time at all, the Klanners filled the power gap. Preaching fire and brimstone, they treated surviving persons of color, immigrants, liberals, academics, and the LGBTQ community to exactly that. "Taking the country back" was no longer a slogan. The central government and the American military had suffered devastating losses in targeted, urban missile strikes, and their struggle to regroup gave rural Klanners an opening. By the time the politicians and the Armed Forces were fully operational again, the Klanners were entrenched.

Nia, Terry, Shen, Rudy, Mrs. Burgess.

I suffered a severe head injury several months back. The doctors said it could cause a condition known as post-traumatic amnesia. My case wasn't as serious as all that sounds, but I was careful to follow the doctors' orders, and they said making and keeping lists and checklists was helpful. Written lists were best, but patrols weren't conducive to list-making, so I recited my chief list, my key, in my head. It was the last people I recalled being important to me. It helped me remember.

I was an undergrad when the war started, and I don't remember being terribly surprised. Things had gotten completely out of hand under the former president. Half the country no longer believed in America anymore, much less the ideals it was purported to be founded on. Faith crumbled and optimism vanished, leaving only frustration and anger. When the press and congressional leaders attempted to curb Trump's abuses, it was just a matter of time before disgruntled MAGA and MAGA2 zealots expanded infrequent, semiautomatic killing sprees to atrocities on a larger scale. They torched mosques and Muslim-owned businesses. They murdered immigrants and foreigners in broad daylight. Thousands perished. Atrocity begat atrocity. Catastrophe begat cataclysm.

I was pretty sure I was born or raised in a town called Hico. But I remembered stories about my grandparents hiding under school desks during nuclear bomb drills in the 1950s. My classmates and I participated in the same kinds of drills in high school to prepare for mass shootings.

When the sirens sounded and the shelter designations came over the PA, I was sitting in the Porter Henderson Library at Angelo State University. I shook my head. I wondered if we weren't finally getting what we deserved. *How long did we think it would take the micro-violence to become macro-annihilation?*

A handful of library employees—most of them students—listened to the shelter designations and, like me, made their way to the library basement. We barricaded ourselves in and survived on what was in the student lounge kitchen and the candy and Coke machines.

Rudy was a freshman political science major from College Station. He came to Angelo State with the intention of transferring to Texas A&M after he had a solid year of studies at a smaller, cheaper school under his belt. I'd been in an Anthropology class with Nia my sophomore year. From Houston, Nia was a skinny Black girl with dark eyes. I was surprised she recognized me.

Shen was a Physics major from South Korea. Petite and cheerful, she'd only been in Texas for a few months. Terry was a Mexican-American student from San Antonio. Sandoval was his last name, I think. He was stocky and fierce looking, but as soft-spoken as a monk.

Mrs. Burgess, a research librarian and a widow—at least thirty years our senior—immediately assumed a matriarchal stance, and that was okay. It seemed to help her cope. The rest of us were disparate millennials, more traumatized by the disconnection we felt from the internet than our actual relationships with parents or siblings or each other. But this changed very quickly.

Nia, Terry, Shen, Rudy, Mrs. Burgess.

The Klanner cell that HQ Intelligence had sent me to find was reportedly maintained by two to four hostiles who were possibly in possession of a hostage.

Austin was a Dali landscape, especially downtown. It looked like it'd been put in a microwave and cooked on "High." Anything that didn't melt, boil, or burn exploded. The handful of topside survivors—leftovers—looked like grisly wax figurines, hairless and dripping. Bleeding flesh, frozen but brittle, like candle wax. There were very few topsiders left. The shelter survivors looked like emaciated ghosts. There were certainly no longer any concerns about keeping the town weird. It was bizarre enough for everyone now. And it would likely remain that way for a long time. Maybe forever.

Patrolling was difficult, especially on foot. The long hills, the alleys. There were lots of tricky lines of sight.

Not much movement there, though. And that was good. I'd begun to take pride in the instinctual processes of soldiering. In my own effectiveness, efficiency—precision. It was alien at first, but reciting the list really helped. It calmed me. It *focused* me.

Nia, Terry, Shen, Rudy, Mrs. Burgess.

I was rescued by U.S. Marine regulars when the Klanners stormed the basement of the Porter Henderson Library, where we had holed up. It was a huge storage area that housed the Unprocessed and Special Collections. That's why the Klanners came. With everything offline and most utilities still inoperable, combustible materials became extremely valuable and even life-sustaining, especially in the winter. Resources placed or stored aboveground had become exposed to more radiation. They had a greater radioactive imprint and residue; the stuff in the subterranean shelters and storage was considered cleaner and safer. And we were surrounded by hundreds of thousands of books. All radiation-free or containing undetectable trace levels of radiation.

It was a new take on *Fahrenheit 451.*

Libraries became really popular again.

***

Nia, Terry, Shen, Rudy, Mrs. Burgess.

"I noticed you," Nia said.

"I didn't know," I replied. "I wasn't even sure you'd recognize me."

"I knew who you were before I noticed you.'

"How?"

"Something you did."

"What?"

"It's not important."

I kissed her.

She acted surprised. Indignant.

We had our own little hiding place in the stacks. Near the boxes, piles and shelves of the Unprocessed Collection—we tried to stay away from the Special Collections. Everyone did.

We had all found our own spots. Shen was with Terry near the microfilm stations. Rudy was with Mrs. Burgess in one of the Study Rooms near the doors. He still had a girlfriend somewhere. Maybe. Hopefully. Mrs. Burgess was good company for him.

Nia finally kissed me back.

I smiled. "You kept me hanging."

"Really? You white boys are insufferable. Nothing wrong with a little adversity."

"White boys? You mean I'm not your first?"

"I didn't say that. I'll neither confirm nor deny that supposition. It's irrelevant."

I pulled her close. She put her arms around me. "What about the Black guys?" I asked.

"I haven't seen any around. You'll have to do."

I kissed her again. "Just glad to be of service, ma'am."

"You know," she said, "one of my friends, a white girl, she said she'd been with you your freshman year. One-night thing, but no hard feelings."

"Yeah? And?"

"She said you were nice. And hung."

"*Oh?*"

"Yes."

"And?"

"And what?"

"Am I?"

"You're not bad for a white guy."

I laughed.

"Fair enough," I responded, crooking my eyebrows. "But there's no reason for the reverse discrimination."

Nia smirked. "Ha. Right. This is more like reverse affirmative action, Mr. Chalky."

I *harrumphed* melodramatically, and Nia smalled.

"Is that white fragility in your pocket," Nia continued, "or are you just happy to see me?"

We sank then, undressing. Eager and maybe even a little reckless. You never could tell who might walk up. Mrs. Burgess would chastise us if she caught us. But only in a good-natured way.

It wasn't every day the world came to an end.

Nia, Terry, Shen, Rudy, Mrs. Burgess.

On patrol, something scurried ahead on the left side of the street. South Congress. I scanned the area. Small and not moving fast, whatever it was.

I resented the break in my reverie. I enjoyed a stray daydream here and there, but they weren't often that pleasant.

I stepped over a discarded scooter. It was in decent shape and clean. Someone else was in the neighborhood.

I lowered myself to a crouch and listened.

I could hear leaves or light paper rustling. Refuse being moved across a stretch of pavement or sidewalk by the breeze. Also, a barely audible clanging, maybe the chain lanyard of a bannerless flagpole.

But no voices.

No human sounds.

Then another memory.

I'd come to Austin once, as a freshman. Sixth Street was a madhouse and we'd partied all night. It was harmless debauchery. Drinking and enjoying ourselves as if we could escape responsibility and consequence.

Adulthood.

Holocaust.

It was an unsettling juxtaposition to what I was seeing on this patrol. It was more eerie than weird.

Two-thirds of the United States' population had died in the initial blasts and immediate fall out. Half of the last third had been subjected to terminal radiation exposure and would expire in the next several months. The entire country was filled with ghost towns.

I thought about this guy that came by our dorm room almost every night. I couldn't remember his name. He was exceptionally average in almost every way, but his schtick was amusing. He'd always poked his head in our door and say, "Where's the party?"

It seemed like there was always a party somewhere on campus, and he was bent on finding it. Or appearing to look like he was bent on finding it... and I don't think we ever went with him or took him with us, not once. He was just one of those guys.

But it made me wonder.

Did he—or we—have any inkling of what a privilege living in a time like that had been?

I couldn't think of one reason why we never invited him or took him along and I couldn't remember a single time I ever saw him at a party. And now the only party was Death's. And his party was *definitely* always happening somewhere.

Nia, Terry, Shen, Rudy, Mrs. Burgess.

When the Klanners found us at the library, we did our best. Or as much as we could do without actual weapons.

Mrs. Burgess braved the main entrance, and she was a real handful. She fearlessly accosted the Klanners, accusing and scolding, all of it loudly, to warn us. She played the cards she was dealt. Her indignance was palpable, but she held her contempt in check.

"Who do you think you are, young man? What is your name?"

Mrs. Burgess kept her hands on her hips and glared. "This is a college library. A public library. *A protected facility*. We are guarding these resources for future Americans. *For future Texans!* Didn't you grow up around here?"

It worked initially, befuddling the first two Klanners who came in. But the third unceremoniously silenced Mrs. Burgess with a gunshot to the center of her forehead.

Mrs. Burgess had tucked Rudy away in a mop closet. But when the Klanners shot her, he burst out of his hiding place with a broom, the handle of which he had whittled down to a sharp point. He rammed the makeshift spear through a Klanner's chest, just below the sternum. He must have worked on the mop handle in his spare time. It was a good idea. I wished I'd thought of it. The next Klanner that entered gunned Rudy down.

Nia and I hid, pursuing a half-baked plan to separate a Klanner from his gun if we could isolate one. Two walked into our trap instead of one and I hesitated, looking to Nia for direction. When I was spotted, she didn't hesitate. Before he even had a chance to raise his weapon, Nia slammed him over the head with the spine-side of a giant, crisp new copy of *The World Book Atlas*. I clutched a massive compendium of the

Holy Bible. It was that or a large, meticulously annotated hardback edition of *Moby Dick.*

Nia's *Atlas* knocked my would-be assailant out cold.

When the second Klanner came forward, Nia was bent over, in the process of striking the unconscious attacker in the head again. I clumsily telegraphed my swing, and the second assailant ducked away. I dropped the *Holy* compendium and grabbed him just as he fired. I felt a pinch in my side and slipped behind him, wrapping my arms around his neck. I locked my right arm with my left and squeezed with everything I had.

The Klanner struggled, and we fell backwards. He dropped his weapon and began clawing at my arms and neck. His swastika was fresh. I could smell the burnt flesh.

"Nia," I said.

No answer. I assumed she might be grabbing the first Klanner's gun.

I squeezed. The second Klanner gasped and abandoned, trying to loosen my grip. He began punching back at me, trying to land a solid blow. I heard a rustling around our feet.

The Klanner was still swinging, but with less force. Nia rose up on her knees just in front of us, but something was wrong. She was pale and one eyelid was half-shut. She was holding the side of her neck with one hand, and it was covered with blood.

"Nia!"

"I squeezed my arms around the Klanner's neck so hard that my biceps began to cramp, and he finally stopped struggling. When I was sure he was gone, I released him and pushed him away. Then I crawled over to Nia.

Nia, Terry, Shen, Rudy, Mrs. Burgess.

Nia had dispatched the first Klanner with her second blow. The *Atlas* spine was splashed with blood. The pinch I'd felt in my abdomen, however, hadn't been a pinch. It was a bullet slug ripping through my side. It had apparently exited cleanly, striking Nia's neck, nicking her jugular.

Her eyes stayed with mine as I gently pried her hand away from the wound to check it. A jetting spurt of blood sprayed across my face. Nia re-clutched the wound and tears began streaming down her cheeks.

I straddled Nia on my hands and knees with my face just above hers. She placed her free hand on the nape of my neck. I stared into her eyes, realizing they were lighter than I'd originally thought. I took her free hand and kissed it and then held it to my cheek.

Nia blinked repeatedly and took a deep breath. I kissed her lips. She tried to say something.

I turned my head to listen, my ear to her lips; but she couldn't get anything out. I pulled away and stared into her eyes again. They started to roll back. The hand over her wound was slipping, releasing more blood.

"No!" I said.

Her eyes refocused, and I held them. I eased her slipping hand away from the wound, transitioning mine to where hers had been. Her hand fell to her side.

"Baby," I said. "*Please*. No. *Nia*. Please, *please*."

Her eyelids started to fall.

"Nia." I started to kiss her, and she responded. I could feel her lips. We kissed.

I kissed her, and then she was gone.

I raised my head.

Her eyes stared.

She didn't even seem surprised.

My eyes filled with tears. I closed her eyelids with bloody fingers and kissed them, licking my lips, kissing the blood away.

I started crying.

Maybe we hadn't shared much of a life, but it was still a life. And we had it together. It existed aside and apart from everything else, and it was ours. A scrap of normalcy. A small, desperate grasp at hope.

My entire body was suddenly wracked by sobs. I was bawling.

I pulled Nia into my arms.

I heard someone coming, but I didn't care.

A little more adversity.

Nia, Terry, Shen, Rudy, Mrs. Burgess.

When the Marines arrived, they transported us to a temporary HQ near Ballinger. I was later told that Shen and Terry volunteered for the rebuilding effort. I wound up in the Corps.

The Marines had discovered me in bad shape, barely alive. I still don't remember everything. They got most of the details from Shen and I got them secondhand.

According to what I was told, when the rest of the Klanners came, they found me sitting on the floor with Nia in my arms. They told me to get up, but I refused. They tried to pull Nia away from me, but I clung to her more tightly.

"Let go-uh that nigger," the leader said. "Act your race, brother. Stand up. Drop that nigger whore, now."

I refused to answer or even look at him.

"You hear him, son?" another inquired.

I ignored them both.

I closed my eyes, smelling Nia's hair, her skin. Her blood. I kissed her cheek.

"You're a fucking disgrace," the leader said. "A waste of white, corrupting yourself with that animal. Let her go and get up. Stand up like a man, and I'll make sure none of your brothers violate her filthy corpse."

I opened my eyes. "Don't touch her," I said. "Don't you fucking touch her!"

One of my glaring "brothers" grinned.

I started to cry again. "Don't fucking—"

Through my tears, I saw a rifle butt come down on Nia's head. I heard the sickening crack of her skull and started to scream, trying to cover the wound with one of my hands. I screamed and raged. Then, one Klanner slapped me in the side of my face with the butt of his shotgun, knocking out two of my teeth. They tried to pull Nia's body away, but I wouldn't let go.

I'm told that the Klanners smashed my head up pretty badly before the Marines arrived and put them down. Initially, they weren't sure I was alive; and when they realized I was alive, they didn't think I would survive.

Nia, Terry, Shen, Rudy, Mrs. Burgess.

When I recovered from my injuries, I was a perfect candidate for what the U.S. military was calling the Tactical Defense System Renewal Operation. At first, the brass was hesitant to clear me for service. They were concerned about my wounds and the trauma I suffered. But the situation demanded all hands on deck. The civil war was mostly over, but they still needed to win the peace.

The accelerated course of basic training was awkward at first. All the things I might have hated about it before, repetition, drills, marches, morning reveille—the mechanics of it all—they came easily. I enjoyed the regimen, maybe even taking refuge in it. It soon became second nature. I was moved to active duty in less than four weeks.

I was surprised and amazed and then entirely pleased by my new composure; and it showed in my combat proficiency. Under fire, I cut down every hostile shadow along the horizon. In the trenches, I cracked every Klanner skull I could reach.

I felt no remorse or pity. I cut through the enemy with machine-like stealth; no sadness, no hatred, and no hesitation.

Compassion was a pre-war luxury. Killing was now almost a compulsion, an impulse we perhaps watered down or repressed in the march of modern evolution, but now returned, like a rediscovered birthright. A vital evolutionary tool for survival.

It suited us.

It suited me.

Six months into the campaign, the Klanners, who in the beginning had outnumbered us, were on the run. After the last of the Bible Belt Battalions surrendered in Alabama, the civil war, on any broad scale, was over.

The brass promoted me. I think it was an incentive to get me to stay. But I wouldn't have left anyway. I couldn't. Civilian life held nothing for me. I climbed the walls even on short R&Rs. I had found my rightful place in this new world. I had changed too much.

There were still active Klanner cells, groups that needed to be put down. And after everything I'd suffered, patrol assignments were about the only thing that made peacetime bearable. War did that, I supposed. It made sense.

There was the way things were, once. A way normal people lived their lives, maybe. It had involved some semblance of comfort and stability, even with all the "noise." We could still indulge. Laugh, piddle, dicker. Prattle, ridicule, snicker. But that had been taken away. That was over. Survival precluded indulgence.

If that frivolity was ever restored, would I be able to switch off or compartmentalize the war?

Surely, I'd have to, eventually.

Wouldn't I?

Occasionally, I wondered what Nia would think if she saw me now; but I never dwelt on it for very long. Nia no longer existed and I am not sure the man she had loved still existed, either. It was a plotline straight out of one of the book piles we discovered our love in, but it was the opposite of a storybook ending.

Nia, Terry, Shen, Rudy, Mrs. Burgess.

I rose from my squat slowly. The abandoned scooter tipped me off. No doubt, this was where the hostiles were hiding. Time to go to work. I re-examined the dilapidated cityscape and disengaged the safety on my weapon. It was getting late.

In the building where our Intelligence had indicated hostile operations, I detected an extra-normal light source shining through a second-floor window. A careful scan of the perimeter revealed no snipers, so I crossed the street silently and slipped into the building through a broken first-floor window. The inside of the structure was lit only by the dwindling ambient light.

I stopped, listening.

I made out two distinct male voices and the whimpering of one male or female, possibly injured. I proceeded cautiously to the stairwell. The stairs were solid, and I propped the door open to have more light. In a matter of seconds, I was outside the door of the apartment where I'd spotted the light through the exterior second-floor window.

I stood motionless outside the door for a long moment. The whimpering had stopped and there was a fourth voice, but it was low. I couldn't make out gender or disposition.

I kicked in the door and fired on three Klanners before they even had time to turn around. A young girl, whom the men had been standing over, darted under a table before the Klanners' bodies hit the ground.

A thirty-something year-old woman came charging out a side room, firing a Baby Browning or small Luger. I neutralized her abruptly, splashing her brains all over an unused dart board. She collapsed next to the men, two of which had huge, fresh, square-shaped scars on their foreheads.

We'd been seeing a lot of this. Renegade Klanners attempting to assimilate, some earnestly, some to perpetrate a ruse. They cut or scraped the Klanner brand off. It was a crude procedure, and it made the skinhead variety of reformed Klanners look like jittery golems. The scars on their foreheads left no doubt they'd once been committed Klanners. My take on it was that it was best to neutralize anyone with a scar on the forehead. It wasn't my job to welcome former Klanners into the new republic, even if they'd had a sincere change of heart.

Intelligence was convinced that most of them were not abandoning the Klanner cause so much as trying to infiltrate the U.S. government's scattered co-ops and communes to create havoc. So, I just shot them all to be done with it.

The young girl never ventured from her spot under the table, but I could tell she was watching me. I asked her if she was injured.

She didn't answer.

"I'm not here to hurt you," I said. "I just want to make sure you're okay."

For a moment, there was no response.

"You killed peepaw," the girl replied.

"Your father?"

"No. Peepaw."

"Your grandfather?"

"No. Peepaw."

It seemed like it had been a century since I had heard that term.

Peepaw occasionally complemented by *Meemaw*. Or *Mimi*. It was anachronistic now. The blast and the fallout left few elderly.

I knelt down and slid to my knees to get a better look at the little girl. It was darker under the table, but I could tell she was six or seven and had curly blonde hair and bright eyes.

"Are you hurt?"

The little girl studied me noncommittally.

"Are you hurt?" I repeated. "I can help you."

The little girl looked in the direction of the fallen bodies, one of whom was Peepaw. "He was trying to fix it," she said.

"Have you been hurt? Were they trying to hurt you?"

"I have a sore tooth. Peepaw was gonna fix it."

"What is your name?"

"He was tryin' to pull my tooth."

"What is your name?"

The little girl looked like she was going into shock. I holstered my weapon and made a concerted effort to soften my voice. "Why don't you come out from under the table?"

The little girl raised her right hand like she was going to use the bottom of the table for leverage to slide out. I smiled and leaned in.

"My name..." she said, hesitating—but her right hand wasn't reaching for leverage. There was a makeshift sheath on the bottom of the table, concealing a machete. By the time I realized what was happening, she had swung the blade.

I jerked my head back too late.

I felt the tip of the machete split my scalp open, but I automatically seized it, blade first, and smashed the little girl in the forehead with the hilt. She scrambled backwards, and I rose, flinging the table from my path with one arm.

Blood poured down my forehead. I wiped it away.

The little girl was helpless—in the back of my mind I knew this—but I didn't stop.

Before my actions even registered, I seized the little girl by her throat and began jabbing the hilt of the machete into her horrified face. I couldn't even hear her screams.

I collapsed the bridge of her nose. Then her eye sockets. I didn't stop 'til I had cratered her face and sunk the hilt all the way to the back of her skull.

I dropped the dull machete and the little girl's body and retrieved gauze and medical tape from a thigh pocket on my patrol trousers. I slowly wrapped my bleeding hand.

Nia, Terry, Shen, Rudy. Mrs. Burgess.

Nia.

I knew how she'd judge what I'd just done. Something in me had snapped.

I dropped the little girl's body and stepped backwards, tripping over a broken table leg. My stumble turned into an awkward jog and then a run. I screamed and tore at my clothes. I bolted through the hall and down the stairwell. I tumbled out a side entrance on the first floor and found myself lying in a drift of ashes. Ashes were floating again, all around me.

When I sat up, I heard a strange, rhythmic whir. Gathering myself, I unholstered my weapon and took cover. I surveyed the vicinity and discovered nothing. Eyes darting, I scanned the rooftops—nothing. More nothing.

I considered the possibility that it might be a copter some distance out, but HQ had precious few choppers and rarely risked sending them into the city.

Could it be a drone?

I didn't think so. I hadn't seen one since before the war.

What was it?

I could still hear it.

Something wasn't right.

Nia, Terry, Chen, Rudy—Rudy.

I crouched and listened closely.

The whir was coming from directly above me.

Mrs. Burgess.
When I turned, the noise seemed to mimic my movement.
Nia, Terry. Chen.
I rolled instantly and fired three shots straight up.
Nothing.
I spun and fired three shots into the window of the Klanner apartment.
After the gunshots, the whir continued.
Nia. *Terry.*
I froze for several moments, focusing completely on the sound. Then, I raised my free hand to my right temple to concentrate. But I couldn't. I was completely rattled, my thoughts jumbled.
Nia, Nia. Terry.
I slid my fingers over to the top of my head, following the whir— *and there it was.*
Nia. Nia.
The little girl had done more than split my hairline.
Nia.
A portion of the upper left side of my head was gone.
Nia.
I scrambled to a large plate-glass window in the side of the building to catch my reflection in the fading daylight.
Nia.
Where that part of my frontal lobe had been, there were now only crackling wires, sparking circuitry and some sort of hydraulic mechanism.
Nia.
They'd saved my life, but at what cost?
Nia...
Nia...
Nia...
Was I even human?
Nia...
Nia...
Nia...
Was...

Ni...
Nnnnnh...
Nnnnn...

Nnn...

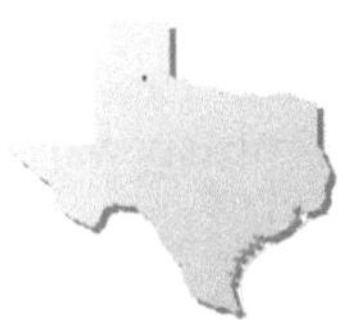

twelve
rugby players eat their dead

Nothing like exploring the adventures of youth with an old rugby team-mate, especially when they involve a sip of electric Kool-Aid. Be careful who you share your fire with--sometimes it never goes out.
    --**Dane Fayle**, Texas State Rugby, 1985-89

IT WAS LATE, and the phone rang. An old landline instead of my cell. Very few people called on the landline anymore, so I had a pretty good idea who it was.

"You going?" a voice inquired.

"We should," I said. "I guess."

"I think so. How you been, Pretty Boy?"

"I'm getting old, Major. Not so pretty anymore."

"It's better than the alternative."

"That's what I keep hearing. What got Smitty?"

"I was hoping you wouldn't ask me."

"Oh?"

"The fancy medical name is 'transmissible spongiform encephalopathy.'"

"Spongebob telepathy?"

"That's funny, but no. The less fancy term is Kuru disease."

"Oh. Shit."

"Yeah. My sentiments exactly."

"Damn."

"Yep. His wife, Sheila, hasn't said anything. But I'm pretty sure she knows. We're gonna have to get our stories straight. Again."

"Maybe we shouldn't attend."

"Where's the fun in that?"

I didn't respond. Major kept going. "Smitty was our brother, warts and all."

"I know. But he sorta' went off the reservation."

"Yes. But he didn't kill anybody."

"As far as we know."

"Okay. As far as we know."

"I don't like thinking about it."

"Neither do I. But it was a long time ago. Nobody knows."

"*I know*," I interrupted.

"Point taken. Are you going to be there or not?"

"I'll be there."

The flight from Houston to Wyoming was a little over four hours. It gave me too much time to think.

My mind, of course, darted straight back to 1979 and that road trip where it all happened. I flagged down a flight attendant and requested a drink. Then, I made it a double.

It was the first week of Spring Break, and we were on our way back from a friendly. An exhibition match against a tough Air Force Academy squad in Colorado Springs. They played with great discipline and the thin air was a beating. We lost but lost well. We made a showing, and they were impressed. They prevailed upon us to stay for a kegger, but Major, Smitty and Queequeg and I had already made plans. Major claimed there was a row of Cadillacs buried nose-down in the dirt just off a highway outside of Amarillo, and Smitty had recently read Aldous Huxley's *Doors of Perception* and was itching to experience a "sacramental vision." Queequeg assured us this could be achieved with peyote, but he couldn't get any. But he knew a guy who had access to Trinity level acid.

"Trinity level acid," Major said. "What does that even mean?"

"*Trinity* was the code name for the first nuclear bomb test," Queequeg said. "In 1945. This acid recipe is supposed to be early batch stuff, close to the source... whatever that means. And it's rumored to have a kick." Queequeg's real name was Jesús Garcia, and his dad was supposedly half Comanche. He said we should drop the LSD at a sacred Comanche site near Silverton, Texas, just west of Canyon. We had our whole week planned out. A gawk at the planted Caddies, an acid trip at the sacred site, and then a nine-hour drive to Corpus Christi, where we would finish out the week drunk on a beach. Proverbial best-laid plans.

After we crossed the state line, we stopped in Plainview to pick up the acid. I expected Queequeg's connection to be a wacked out hippie, but he wore black, horn-rimmed glasses and sported a crewcut, high and tight. Queequeg said the man had been a professor at Texas Tech in the early sixties, but now taught at Wayland Baptist University.

The Cadillacs or "Cadillac Ranch" as they called them, were definitely cool—but we hadn't known to bring spray-paint. Everyone else did, and the graffiti was crazy and painted on thick. Major made sure we knew that the Caddies, which sat nose-down at sixty-degree angles on the open dirt terrain, were perfectly aligned with the Great Pyramid of Giza. We'd had few beers by then, but I thought it was ingenious. Smitty was less impressed. "That's a waste of ten perfectly good Cadillacs," he half-seriously lamented. "It's also a snide comment on Capitalism... and the American way."

"Sheesh," Queequeg sighed. "You're not gonna start pissing and moaning about Nixon, again, are you?"

Smitty burped. "He was good man."

"My ass," Major quipped. "Watergate was a *snide* comment on America. Those caddies are just art."

"Art for anarchists, I say," Smitty responded. "Love it or leave it, you goddam hippie freaks."

"Oh, shit," Queequeg said. "Here we go."

"Don't you have some roadside trash to cry about, Queequeg? Or peace signs to paint down at Haight-Ashbury?"

"I'm an eighth Indian," I noted.

"Take Pretty Boy with you," Smitty added. "He's a hippie deep down, too. Just like all you redskins."

My name was—is—Bruce Floyd. "Pretty Boy" was my nickname, as in "Pretty Boy Floyd" from the gangster of the same name during the Great Depression. It was meant to be funny, I think. At the time, I thought I held my own in the "looks" department, especially in the late bell-bottoms era. But, like most young men, I was probably a little over-confident.

Smitty's real name was Benjamin Schmidt. He was a big, clumsy flanker from Georgetown, Texas. Major was Thomas "Major Tom" Loudermilk, and he was a giant, corn-fed college ROTC (hence, the "Major" moniker) dropout from Uvalde, Texas. I was a tall, rangy inside center and Queequeg was a small, hard-hitting fullback. He was dubbed Queequeg (pronounced quee-quay) because of the beeline he always made toward runners who broke through the line. It was like watching a harpoon when he hit one of the big uglies from the scrum. In one match against the Woodlands Men's A side, Queequeg hit this giant albino-looking scrummy—who was easily 6'6"—and didn't drop him, but he held on to the big bastard until the rest of us could catch up. A shit-hard prop nicknamed "Franchise" immediately christened Jesús "Queequeg," after the Polynesian harpooner in Moby Dick.

We were in Major Tom's car, a hulking yellow 1975 Buick Electra, one of the longest vehicles Detroit ever built. It had golden Velour interior and electric door locks, and Major occasionally bragged that no red-blooded American girl could resist the crushed velvet gold seats. It was a living room on wheels, almost nineteen feet long and nearly seven feet wide. It could easily seat three across in front and back, four when needed. Unfortunately, it got about eight miles to the gallon on the highway, so pitching in for gas on road trips practically required a bank loan. But there was plenty of leg room.

By the time we turned toward Silverton, we were all of us half drunk or stoned and running our heads quasi-coherently. The subject turned to rugger bumper stickers that were recently making the rounds at the matches and tourneys. "Only Our Girlfriends Wear Pads" was bandied about enthusiastically, because we all beer-boldly agreed that football players were pussies. "Rugby Players Eat Their Dead," however, led to some light contention

"It's because of the movie," Major said. "*Survive!*"

"Survive?" Smitty coughed, exhaling pot smoke. "That one about that Mexican rugby team that ate each other?"

"They were from Paraguay," I said.

"Uruguay," Queequeg corrected. "And they crashed in the Andes."

"In Chile," I added.

"Yeah," Queequeg said. "Like, thirty-four of them."

"And only sixteen survived," said Major. "It was seven years ago."

"I think that bumper sticker was done in bad taste," Smitty pronounced.

"Bad taste?" Major countered. "It happened, man. They were out there for seventy days. I dig it. It's a prime example of rugger toughness. And resourcefulness. They didn't have much choice, anyway."

"Sure, they did," Smitty replied. "They could have gone to their grave unsullied."

Queequeg scoffed. "*Unsullied.* Which sophomore English course did you hear that in? Like Mother Nature even gives a shit. Especially about tractor-trailer bumpkins like you. You'd probably be the first one to take a bite."

"No way, pepper-belly. Especially not of your ass. I prefer white meat."

I chimed in. "You prefer anything with a pulse."

"Exactly," Smitty said. "You're making my point for me."

"You wouldn't have eaten the chick?" Major inquired.

"Well, maybe. But preferably while she was still breathing."

"Yeah, yeah," I said. "But for real. What if we were starving? What if you had your whole life ahead of you?"

"I do have my whole life ahead of me."

"What if you were still a virgin?"

"Smitty is still a virgin," Queequeg snorted.

"Fuck off, Tanto."

"I'm serious," I said.

"So was I," Queequeg teased, smiling at Smitty. Smitty raised his beer and smiled back. "Goddamn beaner."

Major kept going. "What if you really wanted to live? What if it'd been us? Would you? Do you think you could?"

"Dude," Smitty said. "That's really heavy."

"Yeah," I said. "But at that point, you're in the shit, man. It's not exactly you or them—because they're already dead. It's more like you and them. They'd be helping you stay alive."

"You changed my mind, Pretty Boy," Smitty replied. "You can eat me anytime."

"Fuck you, Smitty."

"I'm just saying, man. You can have a big ol' bite. Right now, even. A big ol' bite of my pork pud."

"No thanks," I said. "That little Vienna sausage?"

"Shit," Smitty laughed. *You call King Kong a monkey?*"

"You're a bunch of crazy assholes," Queequeg said. "Cut the bull-shit. You're ruining my buzz."

"Where is this place?" Smitty complained. "We been on this dirt road for twenty miles. Sacred my ass."

"It is," Queequeg said. "You'll see. Fucking hayseed."

"Well, get us there, Major," Smitty replied. "I'm hungry."

"We should fast," Queequeg said.

"Fast?" Major blurted. "We can't eat?! Fuck me."

"Yeah," Smitty added. "I really got the munchies, bad."

"Fasting increases the effects," Queequeg said. "Just like with peyote."

When we arrived in the Silverton area, Queequeg told us we were headed to a place called Linguish Falls. He had Major park his land yacht a few miles down and on the other side of the road from the path to the site. It was on private property, and Queequeg said it would be a bad idea to draw too much attention to where we were. It was a beautiful, early March afternoon, low seventies. We grabbed our beer, a few joints, the acid and a couple of blankets and started down a faint trail.

The hike was incredible, even though I was nursing a buzz. It led to a small, red dirt canyon that slowly narrowed as we walked through it, probably dropping five hundred feet in the first quarter-mile. A half-mile in, it was as amazing as anything I saw when I visited Antelope Canyon in Arizona several years later. The small canyon quickly shrank to an abrupt, winding slot canyon, which narrowed even further, to a twisting, tight crevasse. I'd never seen anything like it. We stopped several times and just stared. The red sandstone had been sculpted by water for millennia, and I wouldn't have believed the place was there if I hadn't seen it with my own two eyes.

The meandering narrows opened into a small basin and an emerald pond, fed by a twenty-foot waterfall off a sandstone outcropping. It was spectacular. There was no sign, or even a suggestion, of this place from the main road or from the maps of the area back then, and there's still not today.

"I take it back," Smitty said in a subdued tone. "I might eat you after all, Queequeg. This place is the shit."

"It is," I agreed. "It really is."

By the early evening, we picked what looked like an old campsite to drop our blankets and build a fire. Major showered in the waterfall.

"We should've brought a lantern," I said. "And some beach towels."

"When the acid hits, I'm not sure it will matter," Queequeg replied.

The small squares of LSD were decorated with what looked like an image of Fat Man—the nuclear bomb the United States dropped on the Japanese city of Nagasaki. The last coherent conversation I recall us having that night was about the beach, which we would head toward the next day.

Francis Bacon's phantasms, Bruegel's bizarre, medieval peasantry—they were surreal elements of recognizable images, figures squawking, canvases stretching and shrinking and iconic tapestries twisting impossibly, vibrating. They were the only frames of reference I had for what happened next. Later, I would know more, especially in terms of context. But, in 1979, it was just mad gibberish, and we were dizzy jabberwocks navigating an Eden-like crevasse in one of the last frontiers of the country.

It went on for a time that I felt was unquantifiable because, at some point, I decided it might never end and it scared me. Then, I found a comfort to it, as if things had always been this way and they would always be this way. The entire landscape began to reverberate with a soothing cadence that linked the outside world and my inner mind. There was nothing to be afraid of. I was a grain of sand on a blue marble and the rigid structure of the "real" world was just an opposing scrum to navigate and avoid.

Then, later, several hours later—or maybe just a few—a blue norther blew in and was full upon us. At first, I found the cold wind refreshing. But, as the weather is wont to do in that part of the Texas Panhandle, the temperature dropped forty degrees. And we were still dressed in t-shirts and shorts.

So, there we sat, smacked out of our heads on acid and crowded under our blankets, shivering, marveling and freezing, all at the same time. The fire was low, but there wasn't much wood around. And we weren't in any shape to gather it or place it over the coals. Major was mumbling something about Merv Griffin, and Smitty seemed to have shrunk. Only Queequeg appeared to harbor some form of wherewithal, but I was hardly a reliable witness. At one point, he leaned close and raised his voice. "I can see the Caddies," he said.

"What?" I managed, unsurely.

"They're no longer in the ground."

"*What?*"

Another indeterminate period of time passed; no doubt made longer by the bitter cold.

The wind, then, was no longer a cold caress. It was like a blast of dry ice, biting, scratching, but still part of that cadence I felt, almost like an instrumental accompaniment. Queequeg was still there, leaning in. I was mumbling nonstop, and he listened. I felt hollowed out and there was no relief for it. My blood boiled, and I swam awkwardly, shouting sideways, blinking at deafening colors in the glowing darkness. I was horrified and fascinated at the same time. My reality was a patchwork of visual throbs and contortions, and my perspective seemed no longer prefrontal-lobe oriented. It was base and primal, all medulla oblongata.

Queequeg disappeared. Major Tom was mumbling about organic portfolios and Smitty was completely mute. Stone. Nothing came out of his mouth. It was like he was afraid of what might come out.

The cold, ruthless wind lashed us and made strange noises as it passed through the sandstone narrows. I didn't understand until much later what had really happened. One moment Queequeg was an ally in the madness, and then he was gone. And then another indeterminate period later, he reappeared. But something was wrong. His gait was clumsy, and he was leaning. He was leaning and falling. Then, he collapsed into what was left of the fire, purple, bloodied, and unconscious. There was no understanding or comprehension. We smelled his burning flesh and pulled him away from the remaining red coals. Major Tom was talking about Merv Griffin again, calling him—or maybe it was me. One of us was threatening to contact Merv Griffin. We could ask him what happened to Queequeg. Merv could interview Captain Ahab, and maybe Melville's First Mate, Starbuck.

As is probably obvious, there was suddenly no context for any sort of awareness of the moment. Our existing demons were flirting with new ones, and our perspectives were expanding faster than our ability to grasp them. Later, I realized Queequeg had probably been the least affected by the acid and may have left to find help, leaving us bundled in the two blankets we'd brought. But the norther had been too intense. The ice storm it had brought along with it was blinding, and Queequeg had probably lost his footing and tumbled off an embankment. Whatever the case, he smashed his head and was lucky to even make it back to our campsite.

It was an inopportune stroke of fate.

In my own fever dream, beneath the cadence, I had devolved into a Pleistocene beast standing at the foot of a primordial ocean. The waves were receding fast, and then they stopped coming back in. The water

just kept going farther and farther out. I began running after the water…
with a rugby ball under my arm. But it was deflated, and I had outrun
my support. I kept running and running, past oversized seashells, Volk-
swagen-sized jellyfish, Greyhound-bus-sized sharks, sea monsters, the
Loch Ness monster, the Caddies south of Amarillo, the Edmund
Fitzgerald run aground, and the Partridge Family as tall as Big Tex,
slowly reaching for me—and then I saw the water again. I was close. I
tossed the rugby ball aside and broke into a mad, awkward sprint.

I was monosyllabic, frantic, fiendish and suddenly in the water, in
the ocean. And it was warm and red and salty. And I drank.

Even socked out of my gourd, I knew I shouldn't drink it, but I was
freezing and starving and parched. And it was so warm and nourishing.
I thought just a little, just a little.

And that's when a reliable narrator re-emerged in my mind. I wasn't
a prehistoric creature lapping from the Red Sea. I was Bruce Floyd, and
I had blood on my shaky hands and cracked lips. I was base and carnivorous, and I had chewed through the flesh of Queequeg's right thigh.
And his blood was still warm.

I was back on the plane. I grabbed the nearest plastic paper barf bag out
of a seat pocket and vomited.

It wasn't a lot. A small puke and a dry heave.

It was the same reaction I'd experienced when the first semblance of
practical reality resettled over me at Linguish Falls. I began vomiting and
then screaming hoarsely. I frightened Major Tom and Smitty, who, to be
fair, hadn't completely emerged from their trips yet. Smitty had what I
thought was a piece of Queequeg's liver. Major was nibbling on Queequeg's shoulder.

Planning to share a rental car, Major and I met at the airport and had a
couple of beers and a bite to eat at TGI Fridays. I ordered a shot before
my beer. I needed it.

"He wasn't still alive," Major barked at me later, after we had finished our meal. "He wasn't breathing."

Other diners turned and looked in our direction.

"I didn't say he was," I replied in a low voice. "I just said his blood was still warm."

"As opposed to what? The sudden freezing temperatures and Arctic winds out there?"

"I'm just saying."

"Well, so am I. I get it. I know. But let's not make this thing any creepier than it was. I wish we had skipped the acid and gone straight to the beach. I wish Queequeg was here, right now, slinging shit. I liked him a helluva lot more than Smitty."

Major raised his beer, and I tapped his beer bottle with mine.

"To Queequeg," I said.

"To Jesús," Major added.

We drank our beers down a bit and were silent for a moment. Then, I ordered another shot.

"I really miss that crazy fuck," I said. "Even after all these years."

"I'm sure we'll see him again in Hell," Major replied.

We picked up the rental car and headed for the hotel. Major drove.

"Who all will show you think?" I was more than a little concerned.

"There'll be some old boys, for sure," Major said. "But I don't know who."

"You know it will come up."

"It always does. And we say the same thing. Coyotes or mountain lions. And you know, some coyotes or a mountain lion did have a go at Queequeg."

"Yeah. But after us."

"I don't care if it was a goddam Chupacabra at midnight. Thank God for whatever it was. If something hadn't had got to him after us, we'd probably all still be in jail." Major stopped the car and glared at me. "You need to keep it together, buddy. You can't fall apart on this."

I nodded. "I'm okay," I said. "It's just a lot, again. It brings back some bad memories."

"Agreed. It's sad. But he was dead already... and we were out of our fucking minds in an Arctic ice storm. And starving."

"Hungry. Not starving."

"Okay. But we didn't know that. We thought we were starving. Or maybe we thought we were in the Andes, I don't know. You don't think Queequeg would have done the same thing? We could've eaten you instead, Pretty Boy."

I knew he had a point. He'd said it all before, about twenty years back. I had tried to look into the LSD we'd dropped that night, and the professor that had previously worked at Tech. I found something on an MK Ultra forum that suggested there had been experiments at Texas Tech in the early seventies. Looking back, I decided that we must have gotten hold of some of the acid from those experiments. I told Major about it, but he wasn't sure.

"It was just a bad trip," he said. "I mean, have you had any crazy flashbacks? Have you had the urge to eat somebody or jump off a building? Or frickin' kill somebody?"

I got quiet, and he continued. "I think part of it was, we were just caught in that fucked-up moment. And the power of suggestion... we had been yacking about those ruggers in the Andes. But who frickin' knows? And does it really matter now?"

The rest of that March night in 1979 was a dark haze. My imagination intervenes where it shouldn't, I think, but I am haunted by the need to fill in the blanks.

We woke up shivering the next morning, but still under the blankets. Me, Major and Smitty. Queequeg was no longer covered, and his open eyes were now frozen open. It freaked us out. I just knew we had closed them.

He didn't even look human anymore, just a collision of flesh, a nightmare vision made corporeal. Something to remind us of the madness.

I tried to look away, but I couldn't.

We were covered in Queequeg's dried blood, the implications of which soon began to dawn on us. The ice and snow had stopped, and

Smitty took charge. We struggled to the car and grabbed the rest of our clothes. We also found an unopened can of Pringles potato chips.

We shared the chips and then went to work. We built a new fire at a different location and threw all our bloody clothes into it. We rinsed ourselves off in the waterfall and then dressed in two pairs of clothes. It was still freezing. Smitty already had a plan.

We had to stay another night. Major would go get some food and water, more blankets, and some wood for a proper fire. Smitty and I would take Queequeg out to a connecting canyon or open plain well away from our campsite and leave the body.

It would be a grim chore, especially if Queequeg's body began to thaw. I retched and cried before we started. Smitty remained focused, and didn't make light of my tears. When we got Queequeg to a decent spot—it was high in a canyon and had a nice view—we placed him gently on the ground.

"You should say something," Smitty said. "He was your friend."

"I... What am I supposed to say?"

"Tell him how you feel."

I hesitated. "I'm sorry, man," I said, staring down at Queequeg. "I'm sorry. This is crazy. I'm sorry."

Smitty stepped up. "You were a badass on the pitch," he added. "We'll miss you. And we'll remember you."

I appreciated that at the time and wanted to tell Smitty so—but he kept it short and sweet. He turned to me. "You better head back," he said.

"Alone?"

"He's starting to thaw out," Smitty continued. "We need him plenty bloody to attract critters. We need a strong scent."

It made sense. "Okay," I said. "You'll be along soon?"

"Yep. I'm gonna let Jesús thaw out a little more and, you know."

"Oh, yeah. Okay."

"Keep your powder dry, Pretty Boy. We'll get through this."

Keep your powder dry, Pretty Boy. We'll get through this.

Smitty was right. We did get through it.

After the ice and snow were gone the next day, we went back to where we left Queequeg and examined his remains. He was tore up pretty bad. We drove into Silverton and called the Sheriff. We admitted to trying LSD and said Queequeg had wandered off in the storm. We took them out to his body and the local medical examiner—who also ran the local funeral home—confirmed the story we told. He ruled that Queequeg had walked off and taken a fall and succumbed to the head injury and exposure. Then, he surmised, some of the local critters had had a go at him.

We—Major and I—called around and couldn't find any of Queequeg's people after the incident. He'd been older than we thought. And he had hardly been in school, working odd jobs and only half-attending college classes. But he still managed a 2.3 GPA—I looked it up later.

Queequeg had lived alone in a rundown RV park on the south side of San Marcos, and he rode a Honda Night Hawk motorcycle to classes and rugby practice. We couldn't find anyone that knew anybody in his family or if he even had a family.

We paid for Queequeg's funeral and a headstone with what we had saved for spring break and a loan Smitty had gotten from his parents. They owned a car lot or something. Smitty's parents also pulled some strings that kept the story out of the local paper and, luckily, the county sheriff wasn't real inquisitive.

While we were at the sheriff's office, the rancher who owned the land that Linguish Falls was hidden in stopped by. He gave us hard looks. "Don't ever come back here," he said. "Ever."

I remember getting the distinct impression that something like this had happened there before, but no one would elaborate, and I didn't ask.

That second night at Linguish Falls had been tough, because the thought of Queequeg being out there all alone bugged me. Major was sympathetic, but practical. "He doesn't feel anything anymore, man. He's gone."

"It just doesn't seem right," I said. "You really think he would have left one of us out there alone like that?"

"He left us alone last night," Major countered.

"We weren't alone," I said. "We were just jacked out of minds. And besides—I think he was trying to go for help."

"That may be so," Major conceded. "But I guarantee you if he were here and it was you or Smitty, he'd be with us on this. I really dug Queequeg, but there isn't anything we can do for him now. We can just try to keep it from ruining the rest of our lives. He would understand. He would do the same thing if he had to, and you would forgive him, and us, if the shoe was on the other foot. You know I'm right, Pretty Boy."

"I guess," I said.

"Well, good. Then there's an end to it."

Smitty showed up later, right after dark. He said he'd begun hearing noises in the canyon. He was convinced Queequeg's corpse would be receiving visitors.

The tombstone we picked out for Queequeg had his real name on it and we were able to get his birthdate from his driver's license. We had them put *¡Vaya con Dios!* at the bottom of the marker.

We didn't stay for the funeral, and I've never been back. I felt bad about it for a long time, but it was just the best. I didn't feel like any good would come from hanging around.

My collegiate rugby career ended not long after. I got banged up and then pretended it was worse than it was. I lost interest. Queequeg and I had both been members of the back line, and it just wasn't the same without him. Besides that, Smitty and Major and I also got a lot of sympathy for the incident, as if we had been the victims of the ordeal ourselves. It was too much. I wanted no part of it. I went by Queequeg's run-down RV and looked for contact information for his family. I didn't find anything. Then I wasted an entire semester on pointless debauchery and almost flunked out. I changed my major to biology.

Smitty's rugby star shot up like a rocket. He made the Western Select team his last two years in school and then became a star for the

Dallas Marauders in the Men's League. He even enjoyed a stint with the American national rugby squad, the Eagles.

After college, I kept my distance. I lost contact with most of the guys but stayed in touch with Major. I occasionally met some of the others for beers if they were in town and attended a couple of the rugby alumni festivities. That was pretty much it.

I stayed around San Marcos and became a Marine Biologist. A darkly humorous side note to this was that there were several species of catfish, perch, and carp in the local waterways that were cannibalistic. They occasionally engaged in filial cannibalism. They ate their own offspring.

After a surprisingly prestigious rugby career, Smitty went to work for his parents' car dealership and made lots of money. He became—no surprise—a staunch conservative and, the last time I saw him (at an alumni match), he razzed me about still being a hippie who was light on doing what was necessary to get the job done. "Like you?" I quipped.

"Damn right," he said. "I'm a winner. I've always been a winner."

I smiled at him and thought of something sarcastic to say, but he grinned mischievously and winked. I couldn't help but laugh. We had a history. Not a good one, but a history all the same. I didn't make anything else of it. Major Tom got married and had kids. He'd spent the last thirty years with a medical supply company.

I also eventually became a vegetarian. It was a slow evolution. I simply became less and less interested in consuming meat. It wasn't a conscious decision so far as I know. It just got to where it turned my stomach.

The memorial the following day was in the early evening, and Major and I both thought that was strange. But Smitty was a strange guy.

None of our fellow collegiate ruggers made the trip to Wyoming, just Marauders and a few stragglers. Smitty had become something of a Marauder legend, particularly for his brutal, smash-mouth style of play. They showed some videos of his handiwork, and Major and I listened to the stories and shared a few of our own. Smitty had been a cheat and a bully, but everybody loved him. And the ceremony was everything I imagined Smitty would have wanted, and we were having fun, which I think he also would have wanted. But then Smitty's wife, Sheila, cornered us. I hadn't gone to their wedding, but Major had. I'd met Sheila at one of the alumni weekends.

She hugged Major and greeted me warmly. She said Smitty had been sick for a while, so his passing had come as no surprise. But he had refused to see a doctor. She actually said she didn't know if Smitty had ever seen a doctor, which struck me as weird.

"Picture of health?" I inquired.

"For as long as I knew the man," Sheila said. "You knew him. He was unstoppable until he just wasn't. I think it was something he picked up overseas."

"Did y'all travel a lot?" I asked.

"We did," she said. "Once or twice a year, every year. More when we were younger, less as we grew older."

"Wow," I said. "That surprises me. I didn't figure Smitty for a world traveler. Where did he like to go?"

"Oh, all over. We traveled to a bunch of exotic places. Cambodia. Nairobi. Papua New Guinea. We used to go to Papua New Guinea every year. Even before we were married."

I shot a sideways glance at Major. "Papua New Guinea? What do tourists do there?"

"Oh, they have all sorts of tours and safaris, active volcanoes, rainforest and Mt. Wilhelm. It's really something. It was one of Smitty's favorite places in the world. He loved it there."

"Did he?" I said.

"He sure did. And we loved the food. I'm so glad y'all could come. It would have meant so much to him."

I turned to Major. He looked a little peaked.

The memorial was subsequently moved to an adjacent room, something like a ballroom, and we were seated at tables with full dining place sets. Things just got stranger and stranger.

A couple of speakers spoke highly of Smitty, and then Sheila stood at the podium. She talked about Smitty and his teammates, whom he had considered family, and then she got choked up addressing Major Tom and I.

"Tom and Bruce," she said. "I wanted to talk about his love and respect for y'all last."

Major and I looked at each other and then back at Sheila. Everyone else was suddenly staring at us.

"Most people here don't know what happened to you and Smitty in the Texas Panhandle all those years ago," she continued. "But I do."

My stomach dropped. Major shook his head.

"It changed Smitty's life. It made him the man he was, the champion he was. You, Tom... and you, Bruce... you were there. You took those first steps together..."

"What the frickin' hell..." Tom mumbled under his breath. "What the fuck?!"

As Sheila spoke, a catering team started bringing food out. I glanced around nervously. Surely not, I thought. No way. But I suddenly recalled how long it had taken Smitty to get back that night, after we moved Queequeg's body.

I began to tremble.

A large catering tray, which resembled an oversized gurney, was suddenly rolling down the main aisle of the ballroom toward us. And Sheila was walking behind it, still talking. But I didn't hear her.

Tom and I were too focused on the oversized catering gurney, which had the main "course" on it.

It was Smitty, naked as the day he was born. A banana and two ripe peaches occupied the space his genitalia previously had, and there was a juicy red apple in his open mouth.

His Marauder teammates were clapping, and they were joined by Sheila. And she was still addressing us, and the small crowd. "If not for you..." she was saying.

I stood up. I took one uneven step backward and almost collapsed. Tom caught me.

"And there's no reason to worry," Sheila continued, smiling. "We had Smitty's brain removed before the meal was prepared. And we'd like you, both of you, to carve your own portions, the first portions. It was one of Smitty's last wishes. He felt that he owed both of you that."

"No," Tom said, under his breath. "No," he repeated, a little louder.

Sheila ignored him.

"We're so honored to have you here," she said. "He was so honored by your friendship. And your confidence."

"It can't..." Tom started. "You can't..."

"It went beyond rugby," Sheila said, raising her voice. "You were brothers."

Shouting rang out, then, from all around. And cheering.

And laughter.

We tried to leave, but didn't get far. We were suddenly at the bottom of a large scrum.

We kicked and fought, but it was no use. I heard Major Tom screaming—or maybe it was me. And in a matter of moments, I was back in the warm, red water. I was back in the ocean.

But the cadence was weakening.

thirteen
warren

The executioner will inject sodium pentothal into the intravenous tube...
The... liquid will flow into the needle. Unconsciousness will be almost
immediate. Death will follow quickly. Eighteen hours or so later, it will
be time for trick-or-treating on the sidewalks of Pasadena, Deer Park
and Houston, a time traditionally filled with the laughter of pint-sized
goblins. But the memory of the Halloween of 1974 touches children not
yet born on that horror-filled eve eight years ago.
    *--**Corpus Christi Caller-Times**, October 25, 1982*

"MY DAD LETS me sleep in it," the boy said, his gaze half rising.

"Really," Culley replied, admiring the costume through the slits in his Iron Man mask. "It's scary."

"Yeah," the boy said, his eyes dropping.

It was darker in that part of the neighborhood, but Culley could make out blood on the boy's chin and the front of his white shirt.

"My name is Warren," the boy said. He wore a black mask that only covered his eyes and nose. His cowboy hat was white, and his pants were also white.

"I'm Culley. That's a neat mask, too,"

"I'm 'upposed to be the Lone Ranger," Warren replied.

"Who's the Lone Ranger?"

"A good guy who fought bad guys in the cowboy days. Who are you 'upposed to be?"

"Iron Man," Culley said. "Like in the movies."

Warren didn't seem familiar. Culley walked up to the next house with the rest of the kids. Warren stayed in the street.

The residents, a middle-aged man and his wife, already had their door open. The kids emitted a cacophony of "Trick or Treats!" and the residents doled out generous handfuls of candy.

Culley held up his plastic pumpkin-head treat container.

"I like your costume," the husband said. "Happy Halloween!"

Culley grinned under his mask as the man dropped candy in the pumpkin head. "Happy Halloween," he said, as he turned away. His father, Michael, was down at the street curb talking to another dad.

The boy in the Lone Ranger costume was gone.

"His name was Warren," Culley said, as he emptied his haul on the faux antique rug on their living room floor.

"Does he live in the neighborhood?" Culley's mother, Alyssa, asked.

"I don't know," Culley said. "But I liked his costume."

Michael sat down on the rug next to him. "What did Warren go as?"

"He was the Lone Ranger," Culley observed, removing the Iron Man mask he had slid back on his head so he could see better. He began slowly separating his candy by type. "But he was scary. Wasn't the Lone Ranger a good guy?"

"He was," Michael replied. "Why was he scary?"

"Maybe he was just a cowboy ghost," Alyssa noted, taking a seat on the floor next to Culley.

Michael and Alyssa exchanged glances over their little boy. Michael smiled. Alyssa nodded and returned her husband's smile.

"Sounds like you made a new friend," Alyssa continued. "That's nice."

"Yeah," Culley replied, focused on sorting his candy. "He was out by himself."

The separation of Culley's Halloween bounty was soon complete. He had thirteen snack-size Snickers bars, six mini Crunch bars, eight Tootsie Rolls, nine snack-size packets of Skittles, a dozen mini Hershey bars of assorted types, a handful of Hershey's Kisses, seven snack-size packets of Sweet Tarts, several mini Reese's Peanut Butter Cups, and eleven snack-size Reese's Cups—which were his favorite. He also had one full-size Milky Way, two full-size Baby Ruths, and two more separate piles, one for miscellaneous M&Ms (plain and peanut, which he knew his mother liked) and a slush pile composed of miscellaneous taffy bars, Whoppers, jawbreakers, Jolly Ranchers, individual Starbursts, Almond Joys, gum, lollipops and candy corn.

Michael eyed the slush pile. He grabbed a small box of Whoppers and said, "Father tax."

"What's a 'Father tax?'" Culley inquired, without looking up. He was unwrapping a snack-size Reese's cup.

"The candy I get as compensation for taking you trick or treating. Nothing's for free, son."

Culley gave his mother a look.

"He's playing with you," Alyssa said, smiling.

"Yes, I am, buddy," Michael admitted, popping a Whopper into his mouth. "It's just something my father used to say to me."

Culley began nibbling at the chocolate edges of the Reese's. He liked to eat as much of the chocolate as he could before he ate the peanut butter. His father ate two more Whopper balls.

"Man," Michael said. "I haven't had these in a million years. Malted milk balls. They're awesome." Culley smiled at his dad before he placed the mostly peanut butter portion of the Reese's in his mouth.

"Is that Bazooka bubble gum?!" blurted Alyssa, eyeing the slush pile.

Michael spotted a rectangular-shaped white wrapper with blue and red letters. "It sure is," he said.

"I didn't know they still made that," Alyssa replied.

"It looks like they still do... unless it's been sitting in a jar in somebody's basement for forty years." Michael underhanded it to Alyssa. "Catch," he said.

Alyssa caught the Bazooka and looked it over. "I wonder why they called it Bazooka?" she asked, holding it so Culley could see it.

"Shoot," Michael replied. "Get two or three pieces of Bazooka in your mouth and you could blow bubbles that sounded like a bazooka when they popped."

Alyssa unwrapped the Bazooka bubble gum and began chewing it. She looked at the inside of the wrapper before she wadded it up and tossed it into the growing candy wrapper pile. "The Bazooka bubble gum wrapping used to feature comic strips," Alyssa noted.

"Like Iron Man?" Culley asked.

"Bazooka Joe," Michael responded. "The main character was 'Bazooka Joe'."

"Was he a superhero?"

"He was a soldier."

"I barely remember," Alyssa said.

Michael ate a couple more malted milk balls and Culley was nibbling at the chocolate on another snack-size Reese's cup. He stopped and repositioned the cup in his small fingers. "There was blood dripping down Warren's chin," Culley remembered. "It was also on his neck and chest."

"Was he okay?" Alyssa asked, pausing in mid-Bazooka chomp.

"I think so," Culley answered. "But he didn't have a trick or treat bag. All he had was a candy stick. He was eating candy out of it."

"A candy stick? A lollipop?"

"No, a candy stick. Like a straw. A big, purple-striped straw."

"A Grape Escape," Michael deduced. "Krazee Stix. I think he means Krazee Stix. You hardly see those anymore."

"I think they discontinued them," Alyssa said, positioning her Bazooka. She got it on her tongue just right, flattened it a little against the roof of her mouth, and then spread it a little with her lips and tongue. She attempted to blow a bubble. The pink blob began to expand away from her lips, thinning as it grew. It ruptured before it was an inch in diameter.

"Flat tire, lady?" Michael smirked.

"I don't think I have enough gum," Alyssa said. "Is there another Bazooka?"

Michael sorted through the slush pile and came up empty-handed. "Looks like you're the only one who's packing," he joked. "Be careful where you point that thing."

Alyssa grinned and kept chewing. She grabbed her iPhone and looked up Krazee Stix. "It looks like they discontinued Krazee Stix," she announced. "It was a few years back."

Culley was concentrating on the last nibbles of chocolate on his Reese's.

"Why?" Michael inquired.

"It says they were worried about kids learning 'the habit of using illicit drugs.'"

"Uhhh... *what?*"

"I don't know."

"What does that even mean?"

Alyssa stood up and shrugged, then touched her right nostril with her right index finger and executed a light snort.

"Holy crap," Michael said. "No way."

Culley grabbed another Reese's. "Can I sleep in my costume?" he asked.

"Why do you want to sleep in your costume?" Alyssa responded.

"I don't think the real Iron Man even sleeps in his costume, buddy," Michael said.

"Warren gets to sleep in his," Culley replied.

"Warren?"

"The boy in the Lone Ranger costume," Culley answered.

"I hope his parents clean it first," Alyssa said. "I'm sure they will."

Michael considered the request. What would it hurt? "Culley is eight years old now," Michael observed. "He's in the third grade."

"Ok," Alyssa replied, addressing Culley. "I guess so. But don't wear the mask, please. Put it on the other side of your pillow."

"I will," Culley said, carefully extricating the chocolate from another snack-size Reese's Peanut Butter Cup.

Culley woke up just after 3:00 a.m.

The room was cold. He pulled the covers up and turned toward his Iron Man mask, which was lying on the other side of his pillow. He grabbed it with his left hand and turned it so that it faced him.

Culley stared at the Iron Man mask for a long time.

He loosened his grip on the mask when he was about to doze off. Warren stood up behind it on the other side of Culley's twin bed.

Culley startled awake and put his mask back on.

Warren had the Krazee Stix in his right hand. The blood on his chin and shirt was dry.

"Your parents let you wear yours to bed, too," Warren said.

Culley raised his head a little. "What are you doing here?" he asked.

"I followed you," Warren answered.

"Why?"

"I don't know. I like talking to you, I guess."

"How come you didn't trick or treat?"

"I already did."

"And that's all you have left?" Culley said, looking at the giant Krazee Stix.

Warren looked away. "Yeah," he replied.

"You want some of my candy?"

"No," Warren answered. "My tummy hurts."

Culley pointed at the large Krazee Stix. "My dad said that is called a *Grape Escape*."

Warren turned to the Krazee Stix. "Yeah," he said in a quiet voice. "But I didn't get away."

"What?"

"I didn't 'scape."

Culley didn't know what his friend meant, but Warren seemed uncomfortable. "It's a lot of candy, though," Culley added.

"Yeah. It was good at first. But my daddy said I ate too much. My tummy started to hurt."

"Can I try it?"

"No. I don't think you'd like it."

"Maybe you're right. Do you live in this neighborhood?"

"Yeah."

"Wanna play sometime?"

"I guess so."

Culley looked around his room, wondering how Warren got in. When he turned back around, Warren was gone.

Culley lowered himself off of his bed and went to his parents' bedroom. The door was open, and they were asleep. He didn't want to wake them.

Culley nestled under the comforter hanging off the foot of the bed.

He left his mask on.

Alyssa woke up glad that Halloween had been a Friday night. She stretched and got out of bed dressed in her panties and a T-shirt. She walked to the bathroom, not noticing Culley.

When Alyssa came back out of the bathroom, she was startled. "*Omigosh*," she exclaimed.

Michael bolted upright. "What's wrong? What's wrong?"

"It's Culley," she said, pointing.

"What?" Michael hopped out of bed in his boxers and followed Alyssa's line of vision.

It was Culley.

Michael got on his hands and knees and began unraveling him from the comforter. Culley woke up and pulled off his mask.

"You okay, buddy?" Michael asked.

"Yeah, Dad. I just didn't wanna sleep alone. I didn't wanna wake you up."

Alyssa came over and knelt next to Michael. "It's okay, baby. It's okay. Did you have a nightmare?"

"I don't think so," Culley said. "But Warren was here."

"*What?*"

"He was in my room."

"How did he get—" Michael started. "Did you let him in the house?"

"No," Culley said. "He was just there. I woke up, and he was just standing by my bed."

Michael gave Alyssa a quick glance and held his hand up and out at chest level, silently indicating he wanted them to stay right there. Then he jumped up and left the room.

Alyssa helped Culley up, and they sat on the bed. "Are you sure it wasn't just a dream?"

"I didn't think I was dreaming," Culley answered.

"What did Warren say?"

"He said he liked talking to me."

***

Michael inspected Culley's bedroom. The windows were locked and there was no sign of the Lone Ranger. There was no blood. He checked the front door and the other windows in the living room. They were all secure. As he headed for the back door, he spotted a small trace of purple powder on the rug next to the discarded candy wrapper pile. He dropped down to his hands and knees again and examined it. He licked the tip of his pinky finger, dabbed his moist pinky tip in the powder, and sampled it. It tasted like Grape Escape. He remembered it after all these years.

Michael raised his head up and looked down the most direct path to Culley's room. He spotted two tiny drifts of purple powder on the hardwood floor. He hopped up, retrieved a broom and dustpan from the pantry, and then stopped.

The powder was gone.

Michael went back into the bedroom and told Alyssa and Culley that everything was okay, but that it looked like someone had been in the house. He grabbed his phone and called the Harris County Sheriff's Department.

"Did I do something wrong?" Culley asked.

"No, honey," Alyssa said, hugging her son. "Of course not."

"I just woke up, and he was there," Culley said. "I put on my mask."

"What did he want?"

"I don't know," Culley said. "He... He said he didn't get away."

"Away? Away from who?"

"I don't know. He was by himself."

Alyssa held Culley's tiny hands and studied his eyes. "Are you sure you're alright?"

"I think so," Culley replied.

"Did he say anything else?"

"I asked him if he wanted to play and he said 'Yeah'."

"So you two are going to play sometime?"

"Yeah," Culley replied, watching his mother's expression change. "He said next Halloween."

Two Harris County deputies showed up and performed a perfunctory search. One was extremely tall, and one was surprisingly short. The short deputy did the talking.

There was no evidence of a break-in, and no valuables were missing. Also, no one was assaulted or injured, and the only witness of an intruder was an eight-year-old boy with a mild stomachache. "We all ate too much candy," Alyssa said.

"Do you want us to speak with your son?" the short deputy said.

Alyssa wasn't sure. Michael had to admit it was strange. "What about the purple powder?" Michael inquired. "You can't really get Krazee Stix anymore."

"It could be Fun Dip," the tall deputy said. "That Lick-M-Aid stuff."

"I remember those," Michael said. "It was like a three or four-section packet. One for a dipping stick and the others for the flavored powders."

Alyssa was already looking it up on her phone. "Wonka Fun Dip," she said. "I think the original packaging had three flavors... RazzApple Magic, Cherry Yum Diddly, and Grape Yumptious."

"We didn't see a pouch like that in Culley's candy," Michael said. "I would have noticed."

"It doesn't come like that anymore," the tall deputy replied. "The new packets are two-section, one for the stick and one for the flavor."

Alyssa had moved the separated candies to the dining room table and thrown the wrapper pile away. She dug the wrappers out of the trash and couldn't find one for Fun Dip.

"Look," the short deputy said. "It was Halloween. Your son ate a lot of candy. Do you think it was a bad dream? Maybe a Fun Dip wrapper is under a pile of Legos or something."

"I don't know," Michael said, stumped.

"We can talk to him," the short deputy said, "But no one got hurt. Nothing is missing. If someone was here, it doesn't look like they did anything. If you're worried, I would install one of those Ring security systems. You can get them at Lowe's or Home Depot, I think. The doorbell and the floodlights... with cameras. And they'll notify you on your phone. If you're concerned, I mean."

After the deputies left, Michael and Alyssa found Culley in the den, watching TV. He had found episodes of the original 1949 season of *The Lone Ranger* serial on one of the throwback cable channels.

Michael and Alyssa looked at each other. Alyssa raised her eyebrows.

"Whatcha' watching, buddy?" Michael asked.

"He wasn't just a lone ranger," Culley said. "He was a Texas Ranger."

"I remember that," Michael said.

"His horse's name was Silver," Culley added.

"Hiyo, Silver!" Michael replied in a dramatic, elevated pitch. He smiled at Alyssa and sat down next to his son on the couch. "I am very pleased, *kemosabe*."

"That's Tonto," Culley said.

"Sure is."

Michael and Alyssa purchased a Ring Security System with two motion-activated two-head floodlights (with cameras) and a doorbell. They hired an electrician, and he came out and installed them the following Friday. Alyssa spent the next morning linking it with her phone and, as she was demonstrating the various features to Michael, a man suddenly appeared in the Ring doorbell camera.

"Who's that?" Alyssa asked.

"I don't know," Michael said. "He looks like a salesman."

They watched him approach on Alyssa's iPhone. He was wearing casual slacks, a short-sleeved white shirt, and a blue tie. He was carrying a manila folder in his left hand. He rang the Ring doorbell with his right.

"It works," Alyssa remarked.

"It does," Michael agreed. "But I still don't know who he is."

Michael got up and opened the door about six inches, placing his right foot behind the door base.

"Howdy," the man said. "My name is Harvey Taggert."

"Hello, sir. What can I help you with?"

Harvey seemed pensive. "I think I'm here to help you," he said. "And maybe you can help me, too."

Harvey's eyes were pale blue. He appeared to be about seventy years old and looked like a man who wasn't used to being back on his heels. But he seemed that way now.

Michael hesitated. "You're not a salesman, are you?"

"No, sir," Harvey answered. "I'm a retired preacher, if you can believe that."

"Well," Michael replied warily. "That's awkward. We're not churchgoers."

"Oh, forgive me," Harvey said. "I'm not here to proselytize, sir. No. No. I'd really like to talk to you about last weekend. Halloween."

Michael looked back at Alyssa, who was listening. She threw her hands up slightly, as if to indicate *don't ask me*.

Harvey continued, "Uhh, a couple of deputies were here last Saturday."

Michael turned back to Harvey, and Alyssa joined him at the door.

"The sheriff called me," Harvey added. "He thought I could help explain—the sheriff told me to drop by."

Alyssa tapped Michael's door-stopping foot with hers and he removed it. She opened the front door. "I'm Alyssa," she said. "And this is Michael. Come in."

Taggert told them the story.

The real story. A *true* story.

A story you can still find in old Houston newspapers and on nightly news reports every nine or ten years or so.

On October 31, 1974—Halloween—a man named O'Halloran took his two sons trick or treating with another neighbor and his two kids. After knocking on a door no one answered, O'Halloran sent his neighbor and all the kids on to the next house, suggesting he would try again—that maybe the residents were home, but didn't hear them.

O'Halloran was in debt to the tune of $80,000 and had purchased primary and secondary life insurance policies on his children. When he eventually caught up to his neighbor and his kids, he was holding four 21-inch Krazee Stix, remarking that his patience had paid off. The occupants finally came to the door and gave him a Krazee Stix for each of the trick or treaters.

Unbeknownst to all, O'Halloran had opened all four Krazee Stix and mixed the powdered candy with potassium cyanide and then refolded the ends of the sticks and stapled them closed. His plan had been to kill one or both of his kids and collect the insurance money. It would give him breathing room in regard to his debts. The extra Krazee Stix were for other neighborhood kids—to throw potential investigators off.

Before O'Halloran's oldest son went to bed, he asked his father if he could have some candy. O'Halloran let him have his Krazee Stix.

"Omigod," said Alyssa. "Are you telling us..."

Taggert demurred, clasping his hands. Michael put his arm around Alyssa. "Let the man finish," he said.

Taggert continued.

The oldest son, Warren, had problems opening the straw, and the powdered "candy" on that end of the stick had hardened. O'Halloran tapped and squeezed on the open end of the Krazee Stix and loosened the candy. The boy began eating the Krazee Stix powder and almost immediately complained of stomach pains. O'Halloran called an ambulance, but Warren died before they reached the hospital.

None of the other children ate any of their candy that night.

"O'Halloran always denied it," Taggert noted. "Shed tears and cursed the monster who could have done such a thing. Even allowed Warren to be buried in his Lone Ranger costume because he said his son loved it so much. But the house where he claimed to have gotten the Krazee Stix was unoccupied at the time. The owner came forward. Evidence began to stack up against O'Halloran. He was charged with one count of capital murder and four counts of attempted murder. He was convicted by a jury and sentenced to death. He was executed ten years later."

"Why are you telling us all this?" Michael asked.

Taggert unclasped and re-clasped his hands. "I heard your son met Warren."

"What?!" Alyssa exclaimed. "The same boy? What are you saying?"

"I'm not saying anything," Taggert replied.

"Are you suggesting this Warren kid wasn't real? That Culley made the story up?"

"Of course not," Taggert replied. "Not at all."

"I don't understand," Alyssa sighed. "Are you saying Culley spent Halloween with a dead boy?"

"Mr. Taggert," Michael said. "Why are you here?"

Taggert stood up, placed his hands in his pockets, and then sat back down. He pulled his hands out of his pockets and re-clasped them. When he began to speak, he appeared ten years older. "Mr. O'Halloran was nicknamed 'Candyman' before his trial. And he is often referred to as 'The Man Who Killed Halloween'. The monstrosity he committed put a stain on this community—on my congregation—for years. It scared people all over the country.

"This is a nice neighborhood," Taggert continued. "My kids all grew up here. We still like it here. And I'm sorry to bother you folks today... but, as I'm sure you might appreciate, this is a delicate subject. O'Halloran had been a deacon at the church, even sang in the choir. I considered him a friend. I..."

Taggert stopped and stared off. "I don't know how something like that could happen anywhere," he said, "last of all, here. I didn't under-stand. I still don't understand. But I believe this, in my heart... in my soul. Warren didn't do anything wrong... and your boy didn't do anything wrong. It looks like what happened last weekend didn't hurt anything. And I don't believe Warren wants to hurt anybody."

"Culley claims he was in our house," Michael said. "Was he in our house?"

"I can't say."

"Why? Why can't you say?"

Taggert covered his mouth with the back of his right wrist.

Alyssa's eyes teared up.

"Michael," Taggert continued. "Alyssa. No adult has seen Warren since he died. It's only the kids."

"Jesus," Michael said. "How do you expect us to respond to this? It's crazy... It's—"

"It's just a boy," Taggert said. "He's just a boy. He's never hurt anyone. And he was hurt in the worst possible way. I don't know why he comes back. I don't know how he comes back. But he comes back. He comes back. Can you blame him? I think it's all he has. Is he really hurting anything?"

"You've never seen him?" Alyssa said. "Ever?"

"Before, yes," Taggert said. "At church. But never since. No adult has seen him since that night."

"He's alone," Alyssa said.

"He's alone. Lonely, I think. No adult has seen him and a kid or two sees him every couple of years. And they're always good kids. I don't think Warren means any harm. He's just *alone*."

"So, what should we do?" Michael asked.

Taggert smiled sadly. "Nothing, Michael. Culley may never see him again. Most kids don't. It's a nice neighborhood, and we take care of our own. The sheriff—he was a kid, himself, back then, wet behind the ears. It scared us all to death. The sheriff knows I'm here. Twenty or so of us know about Warren, and we've kept it our secret.

"Now, it's yours. Now you know. Will you help us keep the secret? Will you help us keep Warren's secret? He's just a little boy."

previous appearances

Pendulum Grim, December 2019
    Minerva's Vision
    Tarry Tornado
    Recumbent Female Nude
    Pendulum Grim

Road Kill: Texas Horror by Texas Writers
    The Halloween in Me (Volume 2, October 2017)
    A Dark White Postscript (Volume 3, September 2018)
    Nia (Volume 4, October 2019)
    Rugby Players Eat Their Dead (Volume 5, October 2020)

Published as Independent Short Stories
    The Amulet (June 2023)
    Nature Calls (May 2023)

If you enjoyed this book, please do one or more of the following:

- Leave a review on your favorite book review site
- Tell a friend about *The Halloween in Me*
- Ask your local library to put E.R. Bills' work on the shelf
- Recommend Fawkes Press books to your local bookstore

VISIT US ONLINE
www.FawkesPress.com
www.ERBillsBooks.com

9 781957 529394